**Please return / renew this item by the last date shown above**
Dychwelwch / Adnewyddwch erbyn y dyddiad olaf y nodir yma

# LIQUIDATOR

www.**davidficklingbooks**.com

# ALSO BY ANDY MULLIGAN

*Trash*

*The Boy with 2 Heads*

*Ribblestrop*

*Return to Ribblestrop*

*Ribblestrop Forever*

# LIQUIDATOR

## ANDY MULLIGAN

David Fickling Books
31 Beaumont Street
Oxford OX1 2NP UK

# To Vicky

Liquidator
is a
DAVID FICKLING BOOK

First published in Great Britain in 2015 by
David Fickling Books,
31 Beaumont Street,
Oxford, OX1 2NP

Text © Andy Mulligan, 2015

Hardback edition 978-1-910200-14-8
Trade paperback edition 978-1-910200-94-0

1 3 5 7 9 10 8 6 4 2

David Fickling Books supports the Forest Stewardship Council (FSC), the leading
international forest certification organisation. All our titles that are printed
on Greenpeace-approved FSC-certified paper carry the FSC logo.

DAVID FICKLING BOOKS Reg. No. 8340307

A CIP catalogue record for this book is available from the British Library.

Printed and bound in Great Britain by Clays Ltd, St Ives plc.

# OUR PROMISE TO YOU

It's going to be the truth, the whole truth and nothing but the truth from me. From all of us, in fact, sitting here, hammering this out . . . That's the deal we've made as I pull the records together.

There are bits in this you won't believe, but we don't care. There are bits you shouldn't even read because they're VIOLENT and UPSETTING, but what are we to do? Leave stuff out and censor ourselves? The answer is a straight, resounding:

'NO: NOT POSSIBLE.'

Read on, if you dare! Because we start with the morning the fuse got lit, and life changed for ever.

*Kat Kat xx*  *Eleanor*  *Stagger*

~~*Molly*~~  **EDGAR**  *Ben*

*Michael*

*molly*  *Polly*

*Vicky*

# THE WEEK BEFORE

# Vicky

## 07.03
## Home

Stagger and I have a moped system. The moped in question's called George, and we rescued him together from a skip, right outside our house. He stops and starts and makes strange noises, but we get on pretty well and he doesn't usually let us down.

I jump on first. Stagger slides in ahead of me. I squeeze under his coat, keeping my head well down – then I put my arms round his waist, and off we go like that, with our knees tucked in. We roar through traffic at a blistering, what? – twenty-five to thirty with the wind behind us, steaming downhill! – and yes, it's illegal, we know that . . . but Stagger has no licence anyway and you have to do dodgy things sometimes, or you never get to heaven. Looking back, I should have played it safe, and got the bus – but Dad had been pacing around all night, so I'd slept badly and missed the alarm . . . and that was why

I had to run upstairs to hammer on Stagger's door, and beg for help.

'I need a lift!' I cried.

And at first he just said no.

'You have to, Stag,' I said. 'Please! – it's the big day, the important one . . .'

'Why?'

'They're giving out the placements,' I shouted. 'Give me a ride, Stag! – I'll owe you even more, for ever and ever . . .'

He let me in at last, and I fetched him his jeans. I dragged him down the stairs, and then he didn't have his keys, so I had to run back and get them. Now, my school is forty minutes away, so we were already cutting it fine: it was nine-twenty when we left, which meant I'd already missed assembly, thank God, but at nine-thirty the hooter sounds, and my class would be filing in to meet the most humourless teacher still in service: bald Mr Millington.

That's why I needed to be on time: we had a special, extended tutor period to sort out where we were getting sent. The school had signed up to a brand new three-day scheme called 'Work It Out!!' – and that meant our whole class was to spend Wednesday, Thursday and Friday out of school, in the world of work. Where would we go? We'd put in our requests some time ago, writing to offices, football clubs, hotels and hospitals – there were so many possibilities, but I'd set my heart on our local newspaper, to train as the only thing I've ever really wanted to be: an investigative journalist. I'd been dreaming about it all term, so as we sped onto the main road, getting later, I had a strategy all worked out. I'd jump off George, and race to the side door. I'd skid into the classroom and leap to my desk! Then I'd sit there, ready for business as the rest of the class shuffled in.

I shut my eyes, and felt the ring-road uncoiling . . . all was going well. We went even faster, and Stagger did a bit of weaving through the traffic – George was behaving, and it might all have worked out fine if the fuel pipe hadn't jammed, just off a roundabout. Suddenly we were losing power, and wobbling. I put my nose up out of Stag's jacket, and where had we stopped? I couldn't believe it – it was right outside our brand-new, state-of-the-art police station. And what do you think was turning across our path and pausing in the middle of the road? A fluorescent squad car with two serious-looking officers in the front seats, gazing straight us.

They were not smiling.

Two hours it took.

Two knuckle-gnawing hours in a white-walled waiting room, because as I said, Stagger's illegal, and the only ID I had was a satchel full of schoolbooks and a torn-up bus pass. When they finally let me go, I had to desert Stagger and sprint all the way. The morning was almost over though, and when I slammed open the classroom door, panting for breath, every single head turned to stare, and I could see at once that I'd missed the moment. Everyone had their own envelope. Everyone had a form. The whiteboard showed a grid, with the names next to the placements – and the only empty space was up against mine.

'Oh God, so sorry . . .' I gasped.

Mr Millington raised his eyebrows. 'Late,' he said.

'I know, sir. Ah . . . I so didn't mean to be.'

'We never do, do we? But in the world of work, Vicky – and that's what we're dealing with today – professional work . . . "late" is a four-letter word.'

'But is there anything left?' I said. I was still panting. 'Have you saved something? The newspaper?'

'No. I assumed you weren't interested, Vicky.'

'But I am! You know I am.'

'Because you can always stay at school, and help out with the juniors—'

'I don't want to. I want to take part!'

'Then I just wish you'd organize yourself. Look at the state of you . . .' He stood up slowly, and walked to his desk. 'I don't think there's much in the folder now,' he said. 'I certainly didn't hold anything back, and we're rather scraping the barrel, to be honest.'

I noticed the details then. The grid revealed them in

heartless black and white, and the job I'd wanted most had gone to the twins, Polly and Molly Tuttle. They sat side by side, looking identically pleased with themselves, whilst 'Trainee Librarian' – my second choice – had been given to an illiterate called David who didn't like books, except to dismember. The only other position I'd been remotely interested in was 'Assistant Bookbinder', and that had gone to a little boy called Lewis, who had once been caught in a cupboard, sniffing glue. He was trembling with excitement.

'She could do drains,' said a boy to my left.

'Oh no,' I said.

'They wanted two people, sir – didn't they? She could be with me!'

It was Spud Cropper who'd spoken, and he winked and grinned. His entire family worked in the Water and Sewerage industry, and I'm afraid I shuddered at the thought of being stuck with him. Spud was friendless, and he had the worst haircut in the class – a sort of clumpy wig that suggested his mum's nail scissors. I know it shouldn't matter, but it did – everyone avoided him. I could see his name up there on the list: he'd landed 'Drain Engineer #1'.

Under him I saw Eldon, Eleanor Louise. She wanted to be a vet, and had been awarded 'Dog Walker', which was close enough. When I glanced over at her she was smiling happily, colouring in her envelope with a pink highlighter. Ben Gallagher had 'Computer Programmer', which wasn't surprising as he lived for technology. In fact, the whole class seemed remarkably content.

I was the only one unplaced.

'I'll take anything,' I said. 'Except drains.'

'Will you?' said Mr Millington. 'Good.' He picked up the remaining envelopes, and opened the first. 'There's a Trainee Turnip Checker, out at Hailstone Farm – bit of a drive, and – oh . . . they want a boy.'

'What else?' I said.

'Laundry Assistant – must like washing. That's not one of your passions, is it, Vicky? So the last one . . . this only came in yesterday, in actual fact – some kind of emergency. It's in the catering industry. What do you know about food?'

'I eat it,' I said.

'But are you familiar with its preparation?'

'No, sir.'

'Then this is the one for you – you might find your level here. It's "Assistant Sandwich Maker", Lockson and Lockson. That's a company just out of town, and they need an extra pair of hands in the kitchen. "Overall supplied, and full training given".' He looked at me. 'Eight o'clock start, though. Do you think you can drag yourself out of bed for that?'

'Yes, Mr Millington,' I said. 'I know I can.'

He smiled then, but it was a smile of triumph. Mr Millington was one of those teachers who liked to crush enthusiasm, and he could see that I'd been broken. He knew I'd wanted the journalism job because I'd brought in a special note from my dad, which I'd had to bribe and bully the poor thing to write.

I took my envelope, and I heard someone snigger. Once again everyone was looking at me, and all I wanted to do was get away to the toilets and cry with disappointment. Sandwiches, I thought – for three days of butter-spreading boredom, all because of a beaten-up moped jamming at the wrong place at the wrong time. When the hooter sounded, I was first out into the corridor.

# Vicky

## 12.25
## Girls' toilets

I ran the cold tap and washed my face. The loo door crashed open, and I knew at once who'd followed me.

'Oh, Vee,' said the voice. 'Vee . . . I am so, so sorry. Oh, my love . . . poor you.'

'Hi, Katkat,' I said, and I felt thin arms round my shoulders. I turned into the hug, and scented expensive perfume.

A stick-insect body pressed against mine. 'Oh, I hate him! Mr Millington is so cruel,' she said. 'I just can't believe what he's given you.'

'Well, it was my fault, wasn't it?'

'No! You're sensitive!'

'Not really—'

'Nobody else would go near the sandwich one – you should have stood up to him! I would have supported you, you know I would. You've got to be more assertive!'

She blinked, and a tear bulged prettily from her eyelashes, onto a dark, chiselled cheekbone.

'You're going to be stuck in some kitchen!' she cried. Her voice was trembling. 'Oh God, what's that going to do to your skin? – it's already pale! Your hair too – and look at your shoulders, you're going to be ground down, like a servant . . .'

'Katkat, it'll be over by Saturday.'

'You see? – you're so positive!'

'But who cares, really, in the end?' I said. 'You're the beauty queen, and you've got something really special.'

'That's not even true,' she said. 'And *I* care. I want to help you!'

'You can't, Katkat. Think about your own life – are you ready for stardom?'

'Stardom?' she said, smiling. Her face lit up as she remembered her own placement. 'I don't think so.'

'But it's such an opportunity.'

'I've been lucky, Vee – that's all. And I don't want to talk about me, anyway! You know Edgar's got Fitness Instructor, at the gym?'

'That's no surprise,' I said.

'Well, he does work out. And, Leela, did you see what she's been given? Some smartyboots thing – some doctor or dentist?'

'She wanted a surgeon . . .'

'Yuk! Why?'

'It's good. Katkat – she loves all that. Did Damien get the Fire Service?'

'I think so. Have you noticed his spots lately? – worse than Spud's. I'd say it's leprosy, Vee – I hope no one has to call him in an emergency. Oh, lord – I can't wait till it starts. They're sending a car for me!'

'Who are?'

'I don't know – his people, I imagine.'

'So it's definitely happening? I hoped it would.'

Katkat smiled again. I saw her push a lock of hair behind her ear, and she twirled in front of the mirror. 'Don't tell anyone, all right?' she said. 'But they phoned me up last night, with final instructions. So . . . who knows?'

'You're off to his house?'

She nodded, and clapped her hands. 'I still can't believe it! Dad pulled the strings, Vicky – the school did nothing. But they have to come get me, because of all the security issues. I bet I won't see him, though – not the man himself . . . I'll probably end up in some office out back, doing nothing!' She laughed, and her eyes filled with tears again. 'It'll probably be as awful as sandwich-making, in the end. They'll kick me straight out when they see how dumb I am. Oh, Vicky, maybe we should swap placements! Except you can't really sing, can you? Or dance . . .'

'I'll be fine, Katkat.'

'You could try, though. We should definitely keep in touch!'

I'd better reveal it now, and get it over with.

Katkat Madamba was spending her three days with a ridiculously famous rock star as he prepared for the concert of the century. We'd found out weeks ago, but she'd sworn us to secrecy. How had she managed it? Well, it was all contacts and favours, of course. Her father was a record producer and her mum was in the modelling business. Strings had been pulled, and deals had been done. Katkat, bless her, would be there with the band, making tea at the final rehearsals.

We can't use the star's real name, by the way (for legal reasons) – but you'll know who he is, because his music is everywhere. He's probably the most well-known rock icon of our age, and he's won more awards than you can count, while making more money than he can ever hope to spend. He was the one who organized those giant festivals to end war and inequality. In recent years, however, he'd become a virtual recluse, so how he'd been persuaded to do this particular gig was a total mystery.

He'd agreed to headline 'Africa's Weeping!', which was a huge fund-raiser for poor, sick children in need of help. It had sold out within ninety seconds of ticket release, but he'd refused to do a second night. This would be a one-off special, and you now know who I'm talking about, I'm sure – we'll call him 'Snowy'* – which is the name his intimate friends use because of that famous mane of silver hair.

I should add, by the way, that Katkat is an amazing musician herself – that's only fair. She plays bass guitar in the school's best rock band (boys only, apart from her) and she's had singing lessons since she was about five. Anyone can see that she's destined for fame, and the thing that used to amaze me sometimes was how she'd landed in our ordinary little school. She'd only been with us for a few months, and had often been off sick with dietary problems and anxiety. She hadn't found it easy to fit in.

She looked in the mirror again. 'I won't be allowed near . . . the maestro,' she said. 'Nobody is.'

'I'm sure you will, Katkat,' I said.

'No way.'

'But he loves everyone, doesn't he?'

---

* There are several Snowy biographies, if you want to dig deeper. We can recommend two: *Life At the Top: Let's Tell the Truth*. This one is authorized, so it's great for facts and discographies. The second is called *Is He A God?* – it's a no-holds-barred exploration of Snowy's spiritual journey, and it discusses his life-changing time amongst the animist cults of the Congo.

His own website is a great place to start too – but it may give some of this story away, so don't look at it yet . . .

She shook her head. 'You know the old story. He doesn't let people close any more. He lays a silk circle out, right around him, and you can't step into it unless he personally invites you – he's very superstitious.'

'That's just gossip,' I said.

'It's not!'

'I bet he takes to you. You'll end up best friends.'

She clasped my hands again, and I noticed how thin they were. 'Oh, Vee,' she said. 'You're so encouraging, you know? Let's be buddies, OK? Let's support each other – you need support, you poor thing. You're so alone, what with your poor old dad and . . . that awful boy. What's his name?'

'Stagger.'

'Stagger.' She laughed, and kissed me again. 'I don't know how you cope with your life . . . I couldn't.'

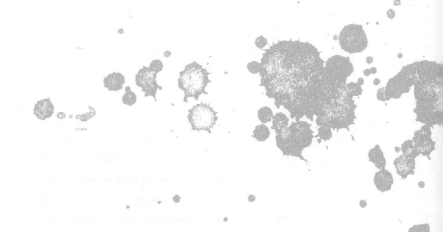

# WEDNESDAY

# Vicky

## 07.02
## Lockson & Lockson kitchens

I will hand over to the others, soon, but it was my placement that caused the first explosion, so I'll hold on for another chapter. When the big day came, I was up before the birds. I dealt with the pets so quickly they looked scared – but I didn't care because I was going to get to the sandwich place *ahead of schedule*.

We'd had a big fight about travel because no buses went in the right direction, and did we dare to use George? I said no, even though he was back on the road. Stagger said it was a risk worth taking, so after a lot of pointless wrangling I agreed. We'd just have to be extra careful. And, oh! – I should emphasize here that despite what Katkat said (and I'm sure she didn't want to be mean), Stagger was the most reliable, trustworthy person in my life, ever since I'd found him, penniless and bleeding, in a car park. I'd just come from the bottle bank, and he was sitting on a bollard having been mugged. I didn't believe his story at first, but I soon learned something important: Stagger doesn't lie.

He's brave too – as you shall see.

Anyway, he had nowhere to go, and he looked so forlorn that Dad let him sleep in our basement, curled up by the washing machine. One night led to a fortnight, and . . . well, he just never moved out. People assume he's my older brother, and I suppose he's become one.

Now we'd had time to do a bit of research, and I was feeling far more positive about my role. It was only *menial sandwich technician* in *lowly, unglamorous kitchen*, but I'd discovered that the company – the Lockson Foundation – was a big, rich law firm. The website had been so full of swirling graphics that it ended up freezing our computer – which is antique. However, I'd got a glimpse of state-of-the-art offices, with teams of serious-looking lawyers. They stared from the screen, lean-jawed and powerful, and it was pretty obvious that whatever sandwiches I made would end up between their perfectly even, pearly-white teeth. This, surely, would mean interesting conversation! – lawyers were educated, literate people who wrote reports and speeches.

What if one of them got stuck for an idea just as I was serving him – or her – lunch? What if some senior partner with failing eyesight wanted a document read aloud? I might end up sitting with him, drafting the response. I'd talked it through with Stagger and we'd agreed: opportunities come to those who are prepared! That was why I set off early, determined to prove Mr Millington wrong about my time-keeping.

When I finally dared to put my head up, I actually gasped. It was like we'd ridden straight into a science-fiction movie: the Lockson building was a great glass rocket, ready for take-off. It was wrapped in strands of steel, rising at least a dozen storeys to a sharp blue snout, and there was a yellow Porsche in the car park. Just beyond that was a waterfall flowing over huge bronze capitals that spelled out the company name.

'Oh, lord . . .' I said.

'What?' said Stagger. 'Don't be intimidated.'

'I'm not. It's wonderful!'

The whole place gleamed with wealth and power, and I would have marched straight up to the revolving door if Stagger hadn't grabbed my arm.

'Look, Vee,' he said. 'Calm down.'

'I'm calm!'

'You're not. And you're in the kitchens, all right? So don't get excited.'

'But it's beautiful, Stagger! Look at it . . .'

'I don't think that's even your entrance. You want the side door. Over there.'

He turned me round and pointed to a small sign.

# KITCHENS →

The arrow pointed me through a hedge, to a cluster of overflowing dustbins. Locating the bell, I pressed it long and hard. Minutes later there was a cranking and squealing, and a shutter rose slowly to reveal a pair of feet. An overall appeared, made of sensible, washable nylon, and at last I found myself looking into the eyes of an old lady, too breathless to speak.

I held up my letter of introduction. 'Are you Mrs Meakin?' I said.

She nodded.

'I'm Vicky,' I said. 'I'm not trained or experienced – but I'm ready to learn.'

# Edgar

## 08.03
## Fitness-Forever! gym

I'm not saying I had any particularly high expectations of any of this, ever, or that I got all caught up in the 'aren't we lucky missing school?' kind of crap, because let's face it, if you want to miss school you don't need someone to tell you can do it, you just do it – but I got signed up to the F-F! gymnasium (me having been stupid enough to say that's the kind of thing I was interested in) – and 'Fitness-Forever!' is a swish new place they just opened, right by a load of fast-food outlets where you stuff your face and screw up your arteries, and then feel guilty about it.

Three girls on Reception.

'Who?' says one, after I'd given my name.

'Ed-gar,' I say, nice and slow.

'Edgar who, love?' says the next. 'What do you want?'

So I showed them my little bit of paper, which had been at the bottom of my pants for about a week, and

I unfolded it under their uninterested noses, smoothing it out and getting the fluff off . . .

'Work experience,' I say. 'I'm with you till Saturday.'

'Oh, I don't think so!' says the first one, looking all panicky.

'You were expecting me, weren't you?'

'Were we?'

'No—'

'I wasn't . . .'

'Oh, dear,' I said, trying to be nice. 'Never mind – I can help out with the training, and I'm OK with presses and weights—'

'Oh no, no!' they all cry. 'Oh God, no – you can't work out front! – health and safety wouldn't allow that.'

'We're not licensed for minors,' says the third. 'Maybe . . . Wait. Could he move the new brochure boxes?'

'Yeah,' says the second. 'Out back, in the annexe?'

'That would be best,' says the first. 'He could sort out the storage shed . . .'


What a wonderful start, Mr Millington – God bless you, sir – moving big boxes off pallets onto shelves, to make way for boxes full of smaller boxes before I break up all the empty boxes and put them in the skip. If I'm good, I get to do the same thing tomorrow too, and who knows? – Friday as well. How ace is that? How fine is my life?

Love from Edgar xxx

# Leela

## 08.30
## East Dean hospital

All I knew was that I had three days with a consultant surgeon: Mr Ahsan. The nurse who signed me in seemed anxious, and she had a card in her hand. I could see spidery writing.

'Do you know him?' she said.

'Not at all.'

'Oh.'

She paused. 'You wrote to him, didn't you? – is he a friend of the family?'

'No,' I said. 'I've never spoken to him.'

The receptionist looked up. 'Who's she with? Mr Ahsan?'

'Yes.'

'Are you serious? Can I see what he's said?'

She took the card, and we all read it together:

*Leela Bhatnagar will be under my personal supervision: please complete all formalities in my name, forwarding access and legal agreements for my personal attention. Permissions and ~~exemptions~~ exemptions will be approved by me – any queries directed to me. L2–6 for 09.00.*

*Thank you.*
*Ahsan*

The receptionist said, 'That's theatre. Are you comfortable with that?'

'With what?' I said.

'How old are you?'

'Thirteen. What's wrong?'

'Nothing. No – he's the best. Just a little . . . unusual.'

# Eleanor

## 08.34
## The park


I got three to start with, just to see if I could cope. There was Brash, who was a dachshund (used to strangers and other dogs, but lacking in confidence). Tommo was a cross between a german shepherd and a border collie, with the collie definitely dominant – also used to other dogs, but scared of horses and lawnmowers. Shogun was a long-haired spaniel, who everyone said was a bit of a challenge, but good as gold once he trusted you – and his main problem (like with so many dogs) was that all his life he'd received contradictory information and mixed messages, to the point where he didn't know what he wanted himself. Brash, Tommo and Shogun: I made index cards for each one so I could record my observations, and got a nice photo too, on my brand-new digital camera. I printed the pictures out small and cut them out so as to stick on their files, which my mum helped me arrange alphabetically.

We set off together, me and the dogs. Short leashes – total control.

# Michael

## 08.56
## Brisley Control Centre

My name is Michael Blake and I have always loved police cars, ambulances and fire engines, and not just because of the lights and sirens. It is the thought that they are rushing to help someone and it might be life or death. All day and all night, whatever the weather . . . 999 is what you call, and you know that from then on someone is dedicated to saving your life.

It will be a calm voice that answers, and you will trust it.

*'What service do you require, please? What is your location?'*

You will tell them, and wait – and in the end you will be OK.

That was the place I was standing outside: the Emergency Vehicle Call and Control Centre. I'd done a dummy run with my dad the previous Sunday, to make sure we'd be on time, and the only thing they'd said to physically bring was ID – so I had my passport and cycling certificate. I'm not going to say I was nervous because that doesn't do justice to how I felt. I was so scared my throat wouldn't work – I'd been sick that morning, in fact, but hadn't told anyone. And it was like someone had spent the night filling my neck up with sand because I could hardly talk – just this awful little squeak, which made me sound like I was seven.

I wasn't in school uniform either, but wearing this suit I'd been bought for a wedding last year, which was so tight I could hardly move my arms. But we got out the car, and there's a great big set of steps, so somehow I got up them, and Dad shook my hand at the top as I rang the bell. I wanted to say, 'You'll stay for a bit, won't you, Dad? – you will wait?' but this woman appeared, in a suit just like mine, and she was holding a clipboard.

'Are you Michael?' she said, and I couldn't even squeak.

They had a copy of my letter, which they checked against the documents I'd brought . . . and then suddenly she scanned in a pass, and these internal barriers slid back, and I was Suddenly inside, and the doors closed behind me, so when I turned round Dad wasn't there any more – he'd just SUDDENLY gone and I was in a long corridor leading to a huge flight of stairs, which we went down and down to some big, grey basement, which is where it all happens – where the phone systems are, so that's when

I started to hear the buzzing and bleeping and the sound of whispering voices . . . and there I was, at the heart of the whole machine and it wasn't even 9.05.

This wasn't made up.

This wasn't my dream.

It was real.

# Vicky

## 10.08
Lockson & Lockson kitchen

Mrs Meakin was extremely patient.

She realized from the start that I was keen but clumsy, and held my hand quite as I explored a brand-new world of sandwich fillings. Time passed as we chatted, and we were doing the smoked salmon and cream cheese, all ready for a lunch-time feast. I'd was telling her about Dad and his problems when I saw her mouth open, and the colour drain from her face. Even her hands went white, and she was still as stone.

'Oh, lord,' she said. 'Vicky, dear – I've been distracted.'

'From what?'

'Coffee,' she said. She whispered it, and started to shake. 'They phoned down earlier – as you arrived! Oh, Vicky! – that was ages ago!'

'Who?' I said.

'She won't like this at all . . .'

'Who won't, Mrs Meakin?'

'Oh, she goes mad, Vicky! She's warned me before, as well—'

'Mrs Meakin, please,' I said. 'Sit down—'

'No!' she cried. 'I should have served it by now – she'll murder me!'

Even as the poor soul said it, a door flew open to reveal a tall, furious woman in green. I thought at first it was a shiny raincoat with matching wellies, so I assumed the weather must have changed. Then I realized her boots were actually dark snakeskin, and the coat was carefully tailored silk. A long throat emerged from a honey-coloured blouse, and the face immediately made me think of a tight, ivory tulip, all closed up with a little purple mouth. There was a roll of silver hair swished over to the right, and the eyes were actually bulging.

I knew at once who it was. We were in the presence of Helen Lockson (LLB, Hons, BCL, D.Phil, Oxon. MA.), and I recognized her from the home page of the Lockson website, where I'd seen her smiling out of the screen with horse-teeth. She wasn't smiling now: she was snarling.

'How dare you!' she hissed.

'I'm sorry, ma'am – honestly, I—'

'Do you realize what's at stake? – do you know how long we've been waiting? Sorry doesn't work today, Mrs Meakin, and I told you it wouldn't!'

'I know, ma'am, but I've had so much going on, and—'

'I've got the directors in!'

'I know, Mrs Lockson—'

'They're gasping for refreshments!' – she was almost shouting. 'Some of them haven't slept for twenty-four hours, and I have to leave the most important meeting of my life to come down here and beg for refreshments!'

'They're on their way! We'll bring them now!'

Mrs Meakin rushed across the kitchen floor. It seemed wrong that an old lady was running, but Mrs Lockson didn't mind. Her phone was ringing, and she was soon hissing into that as her boots clicked across the floor – I half expected to see sparks. Of course, I threw down my tools at once and went to assist, so that together Mrs Meakin and I manoeuvred a large trolley into the middle of the kitchen. We revolved it, as if for inspection: a drinks machine sat on the top shelf, bristling with dials, tubes and switches. Under it, there were a number of compartments for crockery, whilst on the level below that, in nice little wicker baskets, sat the selection of snacks I'd arranged earlier on doilies.

'Get it upstairs,' barked Mrs Lockson. 'We are exhausted . . .'

'Of course, ma'am. Vicky can help—'

'Do it!'

I was putting two and two together, and I must admit, I was excited. Clearly, a whole army of senior staff was hard at work above us, and their coffee break was long overdue. Even more clearly, I was being given my first opportunity to meet the professionals, and make an impression.

We hauled the trolley into a lift, and Mrs Lockson pressed 'eleven'. I was now close enough to smell her perfume, which reminded me of lilies, lavender and possibly bleach – it was a very strange combination, and there was perspiration underneath it too. She was firing off a text, the screen close to her nose, and she was trembling with rage. Then, just as we rose past floor seven, a new disaster struck . . . Mrs Meakin changed colour again, and closed her eyes. There were mirrors everywhere, and I watched helplessly as she gulped and fell backwards. I just managed to grab her arm, and she twisted round to lean on the hand-rail.

'Oh God!' cried Mrs Lockson. 'Not now, please!'

The old lady could hardly speak, and as the doors opened it was obvious she was about to faint. A man in a suit jumped forward to help, supporting her as I dragged the trolley out.

'Send her home!' cried Mrs Lockson. 'Deal with it, Martin!'

With that, the doors closed again, and I heard the lift plunge downwards. I found myself marooned in a long, glass corridor, and as I wondered what I should do and where I should go, a voice behind me said:

'Cappuccino, please.'

'What?' I said.

'We are desperate. You got any pastries, Angel?'

I gaped in terror. In that ten seconds of confusion, a crowd had gathered around me, cutting off my exit. Hopeful eyes looked into mine, but I was paralysed with indecision. After all, Mrs Meakin was sick – I couldn't abandon her. Nor had I been trained to use a complex coffee machine, so how could I satisfy weary executives just as they needed sustenance? On the other hand, Mrs Lockson had made it abundantly clear how urgent the situation was – she'd suggested the meeting was in crisis, so I couldn't walk away . . .

'Espresso for me,' said a woman. 'Hurry it up, though, sweetheart – there's a lot at stake today.'

Jerked to my senses, I picked up a cup. I put it under the snout of the machine, and I scanned the drinks menu. I noticed the encouraging wink of a green light, so I pressed the switch next to it. You can imagine my relief when the motor clicked and a grinder whirred into life. Best of all, there came the swoosh of hot water and a geyser of steam squirted vertically. Seconds later, we had an absolutely perfect cappuccino with a curl of froth on the top – and the whole corridor smelled of fresh coffee. From then on, I moved by instinct. I seized a plate, and found a cinnamon roll – I even folded a napkin next to it. The first man took the cup, and smiled at me. Without delay, I reached for a spoon and saucer.

'Wait!' said a voice.

I froze at once.

'What are you doing out here?'

'Nothing, Mrs Lockson,' I said.

She was staring at me, as if I had a skin infection. Her nose came close to mine. 'Get to the boardroom,' she hissed. 'And look at the state of you! – you can't wear that wretched overall! Get it off, and get moving.'

It was a hideous garment. It came to my ankles, and was the kind of thing you could hose down after use, so I was more than happy to remove it. Fortunately I was wearing a very serviceable school uniform underneath: white short-sleeved shirt over a grey skirt, my hair tied back, no jewellery. My blazer was down in the kitchen, but I was smart enough without it. I was ready for action, determined to serve.

'Don't, for God's sake, scald anybody,' she said.

'I won't,' I said. 'I'm here to help.'

'The last thing we need is extra stress, so take it through and see what people want.'

'Yes, Mrs Lockson, and if you need a document read, or–'

'Go!'

# Vicky

## 10.35
## Lockson & Lockson boardroom

I was totally in charge.

I turned the trolley round, and rolled it carefully forward. We were high above the city, and blue spotlights gave everything a cool, science-fiction glow. I could see rooftops spread out in a great, sunlit curve, but this was no time for admiring scenery; Mrs Lockson's heels clicked ahead of me, and I was ushered through heavy doors into a room packed with yet more executives. There was a splinter of rock down the centre, which served as the table, and it was covered in bottles, folders, laptops, pens and papers. Televisions hung from above, and most people were gazing up at the largest, which was filled by a giant pair of eyes.

'Gerald!' said Mrs Lockson. 'We can't hear you – hold on!'

The eyes blinked, and a voice boomed from hidden speakers, filling the room. '. . . and what time is it there?'

'Wait, please!'

There was a burst of static, and the screen turned to zigzags of lips and nose. They were flipped upside down, and the whole face retreated so we saw a sweaty brow and an unshaven chin.

'Hello? – we've lost track, Helen, but– Can you hear me?'

'Yes, Gerald – go on!'

'We've been working through the night, OK? – same as you. If I look half-dead, it's because I am.'

'How's Chicago?' said a man to my left.

'They're still waiting,' boomed Gerald's face. 'It's Chicago's call – that's what Andy's saying.'

'Andy said that?'

'He's spoken to Bob.'

'Where's Erwin?'

'With Stella.'

'And Joe's on record, so–'

'They're saying their prayers, guys! – all of them. The Africa gig's on Saturday, and the kid . . .'

The eyes blinked again. 'The kid's a risk, still,' said the voice. 'Whether or not it's deniable–'

'He's on his way out,' said someone. 'Last stages.'

'There's people saying we wait six months, though, and–'

There was a storm of protest, and I found myself cringing at the noise. A woman waved her papers angrily, shouting across the table – and that's when I used my initiative. Clearly, nobody could come to the trolley – and yet everyone needed refreshment. I went very quietly to a little bald man, who seemed sunk in misery. 'Would you like a drink, sir?' I said quietly.

'What?' He turned to look at me. 'Oh, wow. Gee. Black coffee, please, honey – strong.'

'Anything to eat?'

'Oh, no!'

He was distracted then, by a buzzing. A technician was fiddling with cables, and a second screen was coming to life at the far end of the room. I moved back to my machine, and pressed the magic button. The grinding was loud, but everyone was far too busy to notice. In fact, the arguments were getting louder, and most people were on their feet. I served the black coffee, and my main worry then was that the man might move his arm and knock it over.

'Anything else you need, sir?' I said.

'No!' he cried. 'The drink is fine!'

'What?'

He shook his head, and I realized he was talking into a mobile, and hadn't even noticed me. I was about to repeat my question, when a thin woman behind me touched my shoulder.

'Tea,' she said. 'Earl Grey, please.'

I nodded, and went for the tea bags.

'Some kind of biscuit?' she said, and I nodded again. It was a problem, however, because there were chocolate digestives, and plainer home-made cookies. I was about to list her options when I noticed that something strange was happening. Everyone was moving, and Mrs Lockson was trying to get control, but failing. I heard someone shout, 'Oh God! – it's coming through!' – and then my machine was nudged to the side, and a tray of snacks fell to the ground. I found myself surrounded, and pushed, so that I ended up in front of the projection screen, unable to retreat. A man was babbling into a mobile, gazing down at us, and his voice was amplified in a squeal of feedback.

'Yes!' he shrieked. 'It's a yes!'

He was waving a bottle.

'What d'you mean?' said someone. 'How's it yes?'

'It's yes!'

'No! Yes to what—?'

'Chicago's a yes, Helen!' cried the man. 'It's yes to the settlement, yes to the plan. The kid's squared and safe, tied up for ever! – he's out of the picture now. Can you hear me?'

'I don't believe it—' said someone.

'God, they're brave! Is he sure?'

'Those are the facts, guys,' said the man. He was wiping his eyes. 'You've got a job to do now – we all have. We've got to make it work, because we go with the product, full-on confidence: go! Stay with the gig, no deviations.'

'Chicago says go?' said Mrs Lockson, and I realized a hush had fallen. Everyone was looking at her. 'Andy, are you serious?'

'I am serious, people,' said Andy – and he held up the bottle, even higher. We all gazed at the label:

# LIQUIDATOR

I wondered why he was showing it to us, and why the room was so hushed and excited. 'What we have,' he said, slowly, 'is a totally safe product. It's always been safe, and OK, we've had a scare – but that's our business! Confidence is restored.'

'And the kid? The boy–?'

'Settled. Silent. Out of the picture.'

'Did you get that, Helen?'

'This is a beautiful drink, guys. Everyone knows it.'

The meeting room was totally silent. The man on the screen was beaming, and I saw tears in his eyes. The bottle he'd been holding was open now, and he let the liquid foam over his fingers. He raised it high, then took a long gulp, and when I turned to Mrs Lockson she had her hands over her mouth.

The man wiped his lips. 'I want to see you smile, Helen,' he said. 'We're behind you, girl, but . . . wow. Close shave . . .'

Mrs Lockson grinned. Then she seemed to retch, but I realized she was laughing. The laughter spread, and turned to applause and cheering. I was surrounded by handshakes, hugs and high-fives, and it took me a full minute to get back to the trolley.

I stood there, cup in hand, ready to serve.

'Andy?' said Mrs Lockson, at last. 'Gerald? – shhh! I am . . . delighted. This is too wonderful! Now, listen, everybody – please! Don't you think it's lunch time? Have we earned a break?'

'We've earned a party,' said someone. 'Where's the champagne?'

'Where's the brandy? I need a bottle . . .'

I smiled happily. I thought of all the sandwiches I'd made, ready and waiting, and I wondered if I should zip down in the lift and get them.

'Excuse me,' I said. 'Shall I –'

'Lunch is on me,' said Mrs Lockson. 'Meet in the lobby – this is a celebration . . .'

With that, they left the building.

It was like a fire drill. They abandoned their coffee cups, and streamed out to the elevators. Seconds later, the top floor was deserted.

'The sandwiches?' I said.

Mrs Lockson stared at me. 'What?'

LIQUIDATOR

'The sandwiches. There's loads, all ready – don't you want them?'

'No.'

'But we made them specially. It's what I was here for – that was my job, Mrs Lockson.'

She walked to the end of the room, and picked up her laptop. 'Are you literate?' she asked.

'Literate?'

'Can you read and write, child? Can you use a telephone?'

'Of course, Mrs Lockson. But I'm just saying, all that food, downstairs . . . Who's going to eat it?'

'Shut up, Vicky.'

'Pardon?'

'That's your name, isn't it? So sit down. Shut up. And listen. I need someone here, do you understand me? – a human being who can answer the phone, and take messages. Can you manage that?'

I nodded. 'Yes, Mrs Lockson.'

'Good. You've been promoted then, haven't you?'

She put a telephone beside me, and laid a pad and a pencil beside that. Then she set the laptop down, just to my right, and tapped out an email. I watched her fire it off. That's when she pushed it towards me, and smiled.

I'm going cold as I write that last sentence, but that's what she did: she pushed it towards me, and smiled . . . The laptop started to chug – and we stood there, looking at it. Neither one of us saw the future – how could we? How could we predict the disaster that was hurtling towards us, meteor-like? But looking back, that was the second crucial moment, the first being the blocked fuel pipe. Helen Lockson put me in a chair in the boardroom, while she went out to lunch. She left me all alone with technology.

I remember the phone display: 11.41 a.m.

I remember the whisper of the lift as it descended, and that strange isolation as I gazed at the mess. There were cans and bottles everywhere and for the first time I wondered why.

# Polly & Molly

## 08.58
## The *Gazette*

What surprised us was that despite a fairly detailed phone conversation, we didn't receive any documentation – and I (Molly) had made the call to request it as soon as the placement was confirmed. I'd got straight through to the editor, whose name was Mr Bickersdyke, and asked what our brief as journalists was likely to be. We have to know our schedule, you see – partly because we train three times a week at a gymnastics club, so we can't afford to waste time.

'Is there work for us to do?' I said.

He laughed. 'Oh, yes,' he said. 'The *Gazette*'s a very busy paper, and we always need new blood.'

'So what's our position?' I said – this being Polly. 'Exactly.'

'Assistant editor.' He laughed again. 'I mean, joint assistants, as there's – ha! – two of you.'

'And there's a job description?'

'No.'

'Oh.'

'I can soon write one, though. I'll knock one out today, and put it in the post. Trust me.'

But he didn't, so from that moment we rather wondered if we could.

What were our first impressions that Wednesday morning? For a start, the nine o'clock meeting we'd anticipated became nine forty-eight, as we sat waiting on the doorstep. Mr Bickersdyke was the only one with keys, and he got to the office late, having stopped en route for coffee: one of his 'little routines', he said. He picked up the mail, most of which was junk, and he then abandoned it on a long table in a damp, dark hall. By the time we'd climbed three flights of stairs to the so-called 'newsdesk', Molly was wanting to leave, and I (Polly) knew I'd have to work hard to keep her on side.

I did want to leave (this is Molly) but my sister always believes we can make things better, which together – (this is both of us) – we usually can. So, when she (Polly) said, 'Mr Bickersdyke?' and he turned round and looked at us, I knew just what she was going to ask for because I'd noticed it too.

'There's only one chair,' I said.

It was a large room, but very empty.

'Well. Yes,' he said. 'I've only ever needed one.' Then

for some reason he started laughing again. 'It's a one-man band, really . . . runs itself.'

'But there's three of us,' we replied.

'True.'

'And we're keen to get started.'

'Of course,' he said. 'Let's see if we can find some furniture.'

What we needed were proper workstations. That meant going all the way down to the basement, and sorting through the rubbish. We found a table wedged between old shelving units, and spent the next hour cleaning it. We then had to organize phone extensions, ID badges, desk lamps and all the basic stationery. Once that was done, we wanted to discuss: (a) the paper's layout; and (b) the actual content. The *Gazette* published every Saturday, so the deadlines were hurtling towards us already. Mr Bickersdyke, sadly, seemed in no hurry to discuss anything. He claimed that 'it ticks along, girls! – leave it be . . .' We found this claim/instruction rather surprising, and told him we'd found recent editions top-heavy with badly laid-out advertising. The headlines, we said, were weary and predictable, and there was a noticeable absence of up-to-the-minute news: there was nothing topical and nothing stimulating. We suggested that the three of us worked through lunch, together, to devise an action plan for the transformation of the paper.

Mr Bickersdyke left the room, looking unwell. I said: 'Polly?'

'No,' she said. 'Let's just wait.'

I said, 'Have we upset him?'

And she nodded, because we knew he was offended.

That afternoon he went home early, and we had the office to ourselves. We cancelled our class, and worked hard. By midnight we had a number of different front-page options, all of which we printed and pinned round the walls ready for a proper news conference in the morning.

We genuinely thought he'd be delighted, and that he wanted new ideas.

# Vicky

## 11.43
## Lockson & Lockson boardroom

The first call came almost at once, and it went brilliantly. The voice was American, and I took the message. The caller seemed satisfied, and even hoped I'd have a nice day. As I put the receiver down, I suddenly remembered that I'd had my own phone turned off, as per Mr Millington's instructions.

Turning it on, I found three texts – two from Stagger, and one from my official 'buddy': Spud Cropper.

The Spud one said:

> You should have done drains!! Call me!!!

– so I deleted it.

Stagger's first said:

> R U ok?

and the second one said,

> Want some pizza?

I texted him back to say,

> How's George?

> George ok no probs,

he replied.

I texted again, and couldn't resist it:

> I am in the boardroom MASSIVE promotion on first morning!!!

I would have gone on, but the Lockson line rang again, and this time it was someone a little more impatient. She explained how urgent something was, but when I asked for her number, she tutted, and hung up. The next caller was Mrs Lockson, checking I was awake and alert, and then there was a period of silence when I did nothing at all.

It was then that I noticed the bottles again, and began to feel thirsty. It occurred to me, suddenly, that I'd been serving drinks, without drinking anything myself – and, as I said, I was surrounded by refreshments. Cans and bottles, bottles and cans . . . they stood there, on the table, glowing in the spot lights.

# LIQUIDATOR

Why had the company bought so much of it? I could see every single flavour.

The logo and slogans were etched in my mind, because the product had only just hit the market. Wherever you went you saw the posters: they yelled at you from hoardings and rolled by on buses. If you watched the television, the ads were burned onto your retinas, and there were jingles on the radio morning, noon and night. We all drank it at school because it was genuinely tasty, and its buzz lifted you right up on to your toes. My mouth was dry, and my fingers tingling. Every flavour was available – for free! – so how could I choose? I sat there, racked with indecision, and that's when the laptop beside me gave an urgent, plaintive bleep.

I turned and lifted the lid.

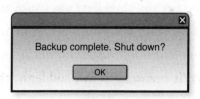

Backup complete. Shut down?

OK

I wondered what to do. It seemed silly to waste Mrs Lockson's battery, but on the other hand I had been told not to touch anything. I decided to follow instructions, and leave it well alone. The priority, after all, was the drink-dilemma.

# Michael

## 11.55
## Brisley Control Centre


A is for Alpha.
B is for Bravo.
C is for Charlie.

That is the NATO phonetic alphabet, and it is there to help us. It goes on like that right up to X-ray, Yankee, Zebra – twenty-six letters, and it's not easy to learn, but my goodness you have to know it, to avoid misunderstandings in critical situations. This is Michael Blake again, and I should have said that I'd been practising it for weeks – they'd told me I'd need to know the whole thing backwards and forwards, fast, and now I know why. You just imagine: if you were a police officer, chasing a getaway car, for example, and needed to radio in the number plate:

'FG23!' you'd say.

'Pardon?' says the controller. 'Did you say F or S? – I didn't hear that, over.'

'F!' shouts the officer. 'Over!'

The controller's nervous now – because nobody likes making mistakes in high-pressure situations. 'What?' he (or she) says. 'Sorry, but "S" for Sugar? Or—'

'No!' screams the officer, who's now getting angry, because the car's getting away and he needs emergency backup right then and there. He needs to scramble a unit, life or death – and time's ticking . . . 'Eff for Freddie!' he says. 'Have you got that? Then it's a "G" for . . . oh God, hurry up, come on! – he's gone, dammit . . . I lost him. Shit.'

That was how it was all explained to me, including the swear word. They'd taken me straight to an examination room. They gave me the sheets, and a book to write in, and a person came in to test me – faster and faster, building up my confidence so that by late morning I had it, even if it wasn't instinctive. That's when a man said, 'I think he's ready.'

'Are you ready, Michael?' asked another.

'What for?' I said.

'You know what for . . .'

I was still having vocal problems. I could hardly breathe, let alone speak, but I followed them out through door after door and then suddenly there I was: the restricted zone. It was a totally circular bombproof bunker, with floor-to-ceiling wraparound screens that showed a constantly moving matrix of road maps, grids and flashing numerals.

There were fifteen operators, all in rotating chairs, and I watched them whispering into their headsets, touching keys.

Lights blinked in a hundred places, and thankfully someone came with a glass of water or I might have just keeled over and caused an emergency of my own. I said a prayer to myself then – and I remember the words:

'Dear God,' I said. 'Thank you for my family and for everything I have, and forgive me for always wanting more – but this is a one-off opportunity, and all I want today, please, is for these people to let me sit in one of those hydraulic chairs. Let me, please, at some point in the future get a headset of my own, and just hear one of those calls. I will never sin again if you allow me this. Amen.'

Well, some people are atheist, I know.

I find that impossible to understand because even as I sent the prayer the man behind me said, 'Michael? Do you think you're ready to start work?' I remember the time exactly, because it was there on the screen: 11.59. I couldn't even squeak. I tried to say yes, but all I could do was nod.

He helped me up, though, and I think I floated down the steps. There was one chair vacant, and they held it as I climbed up and turned myself round. Then I sat, thinking, Am I in heaven? Have I died and ascended? And that's when I felt something touch my ears.

'Would you like to wear these?' said a voice. 'Would you like to hear a call?'

# Ben

## Morning
## Stems & Petals

Rip-off, hoax, swindle or just plain 'misunderstanding' – call it what you will, the old woman was lucky I didn't do something BOTH OF US would have regretted because I signed up to create a new database: that's what I'd been asked to do, and it was a contract signed by us all. That's what my letter said! So I'd gone to the trouble of working out what they needed before I even got there, and downloading the best possible program (which was restricted, by the way – I had to cut through all kinds of permissions to even get at it – because it's state-of-the-art, unlicensed gold dust, amalgamating so many best features while taking up so little memory), and I'd been looking forward to three days of tuning it up and making it work – that was what I signed up for! What did I find, when I actually got there?

The 'garden centre' was a flower shop.

A tiny, dusty, backwater of a crabby, crappy flower shop

with an undertakers on one side and a dodgy little sex shop on the other.

'I'm here to help with the database,' I said.

And what did the old bat show me? What was the 'equipment' she had?

They owned – this is not a joke – a Pentel System 302, which is 1990s. Before I was born. A retarded antique – like the actual woman who ran the shop, in fact: Mrs Robinson, who smiles at me and says, 'Oh no, dearie – we don't want to update anything. It's fine for what we do!' They didn't want to spend money, you see, and as for learning anything new, well, that wasn't going to happen. She said, 'Most of the time we just use pencil and paper. We don't turn the thing on very often . . .'

'So why am I here?' I said.

'Well!' she said – and she grinned at me like I was about five, and was in for a special treat. 'Do you like roses? Do you? Because I can see you making us a nice table decoration. Would you like that, Benji?'

That's what she called me. That's what she suggested – I swear it. And I stood there, unable to speak. I just gaped, and before I knew it she'd got her wrinkly old witch-like hand up and pinched me, right on the cheek. I was so stunned I actually let her touch me . . .

# Katkat

## 11.11
## To the stars!

The car arrived, soon after ten.

It was a gorgeous long black Merc with tinted windows so you couldn't see in, and from the look of it totally bulletproof – I had to assume it was one of the 'Snowy' fleet, built to protect him, as he has to be so super-careful now. Out we shot, way out of town, to his huge great estate, which as you probably know is called 'Yasgar's' but there are absolutely no signs to it, being as it's top secret – people have to know where they're going or they never ever get there.

We turned into the drive, past loads of little tents and even a wigwam where the fans camp – I could see them all gazing at us, wondering who we were, and I'm afraid I stuck my tongue out (not that they could see me!) – but they all looked so moon-faced and hopeful. Then suddenly – *wham!* – we're up against these slow-moving gates, rolling in past video cameras to a gigantic anti-tank barrier, which sinks down into the ground and lets us drive up to the guardhouse, where all the paperwork's done.

High-security, or what?

My letter had a seal stamped onto it, so they took that, photographed me twice, and out of this printer popped the coolest little pass with a close-up of my eyes. It's retina-detection, so I said to the guard (joking): 'I'm glad I use make-up! Ha!' But he didn't even smile, just looked at me as we sped off into the trees.

And oh-my-God what a house it is!

It's a castle, really – a fairy-tale castle with turrets and towers, like Snowy's some knight in shining armour . . . and I half expected a drawbridge over a moat. He'd had the whole place torn down years ago, and shifted half a mile east. Now it sits looking at the lake, on the crossing-point of two long ley lines, which keep 'special energy' bubbling through his studio. I've read all the biographies, you see, so I can tell you everything about it – how it was once a spooky old abbey, full of what Snowy calls 'ancient, primitive spirits', and how he uses all that power stuff for his work.

So was I nervous? I was terrified.

Was I happy too? I couldn't stop smiling, that's for sure – and giggling even, and I was there on the back seat, clapping my hands with my bracelets jangling . . . How many people in the world would ever get to walk into the home of the great, great Snowy? - even if I didn't get to talk to him, they'd let me watch, surely . . .

Anyway, the car stopped by a terrace. We're between the most enormous pots of flowers, so you're breathing perfume, dazzled by the sunshine. There's a tinkling fountain too, and the driver stands there, and I smile and nod, wishing secretly that he'd parked a bit closer to the path because I'm wearing heels that aren't going to find the gravel too easy - but I take a careful step, breathing slow . . . ahhhhh . . . I am determined not to act like a fool. I'm thinking, Slow down, Katkat, you mustn't expect too much! - but who do you think's waiting for me on a little garden bench? Who do you think is there, ready to greet me, with a smile on his face bigger than mine? Who's in the snow-white kaftan with the famous saffron scarf piled around his shoulders and that long silver hair?

Snowy, himself! - in person.

Yes . . . with legs crossed, and a little glass of mint tea - just sitting like a completely normal human being with big Jun, his bodyguard (who's built like a truck, by the way, and has black belts in three different martial arts) - but, wow, Jun's smiling too! Gleaming teeth, and he comes to greet me first, taking both my hands in his.

'Katkat Madamba,' he says.

I can't even speak.

'I'm Jun.'

'I know . . .'

'I'll tell you the rules, baby.' He talks so softly, right in my ear, and all I can do is nod.

'No touching, ever,' he says. 'Keep your voice low, OK? – because the man don't like noise. Other than that, hey . . . just treat him like your grandad.'

How I didn't faint, I do not know. Jun stepped aside and the maestro rose up, and put his head on one side. He doesn't like to use up too much vocal power because 'all sound is music', he says, and it shouldn't ever be wasted. He just said: 'Hi,' in a voice that purred, soft and deep and calm, all gravelly and pure. 'Thanks for coming.'

Jun said, 'Band's ready, boss. Ready to go.'

Snowy nodded. 'Let's do it.'

'Let's start the day,' said Jun.

That's when we heard the most terrible, ear-splitting scream.

# Leela

## 09.00
## East Dean hospital

I was taken to theatre.

All I could see were eyes, between caps and masks, because once you're scrubbed-up and ready almost everyone looks identical. Mr Ahsan was waiting for me, and you can't mistake him – partly because he's small and hunched, and partly because his eyes glitter when they look at you. They seem brighter than the lights above, and everyone was watching him. He took my arm and brought me forward, so that I was right beside the patient, who was already anaesthetized, of course – there on the table. I could hardly tell which way up it was at first, for everything is draped in cloth except the surgical zone, which in this case was a man's chest – a spread of pale flesh, rising and falling, with a line drawn across it in green ink.

A green line, bisecting the ribcage.

'Leela,' he said. 'Meet Mr Gower. He's seventy-two

years old. Cardiovascular complications, thoracic aorta. Our job today is to relieve him by replacing two sections of the artery, and that will mean stopping the heart. For the shortest possible time, of course.'

The chest rose up as he said it. Then it fell again.

'Leela's with us for the rest of the week,' said Mr Ahsan.

Nobody spoke.

'She wants to be a surgeon.'

I wondered then if I was the only one afraid. The eyes above the masks scarcely blinked, and nobody moved. Then, someone pushed a trolley forwards, so that a row of instruments flashed as they caught the light. He picked one up, and felt its weight. I could hear the faint hum of an air conditioner, and one of the anaesthetists said, 'Maintain, even,' very softly.

'The incision should be shallow but firm,' said Mr Ahsan. 'We'll be following the breastbone, towards the navel, so we trace the line and let the cartilage guide us as to depth. Think of it, Leela, as slicing the softest fruit. Cut once, only – always even.'

He was offering me the scalpel.

'You want to be a surgeon, Leela. Help us, if you please.'

'Help you?'

'Yes.'

'To make the cut?'

'Of course.'

'I can't.'

'You must.'

'I can't.'

My arm stayed at my side. He wouldn't let me do it, I knew that – but everything remained still, and quiet, so – at last – I put my hand out. He laid the scalpel onto my palm. It looked no different to the ones we used at school, in biology, but I felt a very different weight, and it was shaped somehow to roll snugly between my finger and thumb, like an expensive pen. The blade was the sharpest thing I have ever seen, and I realized I was cold all over. Mr Ahsan was close to me now, bent forwards, and his head was twisted – staring up at me.

There are times you go to pieces, and I'm sure I've been in situations where I've backed away, or even fled. On this occasion, the stillness went on, as if me and Mr Ahsan, and all those watching, were part of the same, frozen photograph. When I came back to my senses I found my left hand was lying gently on the patient's flesh, and the scalpel – in my right – let itself rest upon that thin, green line as Mr Ahsan's fingers curved over mine.

I tried to say no.

I found that the words wouldn't come. Moments later other hands appeared, with swabs and forceps. The blade's tip touched the skin and I thought of the many things I'd cut before, and why this should be different. Underneath there was a hardness, and as I drew the scalpel down, it was the same as art or calligraphy: I drew firm and hard, and a thin, red line appeared, straight and true. By the time I'd reached the bottom the skin was unfolding and someone else was teasing back the muscle as the blood disappeared and I was looking at what could only be ribs and then, as somebody else cut deeper, I saw the ribcage.

Hands touched my shoulders, easing me back, and the whine of a saw reminded me of the dentist's drill. Then the bone I'd exposed was cut neatly in two, the blade following the same line as my incision – it was all so fast! Four more hands eased what's called a 'separator' into the crack, and springs pushed it apart slowly, and the ribs were strained open to let light shine deep into that most secret chamber of the body – the chest – where no light's ever been.

The ribcage opened before my eyes, and I was staring into a man's guts – and there I saw what I can only describe as dark matter. And, oh God, nestling amongst layers of membrane, there it was! – a beating heart, snug in its nest, lit up for the first time ever, and pulsing over and over – the engine in us all! It jumped once, twice, and on and on, determined never to stop despite the violation, so that old Mr Gower's blood would flow and keep him nourished and alive even as we tore him open . . .

*

Mr Ahsan found me in the ante-room, almost three hours later, and I was numb. He said, 'Well done.' I went to say something and he raised his finger. 'No,' he said. 'Don't speak.'

He pulled up a chair, and dropped into it, wincing with pain – then he drew himself closer and I was honestly not sure if he was grimacing or smiling, and his little round spectacles caught the light so they were two discs of whiteness as he bent forward and looked up at me.

We sat in silence for a while, until at last, he said: 'The first time is critical. Usually we know – once we've cut for the first time. I think you know now, Leela – don't you? But don't try to find the words.' His teeth are nicotine-stained, as are his fingers. His hair is dyed jet black, but I could see the grey at the roots. His smile is insane.

'Good old life,' he said. 'Did you feel it?'

'What?'

'Life.'

I nodded.

Then I went to speak, but again he interrupted me. 'That ugly thing, that leathery old heart – how many beats so far, in your body? How old are you? – thirteen, according to your beautiful letter. So, already . . . let me see, five hundred and forty-six million heartbeats, and so many million more, God willing! – drumming away now, getting faster, perhaps, without you asking or appreciating, even acknowledging – is that what you were thinking, as we lifted it, eh? I'm sure you were.' He took the sleeve of my cardigan, and pulled at a thread. 'You will be a surgeon, Leela. Your letter spoke to me.'

'How?'

'Ha! Let's just say it arrived at this critical time. Why a surgeon, though? Tell me.'

I said: 'To make people well.'

'Oh yes. What else?'

'To stop pain?'

'Good, though it won't ever stop. That's good, again.'

'Also, to help. To cure people, and give them longer. To preserve life.'

'Yes. There are no better reasons, but I do have further questions. Questions I must ask.'

'What?'

He smiled. 'You know about life. You saw it stop and start.'

'Yes.'

'How much do you know about death?'

I thought hard, and after some time I said: 'Nothing.'

'No?' said Mr Ahsan. 'You've never seen it?'

'No.'

'Oh.'

He nodded, and gritted his teeth as he slowly, painfully

stood up. 'You can't know life without meeting death. We're going downstairs now, because we have just three precious days together. I want you to see our mortuary, Leela. The mortuary is key.'

# Vicky

## 12.07
## Lockson & Lockson boardroom

I stood up.

There was 'Tropical', with its range of jungle flavours, and there was 'Moroccan Mint', with its juice from Arabia. To be honest, I had the same awful indecision every time I went into a shop, so I picked up a can of each.

That's when I noticed 'Coconut Cocktail', which was Stagger's favourite. It was at the end of a row, so I set the 'Tropical' down again, and took that instead. Even as my fingers touched the rim the phone rang, loud and long – just like a burglar alarm.

The cans tumbled onto the table, rolling in different directions. One bounced straight to the floor, and the other somersaulted off a chair. By the time I'd retrieved them the answerphone was cutting in, so I hurriedly snatched up the receiver. An automated sales-voice asked me if I felt I was properly insured, so I hung up at once, and got down on my knees to pick them up. 'Moroccan Mint' or 'Tropical'? It had to be the second, because the fruit rose in a kind of fizzy surf – it went up your nose to the back of your eyes. I looked at the side and saw the famous slogan picked out in bubbles –

### 'FOR THOSE WHO WANNA WIN . . .'

– and, as usual, I found myself craving it. The drink made you feel fitter, and the TV ads always featured kids doing action sports. The most dazzling showed a kung-fu expert of about my age, and she was just a blur of elbows, feet and hands, smashing her way through solid walls. When she burst through the last, she snatched up a bottle and glugged it down. The foam said:

# LIQUIDATOR

### 'DON'T **YOU** WANNA WIN?'

The girl stared right at you, and wiped her lips. She was as thin as Katkat, and just as beautiful – and even as I remembered her, I found my right hand had moved to the ring pull. I yanked it decisively, and of course, the thing exploded like a grenade.

I had forgotten that I'd dropped it.

It had been violently shaken, so the liquid rose in a foaming geyser of sugary spray. I leaped back, and dropped it a second time. Where did it land? Oh-my-God, it landed in the worst place possible – right on the keyboard of Mrs Lockson's thin silver laptop, which stood open on the desk! I snatched at the can, but only managed to spin it – then I batted it away.

It was all way, way too late, though: half the liquid had glugged over the keyboard, and though I grabbed a tissue there was nothing I could do. I watched the bubbles sink between the keys, and I stood there waiting for sparks and flashes. There was no sound at all at first, for the chugging had stopped. I leaned in, and then I heard a series of clicks and sighs. I stood there with my mouth open in horror.

The clicks turned into a rattle.

All the lights faded.

The screen went black and there was silence.It was as if I'd killed a precious, living thing, and I just didn't know what to do. When the phone rang, I actually screamed. I let it ring five or six times, and then picked it up, praying it wouldn't be Mrs Lockson.

It wasn't – it was some friendly buffoon who wanted to get a message to someone, but also seemed to want a chat. I got rid of him, and I sat down to stare at the dead, sticky laptop. It seemed such a terrible act of vandalism . . . it had been so pure and clean, so silver and slender and part of the glorious future. Now it was coated in juice and its precious little circuit-board soul had been corrupted and destroyed.

I touched it. It felt cold and useless, and it now stank of fruit. My own phone rang then, and I heard the one voice that could make the world seem better. It was my trusted friend and adviser, Stagger, congratulating me on my promotion. I started crying immediately.

That's something that's changed, by the way: I used to cry very easily. Now I don't.

# Vicky

## 12.08
## Across town . . .

Stagger listened to my story in silence.

He thought hard, and said that the best and obvious thing would be to admit I'd had an accident and accept the consequences. I explained that this was not possible – that I would probably be put through a Lockson shredder. If they didn't actually kill me, then I could certainly expect to be crippled or maimed.

He calmed me down again and said that the alternative was to get the laptop fixed, because the damage was probably not so terrible. Liquidator was a healthy, organic drink and there were things that you could buy to treat any computer parts that had been damaged. He was very sensible, and said that the only real danger was that Mrs Lockson might, possibly, have lost some important data.

That's what she would be most worried about, so that's what we should try to sort out. George could save us, he

said. We'd bike over to a shop he knew and get back within the hour. Looking back, it was just the next moment in the chain of disasters – a crazy decision when I should have simply fled the building and never gone back. Instead, I wrapped the laptop in paper, and I answered the phone twice more before Stagger texted to say he was approaching. I left a note in case we were delayed:

*Minor accident!! Getting it sorted.*
*Back soon, so please don't worry!!*
*Vicky xx ☺*

I then climbed down endless stairs to the reception hall, and got through into the car park. Stagger had just arrived, and we laid the laptop carefully in George's top-box. I squeezed under his jacket, praying there'd be no problems, because if the police stopped us this time we'd be incarcerated!

The first disappointment was that Stagger's repair shop didn't exist any more.

There were boards over the windows, and litter in the doorway. That was when I remembered my most trusted classmate – Ben Gallagher, the computer genius I mentioned earlier. At once, my spirits soared, and I wondered why I hadn't thought of him straightaway. Ben was the fourth cleverest in our class, after Leela and the

Tuttle twins. He could seem rude and sexist, and he didn't seem to want friends very much – but that was only because he operated at a different level to those around him.

Ben actually built computers from scratch. He programmed them, designed applications and knew more than all his teachers put together. I remembered where his work placement was, so we headed there and opened the door quietly. If anyone could help us, it was Ben.

He was sitting on the floor.

He sat cross-legged in his school uniform, in a trance of misery. He was forcing a rosebush into a little china vase, and he was all alone. We stood there, staring at him, and he didn't even look up.

'Ben?' I said quietly.

He jumped then, and gazed at me.

'What are you doing?' I said, and I thought he was going to burst into tears because he went from white to pink, and his eyes blinked helplessly. His face was soon redder than the roses.

'Oh God, Vicky,' he said – and then he swore.

'Ben, what's happening?' I said. 'You're arranging flowers!'

'So what?' he cried.

'Nothing, but—'

'Leave me alone! You tell anyone, Vicky, and I will bust your nose—'

'Ben, no, listen—'

'What?' he hissed. 'What do you want?'

'I thought you were doing a computer project!'

'So did I!' he cried. 'That's what I was told, and . . . she's got me doing *this*!'

'Who?'

'The witch! That . . . woman!' He swore again, and this time I thought he was going to scream and smash the vase.

The florist came in from the back just then, hearing the commotion, and gave us all the most dazzling, twinkling smile. She was like the grandmother in Little Red Riding Hood, rubbing plump little hands in delight. 'Oh well, look at all this!' she chirped. 'You've got visitors, Benji! Are these your friends?'

I gazed at Ben in horror.

'Er, yes,' said Stagger. 'We're, um . . . supposed to check up on each other.'

'Oh! From the same school then, are you? How lovely.' She patted Ben's shoulder, and I saw him jolt, as if he'd been electrocuted. 'He's coming on really well, isn't he? Lovely display, that . . .' Her eyes went crinkly, and she started to chuckle. 'I've said, this afternoon, if he's good, he can try out with a few lilies!' She actually stroked his hair, and I thought for an awful moment Ben was going to bite her – his teeth were bared like a dog's.

'No, Ben!' I cried, and he just managed to pull back.

'Can I go now, please, Mrs Robinson?' he said in a strangled voice. 'It's . . . nearly one o'clock . . . it must be lunchtime, maybe . . . isn't it?' He had the vase in both hands and if she'd said no he would have cracked it over her skull, no doubt about it.

'You go when you want, love,' said the old lady. 'Put your blazer on, though – there's a chilly wind out there.'

I snatched it from a peg.

'You want my umbrella, dear?'

'No,' whispered Ben. 'No!'

'Then you take your time, duck. Come back when you're ready.'

When we got outside, Ben exploded. He rushed over to a wall and smashed both fists against it. Then he pressed his whole body up against the bricks, and gave an animal howl.

'What the hell am I doing in there?' he moaned.

'Ben,' I said. 'Take it easy—'

'What kind of crap is this about, Vicky? I'm going (bleeping) crazy.' He turned to look at me, wild-eyed. 'I can't go back there. I'll end up in jail. There's a big pair of scissors on the table, and all morning I've had visions of stabbing her, cutting, slicing—'

'Ben! Please!' I said.

'I'll cut her eyes out! I can't go back – don't make me!'

'Ben,' I said, and I put my hand on his arm. He was shaking all over. 'You don't have to, I'm sure, but—'

'I'd rather do that sewer thing – with Spud! If she touches me one more time, Vicky . . .' He put his hands over his eyes and dropped into a crouch.

Stagger, thank goodness, saw exactly what was needed.

He had the laptop ready, and he unwrapped it right under Ben's nose.

When Ben finally took his hands down, it was the first thing he focused on, and the change was instantaneous. 'Oh,' he said softly. 'Wow.'

'Ben,' said Stagger, kneeling beside him. 'It's broken.'

Ben's eyes widened, then went warm and dreamy. He took the laptop like it was a new-born baby – tenderly, respectfully – and he opened it. I saw his nostrils twitch, as if he was breathing its scent, and all the rage was gone.

'Oh, my goodness,' he said.

'Ben,' said Stagger quietly. 'Can you fix it?'

'It's a Star-Book Professional,' he whispered.

'Is it?'

'Yes.'

'Can you mend it?'

'Where did you get this? Oh my, look at it . . .'

'It's not ours.'

'Oh, Stag . . . what a beauty. Star-Book Utopia. US, converted. Wow . . .'

'I spilled a drink,' I said. 'Have I ruined it?'

Ben ran his fingers over the keyboard, and we all saw

the stickiness. We were still on the pavement, but it didn't matter: this was too important. He turned the machine over, so gently, and felt for signs of life. 'You spilled a drink?' he said. 'Oh, Vicky . . . no. You don't spill drinks on a Star-Book.'

'It wasn't on purpose—'

'You don't bring drinks *near* a Star-Book.'

'I really wish I hadn't. Can you repair it?'

'I don't know. I do not know . . . ohhhh, look, this is brand-new – it's just a few weeks old!'

'I'd really like you to try,' I said. 'It might just save my life.'

'Limited edition, isn't it? This is beyond upgraded, I'd say. This is . . . special.'

I nodded. 'Have I wrecked it, Ben?'

'Electrical shutdown, that's obvious. I would imagine it's hibernating . . . the circuits will have protected themselves. But . . . oh, God. This will have cost a fortune.'

'Really?'

'I just can't believe you spilled a drink on it. Where did you get it?'

'It belongs to my boss. She left it on the table, right next to me.'

He looked at me, and now there was a strange horror in his eyes. 'I'm not sure I should help you, Vee. You've committed a pretty serious crime. A crime against humanity, actually. You should face the death penalty.'

I hung my head.

'Look,' he said, sighing. 'I'll see what I can do. Apart from anything, I would love to get inside – we'd better go back to my place. Don't touch it, Vee! – I'll carry it.'

Mercifully, Ben's home wasn't too far. I walked behind, and Stagger went back to get George.

We met by Ben's front door, which opened onto a staircase leading up to a tiny flat. We all took off our shoes, and went into his bedroom. There was a narrow bed in one corner: everywhere else it was shelves and work surfaces. You could hardly see the carpet for cable, and the wallpaper was invisible behind rack after rack of spare parts. It was as if he lived and slept inside machinery, and there was no sign of his mum.

'Can I make tea?' I said, wanting to be useful.

Ben nodded. He stripped off his tie, and rolled his sleeves up. Then he laid the precious laptop on a bench, having unrolled a little rug of felt. Stagger kept respectfully silent, and I padded round to the kitchen. When I returned to Ben's room, he said, 'You keep that stuff well away, Vicky! All right?'

I nodded.

'What the hell did you (bleep) do . . . ?' he muttered.

It's always a bit of a shock to see something as elegant

as a laptop with its guts exposed. I suppose it was the same experience Leela had hoped to have in the operating theatre, for Ben had drawn a bright light over the desk, and he was working with a tiny screwdriver and a pair of tweezers.

He was perched on a stool, and he had a glass in one eye. The Star-Book was attached to a kind of life-support system: three cables were feeding it, and I found I was listening for the sound of breathing. I watched him work, keeping well back. Stagger stood beside me, sipping his drink. 'Any hope?' he said.

'She's destroyed it,' said Ben at last. 'The logic's been shorted – and they're built not to do that, so . . .'

'Can you fix it?'

'No.'

'Replace it?' said Stagger. 'At least get it switched on?'

'Maybe. The best thing . . .' He put down his tweezers and picked up a fine, metal probe. He pressed something deep in the innards, and a tiny tray of solder-worms emerged. 'What the (bleep) did you spill? Acid?'

'Liquidator. Tropical.'

'How? It's burned out half the circuits, so you're going to have to replace them and reload most of the applications. It's not going to boot, and quite honestly . . .' He looked at me, and with the big lens stuck in his eye I thought of one of those medics who looks up from the body and says,

'*There's nothing we can do. She's gone.*' What he actually said was, 'The best thing would be to see if it's under guarantee still, and send it back to where it was bought. I mean, a Star-Book – it's bound to be covered.'

'What about all the data?' said Stagger.

'The data's fine. The backup completed ages ago.'

I felt a surge of hope. 'That was my main worry,' I said. 'I thought I might have lost everything.'

Ben shook his head, and removed his eyepiece. 'It's like the black box on a plane,' he said. 'They're designed to withstand massive abuse, and they back up online as well. All her files will be automatically uploading, so you might have cost your boss money, but you just need to ask her when she bought it . . . I can check that, actually. Hang on.' He picked up a thin rectangular piece of plastic, and pushed it into a slot. He tapped at another keyboard, and his own computer came to life, and displayed bright columns of data in green. 'Less than three months ago,' he said. 'It'll still have a warranty. It's a pretty full drive, and as far as I can see . . .'

'What?' I said.

'It's all triple-encrypted. Why is that?'

'Why is what?'

'Wow,' he said. 'Your boss doesn't want anyone to read her stuff, does she? And . . . ooh, this is interesting. She's *not* backing up online, that function's suspended. Which *is* weird – you didn't touch it?'

'No!'

'She's encoding everything three times over, but nothing's saved to the web. Is she a privacy nutcase?'

'Look, Ben,' I said, 'I don't know what you're talking about.'

'It's very simple. If you don't want people looking at your files, you encrypt them – yes? Then if your laptop gets stolen, no one gets access. What your boss has done is apply encryption, MI5-standard. This is going to be quite a test . . .'

I saw him plug in a different lead, and tap the keyboard of his own computer. At once, another screen came to life, and we saw thousands of numbers scrolling upwards.

'That's the Mikron,' said Ben. 'Decodes virtually anything. You can get viruses it can't deal with, but not many. Look at that.'

'What?'

'I'm in. It's safe.'

'Safe, meaning what?' said Stagger. 'Are you saying it's OK, or . . . ?'

'I think it's fine – it's protected. The files are stacking – no corruption.'

'Oh, thank God!' I said. 'I mean, seriously, Ben – you think it's all right?'

'I'll back it up again, just in case. Flush it through. You can return it to her tomorrow and beg for mercy.' He looked at his own screen again, which was still scrolling numbers. 'Wow,' he said. 'There's a lot of stuff here. Who's Jamie Song?'

'I don't know.'

'"Jamie Song: confidential." Interesting . . . What kind of firm is it?'

'It's a law firm.'

'Liquidator. Jamie Song.'

'I think they must work with the drinks company—'

'She is *paranoid*, wow . . .'

An hour later – at five past two, to be exact – Ben had put the laptop back together, and it was nestling in George's pizza box. I thanked him as much as I could, and we agreed to exchange numbers, in case there were further problems. That was when I turned my phone back on, which reminded Stagger to look at his. He'd been avoiding the calls of his angry pizza boss, of course, and I'd been avoiding the Locksons. I had eight missed calls and eleven texts. Stagger had missed six and he had three messages. Then, just as I was opening the first, my phone rang, loud in my hand, and I saw at once that it was Dad.

'Vicky,' he said. 'Where are you?'

His voice was shaky – far more shaky than usual – and my first thought was that he'd had another turn. He very rarely called me because he hated phones as much as he hated television.

'Dad,' I said. 'I'm with Stagger.'

'Where, exactly?'

'In town. Are you all right?'

'Vicky?' said another voice. It was deep, and gentle, with a London edge, but the phone seemed suddenly full of dangerous voltage.

'Yes,' I said. 'What's happened? Who—'

'Do you have a laptop belonging to a Mrs Lockson?'

'Yes. I've got it here, I'm—'

'We're waiting at your house. We need it back.'

'Did she get my note?' I said. 'We had an accident, you see, but—'

'Come home, Vicky. We're waiting for you.'

That was the first moment I realized that I might have stumbled into something serious. Stagger looked at me, and so did Ben – they'd both heard the voice and it had scared them – it was too calm, and too controlled.

We were silent for a moment, and then Stagger said: 'At least we tried. We did our best, didn't we? – so . . . tell the truth.'

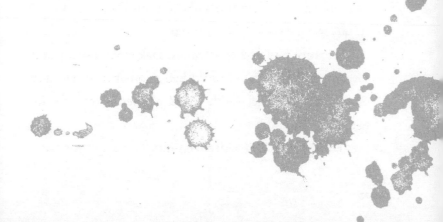

# Stagger

## 14.44
## Home

I'm going to bust in here for the first time, just before things get really bad, and tell you a bit about Vicky's dad. You need to know it, I think, because the man was (and is) a journalistic legend who flew ALL OVER THE WORLD working for a certain daily newspaper. It was his job to report the crazy stuff – and I mean the wars and the earthquakes and the famines . . . all the horror that goes on in the most screwed-up corners of the earth. Out he went, for months at a time, and his partner, a guy called Jake, took the photos. They were the A-team, by the sound of it, but when Vee was about seven years old poor old Jake got blown to bits in a bomb blast, and it was pure luck it didn't get them both. I don't know the details, and nor does Vicky – but her dad had stepped outside the cafe for some reason, and that's when the place went up.

The only time he ever mentions it is when he can't

sleep and his brain gets fixated. We have to talk him down, me and Vee, and I've spent long, shaky nights with him in tears – and he still can't deal with the details. Vee's mum had split a while before that, meaning Vicky got looked after by nannies and friends when he was away, which might have been fun – it didn't do her any harm, anyway – but after that bomb her dad refused to travel, and his writing stopped.

'What's the point in telling people?' he'd say. 'No one wants to listen.'

As for newspapers, he won't have them in the house. He got a job on the local rag for a while – the *Gazette* – but that couldn't last, partly because of the editor, who's a jerk, but also because by this time he was hitting the sauce. That's the word we use for booze, or alcohol, to make it sound harmless. We know it isn't, of course, and Vicky and me spend a fair bit of time trying to get it off him – trying to keep him alive, I suppose – and trying to pretend we don't smell it on his breath, or on his clothes and even in the poor man's sweat. There's a clinic that looks after him, and we walk him round to some therapy-club twice a week. We try to keep to routines and not get him panicked – that's why it was obvious on the phone that something was not just wrong, but *badly* wrong – we could both feel it. I pushed George as hard as I dared, and we got back in just over thirty minutes.

The first thing we saw was a silver-grey car squeezed

behind our neighbour's van, way too swish for our street – so I got off the bike and parked it. That's when a man appeared straight out of nowhere, and the man was head to foot in black.

'Give me the keys,' he says.

I said, 'Keys to what?' – and that was all it needed, because he steps into me, quick, and grabs my throat. He lifts me up, pushing at the same time, and I'm stick-thin and no fighter – I'm in the air, scared to death. I heard Vicky scream, and I try to push back but the guy knows just what he's doing and he hits me, hard, between the legs. That doubles me over, and he sends me smashing into Vee so we're both on the pavement. Someone's shouting, 'No need for that!' but the guy kicks me anyway – and he has the keys now which have spun out into the gutter – and I feel myself carried like a kid, arms behind my back, and someone's got Vicky too.

We're marched into the house, and my head's slammed against the wall at some point, so I'm thinking, Stay conscious! This is bad! We go in up the hallway, and I'm chucked at the cooker, hard. I bounce off and end up on the floor with a nose that's pumping blood and a shoulder I swear is dislocated.

Vicky's been pushed onto a chair, next to her dad. He's got his hands in the air, trying to calm the situation down. He's shouting, 'No! Stop!' – and things like that, until after a while everything's quiet. That's when I see the biggest guy I've ever seen, sitting casually at our kitchen table like he's a guest. He makes the whole room seem tiny as a doll's house, and he's wearing smart suit, dark tie, cufflinks – and he's muttering into a phone, so he hardly looks at us.

He clicks it off at last. 'So, guys,' he says – and it's that London voice again, I recognize it. Gentle and polite, but so serious. 'Where is it, and where has it been?'

As he says it, it appears. One of the guys sets it on the table, and the big man switches it on.

'It's broken,' said Vicky. 'That's what we—'

'Shut your mouth,' said someone.

'What were you kids doing?' says the man in the suit. He sounded tired, but friendly – and I couldn't stop staring at his huge hands.

'When?' says Vicky. 'What do you mean?'

'Why did you take it? Where have you been?'

'I was having a drink,' says Vicky. 'I was thirsty, and I dropped it, and—'

'You spilled your drink?'

'Yes.'

'And damaged the laptop. Right. Yes: I can see the mess.'

The kitchen is now packed with people – lean, tough-looking guys, with little transmitters clipped behind their ears. They look like ex-soldiers to me – some kind of security firm. And they're all wearing boots.

'Where did you go?' says the man in the suit.

Vicky's dad interrupts here, still scared to death. 'Tell the truth,' he says. 'They just want the truth – that's what we all want.'

'We certainly do, sir. Now, Vicky – why did you have your phone off?'

'I was scared,' says Vicky.

'What of?'

'Because I'd damaged the laptop. We wanted to find a repair shop, and get it fixed.'

'That makes sense. And did you succeed?'

'No, we didn't. It was closed.'

'Really?'

I took over then. My nose was still dripping, but I ignored it, thinking ahead. I thought, *Keep it calm, and keep it clear*. I kept my arms round my knees, and I tried just to give them the facts. You could feel it in the air: one stupid remark and the guy who'd hit me already would come for me again.

I told them about the shop that had closed. I said we weren't sure what to do. I said we'd remembered another place, and asked someone for directions . . . and that's when I knew the facts were going to be hard work, because if the laptop was so precious and important, how were they going to feel when I mentioned Ben? That's when I knew I'd have to lie: I said we'd driven across town.

I told him that the bike had played up, which was nearly true – and we'd wasted an hour mucking about with that. We'd had our lunch, I said, and only then remembered we'd turned off our phones, which we'd only done so we wouldn't get yelled at.

All the time I'm looking at the big guy, but I was trying to send a message out to Vee, clear as I could. *Don't mention him* I was saying, in my head. *Whatever you add, Vicky – whatever they ask, and even if they separate us, start in on us and bring out the baseball bats –* WHATEVER YOU DO *– Don't. Mention. Ben. He's dead if you do.*

# Vicky

**Continued ▶**

And the weird thing was, I knew it.

Stagger was lying his head off, and they tried to trip him up with a few questions, but he's one hell of an actor when he wants to be. 'Don't mention Ben!' – I knew that's what he was thinking, and I didn't have to be a genius to know why. I understood perfectly: if they found out we'd been to Ben's flat, and if they knew he'd got inside the laptop and backed up files . . . I mean, maybe they'd find out anyway, at once, as soon as they checked the data. But I had that feeling just as strong as Stagger: if we tell them about Ben, they'll tear his room apart and kill him.

The man in the suit looked over at me. 'How did that take two hours thirty-four minutes?' he said.

'It just did, sir,' I said. 'We lost track of time.'

'Oh,' said the man. 'You lost track of time.'

He flipped up his phone again, and tapped in a

number. A high-pitched voice answered at once: one tight syllable, and the man replied to it, slowly and carefully: 'The item's been returned, ma'am,' he said. 'False alarm.'

A woman's voice snarled into his ear, and the man listened hard. At last, he turned to me again, and gazed into my eyes. I swear he didn't blink for a whole, long minute.

'One little thing,' he said – and he was so quiet. 'Did you look inside it?'

'The laptop?' I said.

He nodded.

'No.'

'You're sure about that?'

'It doesn't work,' said Stagger. 'We just wanted to fix it, honestly, so when we realized we couldn't–'

'Did anyone look inside it? In their efforts to assist you?'

'No.'

'Because if you did, Vicky. And what's your name? – Stagger? If you so much as–'

'We just wanted to help!' I cried – and I could feel the tears rolling down my cheeks. I was grateful for them because they made me look weak, silly and helpless.

My dad hugged me tighter, but the man simply stared.

'It's all right, love,' said my dad. 'You didn't know.'

'I'm so sorry,' I said, through all the snot and mucus, and I was aware of the man getting up at last. He seemed to fill the kitchen, and when he came towards me he blotted out the light. He touched my chin with one finger, and lifted my head so we were gazing right into each other's eyes. Like Stagger said, his hands were huge.

'Nobody looked at the laptop?' he said.

'No, sir.'

'Good.'

He smiled at me. 'I'm going to take your word as truth,' he said. 'We've had a mix-up, and I believe you. But, oh my . . . if we discover, some way down the line, that you haven't been frank. If we find out that there was a third party, so to speak – and someone's . . . been peeping. You'll see me again, and I won't be so friendly. In fact, Vicky – I'll be downright dangerous.'

The kitchen emptied then. There were boots and shoes down the hallway, and we sat motionless. We heard the front door slam so hard we waited for the glass to break. Then, after some time, we heard the rich, throaty roar of their high-performance cars. When everything was quiet, Dad said, 'What was that about?'

'I don't know,' I said.

'What was on that computer?'

'I don't know. It was broken.'

Stagger said: 'Maybe they have sensitive files.'

'What do they do, those people? What did you see?'

'Nothing!'

'Lockson and Lockson. Who do they work with?'

'I don't know, Dad. I just spilled a drink . . .'

He paused, and I could see how shaken he was. He was trembling. 'I'm sorry,' he said, at last. 'They just barged their way in, and it was . . . like being out East again. I opened the door and . . . well, you have no comeback. There's nothing you can do, you see.'

'Should we phone the police?' asked Stagger.

'What?' Dad laughed a savage laugh and I went cold all over. 'If we wanted to waste everybody's time, we could certainly call the police. And we'd get very badly hurt into the bargain – all of us. You heard what he said, didn't you?'

'Yes.'

'You don't *deal* with people like that, Stagger. You *avoid* them.'

'Were they violent to you?' I said.

He shook his head, but there were tears in his eyes. 'No need,' he said.

'And it's over, d'you think? They won't come back?'

'Vicky, were you telling the truth?'

'Yes.'

'Because they'll know if you weren't. If you opened any files, God help us: they'll find out.'

That was when my phone buzzed in my pocket.

Stagger said, 'I'll make us some tea.'

'Did you open anything, Vicky? Tell me.'

'No, Dad!' I cried. 'No.'

Because I knew who was texting, and I was frightened to look. There are times you just know when someone wants to get hold of you urgently – it's like you can hear them breathing in your ear. I knew it was Ben Gallagher, and I knew the message was going to take us to a totally new place, and that things were going to get a lot more dangerous and complicated and frightening.

> We need to meet now hurry you wont believe the stuff I am reading where can we meet this is amazing dont tell anyone anything just you and stag call me but be careful this is big

# Katkat

## 12.04
## In the Stars!

You may remember that the last time you heard from me, I'd arrived at Snowy's studio-paradise only to be scared out of my wits by a high-pitched howling scream, echoing from the top of the stairs. It was followed by total silence.

Jun leaped into the house, and I peered in after him, but I couldn't see what was wrong. There were people everywhere – the musicians, I presumed – and they were all standing still as statues, gazing up at the top of a staircase where a girl about the same age as me was clutching her stomach. Jun bounded towards her, and was in just in time! – she fainted clean away, and dropped into his arms.

'Call an ambulance!' he cried.

Snowy was soon beside her. 'Rosie?' he said. 'What's wrong?'

She couldn't speak, though, and I saw people pulling out their phones, as Jun brought her down.

'She was in pain last night,' said someone. 'This is bad . . .'

'She's dying!' said Snowy. 'Help her!'

I knew who the girl was then! – it was his own adopted daughter and his support vocalist.

She opened her eyes and said, 'No!' very faintly. 'It's here . . . my side! It hurts . . .'

'Something she ate,' said someone. 'Let's get the chopper!'

'Quiet!' said Jun. He'd dialled a number, even as he held her, and the phone was pressed to his ear. 'I need an ambulance,' he said slowly. 'Quick as you can.'

# Michael

## 12.04
## Brisley Control Centre

That was the first call I listened to, there in my chair with my headset on – and I heard the whole thing . . .

'You're through,' said the operator. 'Which service—?'

And a man said firmly: 'I need an ambulance. Quick as you can!'

'OK, sir—'

'It's not OK!' said the man. 'Hurry, will you? Please! – we got a catastrophe here . . .'

You can see the problem, I'm sure. People don't realize that panic is the enemy of efficiency. If you don't explain your situation calmly, you actually waste precious time. That's why it's our job to be clear and precise whatever the circumstances.

'Where are you calling from, sir?' said the operator.

She was wonderful, and I could hardly breathe. Information is key, of course – the facts are vital. But

97

sometimes, you see, people can't really think straight, and all we heard was the man saying a word I'd never heard before: 'Hasgar' or 'Asgard'. Another voice said, 'Snowy's place, out in the woods . . .' – and we heard what sounded like a child moaning.

The operator had to do something then that nobody likes doing. She had to interrupt:

'Listen to me, sir.'

'What?'

'Keep calm. What I need is your postcode.'

# Katkat

## 12.24
## In the Stars!

It was so dreadfully confused . . .

The whole band was crowding round Rosie, who was twisted up in Jun's arms. He dropped the phone, but mercifully a big guy called Jesse was beside him, and managed to catch it – he's Snowy's saxophonist, and gave the right information. By that time, though, poor Rosie was half-unconscious and fading fast. Snowy had backed off into a corner and looked ashen.

'Hurry,' said Jesse. 'Please! Shh! Guys, I can't understand . . . what are you saying?'

A silence fell, but all we could hear were meaningless words: 'charlie', 'foxtrot', and things like that. Ten agonizing seconds ticked by, and at last we heard a woman say: 'OK, confirmed.'

'What is?' said Jun.

'Ambulance, sir—'

'It's coming?'

'It's on its way,' said the voice. 'Stand by to receive it – check the access, keep the casualty calm. Is there anyone there with medical knowledge?'

There wasn't, but we all did our best. We laid Rosie on a rug, and Snowy held her head. The ambulance arrived in minutes, thank goodness, and all we could do was watch as the poor girl was loaded onto a stretcher. That's when Snowy tried to get into the vehicle with her, but the band wouldn't let him – a couple of the crew went instead, and we stood there as the blue flashing lights disappeared into the trees.

Everyone was totally and utterly stunned, and I saw Snowy was inconsolable. He sank down onto the floor again, his hands over his face. One by one everyone followed suit, and nobody spoke. How could anyone rehearse after a shock like that?

That's when I heard a voice, very soft – right in my ear.

'Katkat?' it said.

I didn't answer at first, because I felt so awful. I had my eyes closed, but the voice came again.

'Katkat? Listen to me.'

I felt a hand on my arm, and I when I looked up I saw it was Jun, crouching right by my side, and he had tears in his eyes. 'This is bad,' he said. 'This is disaster, baby. You realize that?'

'What was wrong with her?' I said.

'I don't know what's wrong, but you know that girl's part of the group.'

'Is she?'

'Yes. She's a singer.'

'Oh, no . . .'

'She's a pretty damn special singer, Katkat. She's the man's daughter too, you understand?' I nodded. 'He's going to think the gig is jinxed now, and Katkat – he's going to cancel it all, and shut things down.'

'What? Cancel the concert?' I cried. 'Why?'

'He'll see this as a sign. It's happened before.'

'He can't!'

'She's *the* singer, Katkat! Stands right beside him, keeps him going – does the big solo: "Tell the Truth". She's the beating heart of this band.'

'Then maybe she'll be OK,' I said. 'It might just be tummy-ache – or a bug–'

'It's appendicitis, I reckon. She's out of it, girl – and this is a crisis.'

'Jun,' I said. 'I wish there was something I could do.'

'I think there is.'

'What? Tell me!'

'You sing, don't you? That's what I was told, before you got here.'

'Well, yes, but not seriously–'

'We can't waste time,' he hissed. 'The whole thing's in the balance now – you understand that? I'm more scared than I've ever been, baby. This man might never go on stage again!'

'I realize that,' I said. 'But, Jun, listen—'

'Seventy-two hours and it's "Africa's Weeping!" – that's a live transmission, all over the world, for the poorest kids on the planet. The Snowman's down, child – we've got to pick him up and turn him round.'

'Jun,' I said – but he put his finger to my lips.

'Fate, Katkat,' he said. 'That's what he believes in, as you know. We've got to show him there's a new singer, ready to go: one that's been sent to us, to lead us out of the darkness.'

Five minutes later, guess what? I'm in the studio. We filed down together – the whole band – and someone lit candles. I was aware of incense too, and Snowy's shaman was on his knees, saying prayers. The keyboard man came forward – that's Taffy Bozo – and led me to the biggest grand piano I'd ever seen, and put music in front of me. They fixed up a mic and when I looked at what they wanted me to sing I nearly collapsed – it was one of Snowy's most beautiful songs, and I'd been listening to it since I was tiny. It was called 'Hold Me In Heaven'.

Everyone knows it. It had earned Snowy his seventh

Grammy Award, and it was the song NASA bought the rights to, five years ago, so they could beam it for ever into deep space. It's the tune other life-forms may be listening to, even now! – and I had to wipe my eyes just to see the words, I was that emotional. I had to clench my fists and screw up every inch of courage because they wanted me to sing it right then and there – an audition, I guess! – with its creator himself gazing right at me.

He was scared too, but Jun guided him gently to the Dome of Sound. That's in the centre of the room, and was part of an old temple he had shipped in from somewhere foreign, and rebuilt, to amplify the 'organic beauty of the human voice'. Snowy stood there, under it, and nobody spoke. We just breathed in together, and then Crazy Louie, the percussionist, brought in the beat.

To be honest, I didn't need the music – I knew that song backwards, from the marimba opening to when the nose-flutes come in – and soon I was moving slowly, picking up the rhythm. The two backing singers were smiling at me, thank goodness, helping me – just wanting it to work!

When Snowy started to sing, I came straight in with the harmony – I closed my eyes, and just threw myself at it – what else could I do? And I don't know where the magic came from, but it was like I was taken over – before I knew it, I was improvising, and our voices were intertwined! Snowy looked at me, and I saw the fear and worry turn into concentration, and a little, teeny-tiny smidgen of hope. After the first verse, he smiled too – and that gave me the confidence to keep at it, trying things out. Before we knew it we'd done the whole eight-minute version, start to finish.

Then we just stood there, waiting.

Snowy says you have to wait, until every sound particle has settled and the earth is still again. So after maybe . . . forty-five seconds, people were clapping. That turned into cheering, and Snowy just came right up to me and gave me this great big hug – which he hardly ever does: touch people, I mean – and Jun couldn't believe it. He turned to everyone, lifting up my hand – and do you know what he said?

He said: 'Guys? She's in the band!

# Spud

## 18.00
## City drains

Everyone needs them, and nobody likes them. But: think about it! – a well-constructed, properly functioning drain is a very beautiful thing, doing a very important job, not unlike the pipes in your body. They've always been part of the Cropper family since they were first ever thought of and dug, which is hundreds of years ago: that's why I had no hesitation in choosing them for my 'Work It Out!!' placement.

But I didn't start Wednesday morning, like most people at school. Oh, no! – me and Damien signed up with the E.N.S. (Emergency Night Squad): Special Service. Damien had lasted just half a day with the Fire Service, because they wouldn't let him touch a hosepipe, let alone wear a helmet or go in the engine. 'Health and Safety,' they kept saying, so he walked out at lunchtime, and my dad pulled some strings to get him in with me. First shift, six o'clock p.m.

Hard hat, oilskins, waders and boots. Tool kit (basic), rechargeable torch. High-visibility waistcoat with flotation device, first-aid box, whistle and emergency flare. Radio with spare battery, satellite navigation system, ladder-pack and pocket-knife. That's 20kg of kit checked out every evening, and that's what you carry. Check it back when you're done, and keep it clean – your life can depend on any one of those items, as can the lives of your mates. Outsiders won't ever understand, but down in the dark you're a band of brothers and you never stop learning.

Me and Damien? We were ready to go.

# Ben

## 17.04
## Leisure centre

I told them to meet me at the local leisure centre.

For one thing, it has a cafe you can sit in, which is normally crowded with kids, and whilst that can sometimes be a major pain in the arse, and you're jammed in between buggies and squealing babies . . . what I wanted was a SAFE, PUBLIC SPACE where nobody could bug us or worse still jump us – and if you think I've been watching too many movies, think again, because what I knew already, for sure, was that we'd walked into something that could get us killed. The second thing was that the Leisure Centre had good Wi-Fi, which was going to be essential: I had things to show them.

I'd also done a fair bit of printing.

I'd sorted out a folder of essential information, and I called Edgar in too, thinking if anyone could watch our backs and protect us, he was the one. Then I locked up the flat, but not before laying out hairs and breadcrumbs – putting them in crucial places, like the doorstep and door-handle. I had a feeling it was only a question of time before someone would be calling . . . and I didn't want to walk into my own house to find it full of dangerous strangers.

That's how worried I was.

Anyway, I got to the car park right on time. Vicky and Stagger decided to be late.

# Vicky & Stagger

## Continued ▶

We didn't mean to be.

We were nervous wrecks as well, don't forget, so we decided to go the weirdest way we could, circling twice round roundabouts and cutting down alleyways. We weren't worried about the police any more – oh, no. We were worried about being tailed. We ran out of fuel after ten minutes, and had to push George to the nearest garage. Then the engine got flooded, and the battery started playing up – we had to take all kinds of risks to get there at all. But that was our life now – a long series of risks, and we rolled in with the headlamp dying.

Ben was sitting in the car park with a hoodie drawn over his head, and by total coincidence he'd met up with Eleanor, the would-be vet. She was holding the leash of a very fat basset hound, and was breathless, just from listening.

'Ben's just told me what you did, Vee,' she said.

'You don't half have bad luck! Is Ben right? – is he going to die?'

'Who?'

'Shut up,' said Ben. 'Get inside, and say nothing.'

We all did as we were told.

We were amazed that Ben had shared things with Eleanor, and he admitted later that if he'd thought about it, he'd have told her to get lost. She's so direct, though – she has a habit of asking the most blunt questions, and gazing at you out of big eyes. There was another factor too: Ben was so fired up and worried, he needed a dog to stroke and someone to talk to. Eleanor was sworn to secrecy and brought on board.

'We've got decisions to make,' said Ben, as soon as we were inside, and there were people around us. 'This is . . . nuclear. What happened to your face, Stagger?'

'We had visitors,' I said. And I told him.

'Who were they?'

'I don't know. Security of some kind . . .'

'This confirms everything. This is bad.'

'What?'

Ben's mouth was dry and he kept looking around him. 'Damn it,' he said. 'I'm not sure we should be sitting here. We should go to the police, now–'

'Why? What have you found out?'

He pulled off his backpack. 'You're sure you want to know?' he said.

'Obviously.'

'Then, OK – but listen. The first thing to emphasize is that we could be under surveillance – even now. We are going to have to watch our backs twenty-four seven.'

'I know that. We are.'

'But we're sitting on dynamite, and you don't know what you've got us into. Edgar's on his way, all right? – so let's just wait for him.'

'Why d'you get him involved?' I said.

Ben looked at us, shaking his head. 'Vicky . . . Stagger. We're going to *need* someone like Edgar – just to get home.'

At that very moment, we saw him approaching. Edgar was in tight jeans and bomber jacket, and his baseball cap was back-to-front. He looks tough because he is tough, and it was obvious then that Ben was deadly serious about protection. OK, Edgar's only fourteen, but nobody messes with him twice – not even guys twice his size. He saw us at once, and was soon sitting with a Liquidator in his hand, leaning back in his seat and smiling.

'You are a clumsy cow, Vicky,' he said, when he heard the story. He laughed then, and I believe it was the last innocent laugh we heard for quite some time. I remember his grinning lips, stained with cherry – and it looked just like blood.

'What's the deal?' he said. 'Why am I here?'

Ben pulled out his laptop, and a cardboard folder, dead

111

centre. He'd pasted a large photograph, dead-centre, and we saw the face of a boy who was maybe eight or nine years old – he was smiling up at us. He had wide, laughing eyes and his hair was a mass of braids – an explosion, really – so you found yourself smiling back at him. He looked happy, healthy and wild.

Under his chin Ben had written three words, in clear capitals:

**JAMIE SONG – VICTIM**

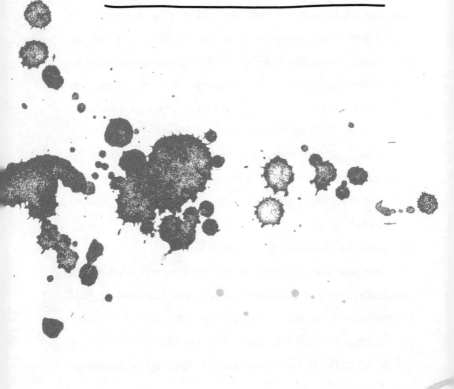

# Ben

## Continued ▶

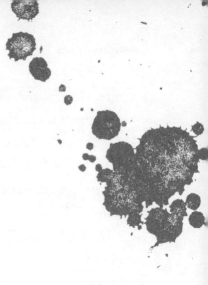

We had a lot to get through, and I didn't know how much they knew already – or how much they could really take in. They were looking at the kid's face, but I told them not to open the file. I wanted to go through it, step by step, but first I needed to show them the drinks companys website. I tapped in 'LIQUIDATOR', and up it came.

'Nice,' said Eleanor, as it loaded. 'Do you want a can? – I can buy you one.'

'Never again,' I said.

'Why?'

'Don't talk. Look, and learn.'

We saw the familiar images – we'd all seen them endlessly, on the TV and on posters. There were kids jumping and running, and blurring into each other – hi-tech edits with CGI – it was sophisticated stuff. Their faces swam up to the front, surrounded by the familiar graphics:

# DON'T YOU WANNA WIN? SEVEN AMAZING TASTES! WHICH DO **YOU** PREFER?

Every child they use is some kind of athlete, and the last one was Vicky's favourite – the little kung-fu girl who blasts her way through brick walls and concrete before swigging long and deep from a can that catches the light and flashes at you. It made you thirsty, just staring at it.

Stagger said: 'Come on, Ben. Why are we looking at this?'

'It's a tasty drink,' I said.

'We know that.'

'It's just hit the market, and everyone wants one. You were dead right, Vicky: your friend Mrs Lockson works for the company that makes it. Gleeson Holdings.'

'Which is why they had so much of it there,' said Vicky.

'Correct. She heads up the legal team, sorting out the licences. That drink's been her only client for about three years. That whole building works for Gleeson, and Liquidator is making everyone a fortune.'

'And it's a nice drink,' said Edgar. 'What's the problem?'

I think I just stared at him, and he stared right back at me.

'What?' he said.

'How many do you get through in a normal day.'

'Two or three. Sometimes more – I don't know.'

'You find you need them?'

'They give me energy. Yes. They give you a real boost.'

I spoke quietly then – and checked around the cafe. 'I know they do,' I said. 'But what if it's not what it seems, guys? Just let me ask a question here: Vicky – you were in the boardroom, right? With all the executives?'

'You know I was.'

'Did they mention that name on my folder. "Jamie Song"?'

'The little boy? I don't remember.'

'Think.'

She turned back to the photo, and shook her head. 'I know the name from somewhere, but I can't remember how. It was a special meeting, and they were arguing a lot. There was some big celebration—'

'OK, let's open the cover. I want you to meet him . . .'

'Why?'

'Do as I say.'

I turned over, and even though it was a noisy cafe it felt like we were in total silence – they were all huddled over the folder, pressed together. I'd printed in hi-res colour, 400dpi – and the first page was a lush, lovely jungle of palm trees and tangled bush, all emerald greens under a bright blue sky. You could see tatty buildings at the bottom, but it was a tropical paradise. I'd put in an inset which showed them what it was: a little tumbledown school, and you could just make out the sign-board, surrounded by purple flowers:

---

**THE HOLY INFANT JESUS
SCHOOL OF HAPPINESS AND HOPE**
Established 1976

---

'Turn over,' I said. 'Page two.'

'Is this all from her laptop?' said Vicky.

'You bet.'

Page two took them inside the school walls, and we were looking at happy kids playing under a crummy old basketball hoop. You could see laughing faces – maybe thirty boys and girls, and everyone was barefoot, chasing over hard earth, either topless or in too-big T-shirts. You could almost hear the laughter.

'Look at the little one,' I said. And I put my finger on him.

'OK,' said Stagger. 'That's Jamie again.'

'Correct.' I said. 'Normal kid. Having fun. Let me show you on the laptop now – there was a whole file of images. You wait . . .'

I called up more photos, and it was easier to zoom in, and follow the kid closely. We saw him stretching for the ball, getting higher than anyone – his long hair was sprayed out and he always seemed to be laughing. I showed them a team photo, with everyone posing and hugging each other. Jamie was right in the middle, with an older girl cuddling him as he twisted away, giggling. In the one after that he was on some other kid's shoulders, stretching the edge of a banner. The banner sagged, but we could still read the last three words:

## '. . . WHO WANNA WIN!'

That was the logo on the T-shirts too: the jagged lightning of Liquidator. I showed them five more shots, and in every one little Jamie was running, jumping, fighting, or even dancing. I'm telling you: in every scene he was glowing with health and happiness.

'Where is this?' said Edgar.

'Kenya. A village called Tiwi, by the sea.'

'Were they making one of those advertisements?' said Eleanor.

'No,' I said. 'This was before the ads. These guys were helping with drink development. They were part of the trials.'

Edgar looked at me then, and grabbed my wrist. I was about to pull up a new file, but he stopped me, and he was squeezing hard.

'Ben,' he said. 'I'm not understanding you.'

'No? Let go, and I'll show you—'

'Trials for what, Ben? What's "drink development"? – and what's happened to the boy?'

# Edgar

## Continued ▶

And that's always the thing with Ben – he forgets not everyone's brain is as big as his, and not everyone holds information the way he does, and to be honest I was getting a bit frustrated looking from folder to laptop and then back to him, like we're all at school and he's the big, clever teacher about to tell us something amazing. So I didn't let go, and I said it again: 'What happened to him?' – because the thing that was spooking me was that Jamie Song looked just like my little brother, who's on my mind at the moment anyway, being as he's not living with us right now – and I could feel from the way Ben was talking that something bad was coming.

I was getting ready to be mad.

He said, 'Let me explain "drink development".'

'Go on then,' I said.

Drink development, it turns out, is when some

company tests its product, before it gets a licence and before the product hits the shops. What they did in Kenya was find out how to make it tasty – which all sounded fine, and I think it was Eleanor who said, 'Wow, those kids were lucky!' – which made Ben shake his head and swear.

'No,' he said. 'Luck is not the word.'

So I said, 'Ben? Tell us what happened.'

'I'm trying to,' he said. 'They tested the drink. They loaded in the sugars, and the caffeine – and nicotine even. Oh, yes – they were playing with all kinds of things, and–'

'Making Jamie drink it?' I said. 'Just him, or–?'

'All of them,' says Ben. 'They were doing it for months, changing the mix, altering the flavour. You saw the kind of school it is: it's a bush-school, way out in the middle of nowhere, where nobody's going to know what's going on. The governor's been bribed, so they can run what tests they like–'

And I interrupted again. I said: 'Ben?'

'What? Wait.'

'No.'

I was feeling scared. Every time you looked into Jamie's eyes, they looked straight back – and his smile, I'm telling you . . . it was just like little Rio's (my brother), and I knew for a fact that Rio wouldn't care what you gave him to drink, as long as it was sweet. He'd guzzle down anything till he was sick, and he's kept me up so many times with tummy-ache or headache, or maybe just wanting attention because he loves being held, and he gets scared too – scared of the dark and scared of his dreams. So I was getting very worked up, and I tried to calm right down again. I said, 'Ben – just cut the crap, will you?'

'What crap?'

'Tell. Us. What. Happened.'

'It won't make sense without the background,' says Ben. 'What the Liquidator people didn't realize – or chose to ignore, I don't know – was that Jamie was diabetic. And they got him drinking and drinking – as they ran trial after trial – because they were working out how to up the steroid level, and get more gunk into it. I mean, it's full of flavourings and additives—'

'It can't be!' said Vicky. 'It's a nice drink!'

'Because it's full of sugar,' says Ben. 'It's addictive, yes? All these sugars are modified so they can under-declare them. They worked out the best formula on kids like Jamie, and went into production. Then just as he's getting sick – and I mean really sick, by the way – I mean weight loss, blood pressure . . . you name it. Just as Jamie needs them most, because his systems are collapsing – that's when the Liquidator people pack up and go home. The circus left town, guys, and I expect you can imagine – the hospitals out in Tiwi aren't too good for complicated disorders caused by massive chemical imbalances. You need specialist care.

So, if you turn over and look at the next page – you can see what five hundred cans of chemical crap does to a little boy five thousand miles away. I'm done now, Edgar – the lecture's over. Turn the page, and take a look.'

But of course I didn't want to, then. Because I knew from the build-up that poor little Jamie was dead, and we were going to see a coffin or a grave.

# Eleanor

**Continued ▶**

But we didn't, thank God – Edgar was wrong.

Even so, the next page was the most awful, horrible thing I've ever seen, and such a terrible shock because I ought to add that Jamie was the most beautiful little boy, and you couldn't stop smiling when you looked at him. To see the state of him in the last pictures made me actually gasp out loud – everyone did . . .

I wasn't even sure it was him, at first.

He was on a bed, but like Ben said, he'd lost weight. In fact, he hadn't just lost weight, that's not accurate: he was a skeleton. You could see his bones, and he's just wearing a little pair of shorts so I could count his ribs, and see the knobs of his elbows and knees, and you're thinking, Where's all his flesh gone? What's happened to him? The skin was  stretched tight, and he was sitting up but only because someone – a grown-up – was holding him that way, for the camera. And maybe the flash had been too bright, but his skin was shiny, like he was covered in sweat, and then . . .

Ben made us turn over again.

Vicky turned the page, and I'm afraid I just started crying. He wasn't dead, no – he was still alive, but this was a close-up of his face and it was a skull, and he was obviously dying. There were gaps between his teeth where his gums had shrunk, and his eye-sockets were way too big. They were grey round the rims and I thought at first it was a little old man, but it wasn't – it was him.

Someone had put a card up, under his chin, with the date and a pathetic little message:

JAMIE SONG.
HELP US.

The words were written in these spidery capitals, and while the little boy's eyes were still staring, the light was dim – you could almost see it fading. Worst of all, they'd cut all his hair off, or it had just fallen out, maybe – you couldn't tell. But he was bald, and so sick – so as I said, I started crying – but Edgar . . . oh my God. Edgar was suddenly on his feet, and he went crazy. He grabbed Ben and dragged him out of his chair so everyone's getting up, and I thought he was going to punch him!

Stagger jumped up too, of course – so there's chairs going over, and he grabbed Edgar, but Edgar threw him. That scared everyone, and then Edgar's pushed Ben up against a post – I really thought he was going to murder him, but poor Edgar, he suddenly just went limp, and turned round and I realized then that he was in a worse way than me. His whole face was twisted up and his hands were like claws, not knowing what to do with them, so Stagger gets up again, and puts his arms round him – everyone's staring at us, of course, and we realize then that we'd better get out of the cafe before we get thrown out. The manager was coming over, and babies are crying, and Edgar's saying, 'No – no way, no!' – over and over again in this quiet voice, looking plain furious.

Wow.

Vicky, bless her, did the obvious thing, and steered us all out, fast, through one of the emergency exits. She just pushed through, and Ben grabbed his laptop, and we found ourselves outside, in the cold, fresh air with the exit doors slamming closed again.

# Vicky

## 17.36
## Outside the cafe

And it was so lucky we left when we did.

As Eleanor says, we found ourselves outside, on a grass verge that looked down onto the car park, where we'd met. And what did I see, just as we stood there? – I saw a car rolling past and stopping at the main entrance. One big, swish, silver thing, and yes: it was the very same one that had parked outside our house. I might not have noticed if the doors weren't opening all together, before it was even still. There were men getting out, in black jeans and black jackets, and I knew straight away who they were looking for.

Stagger saw them too. 'Keep moving,' he said.

'Why?' said Ben. 'Where?'

People always ask questions like that, just as you're saving their life! When you have to move fast, you're better off shutting up and getting out – so I shushed him, and set off. Eleanor had to grab her dog, of course, but she caught up with us down the road a bit, and we started to run. Ten minutes later we found a playground, with swings and a slide – it was in a park, round the back of some houses.

'You were right, Ben,' said Stagger. 'They're after us. That was them, the same guys.'

'The same?' said Ben.

'Yes.'

'The ones who assaulted you?'

Stagger and I both nodded.

'Damn. How quick is that? That's . . . a few hours.'

'How could they know where we were?' said Stagger. 'We weren't followed, I'm sure we weren't.'

'Could they have bugged George?' I said.

Ben was shaking his head. He was taking shallow breaths, and blinking.

'I don't believe it,' he said.

'What?' said Edgar.

'I can't believe they'd be so fast. I mean: OK, they've looked at the laptop by now – the one we tried to fix. But they can't have had time to really analyse anything—'

'Would they know you'd been inside it?' said Stagger.

'No!'

'Are you sure?'

'I covered my tracks. I was so careful.' Ben closed his eyes, and I suddenly realized how scared he was. 'I didn't leave a trace,' he said. 'I did all the things you do – I cleared history, I suspended the supervisor, and with all the damage . . . They couldn't be sure, but – I suppose. If they had someone good looking at it, then . . .'

'What?' said Edgar. 'What would they see?'

'There's always a clue.'

'But they knew exactly where to find us,' said Eleanor.

'Yes.'

'How?'

Ben swallowed. 'I was online, wasn't I?' he said. 'I was on the Lockson website, leaving a trail. I was using my phone, earlier, to look up stuff, and cross-reference. There's a report I downloaded, full of accusations, and I looked up the boy's school, and I pulled up maps. I pulled up his medical history – that was on the laptop, and I did a search to understand the chemistry. If they got into my searches, then they'd know I was on their trail.'

'Wait,' said Stagger. 'They can't instantly know when someone hits on a website, that's impossible–'

'It's not.'

'Isn't it?'

'I don't know how else they'd do it!' said Ben. 'They call it "shadowing". If they've set up an alert, an online trigger feeds them instant information about . . . local hits. Christ, Edgar – *I can't go home.*'

Edgar put his arm round him. 'Where's your mum?' he said.

'Away. Away until Sunday, but—'

'You stay with me. You don't go anywhere near your flat. Where are you tomorrow?'

'That flower shop.'

'I'll go there with you. You'll be safe.'

'We should call the police, though. Right now.'

Stagger laughed. 'To say what, Ben? To say we saw three threatening-looking guys drive into the leisure centre car park and do absolutely nothing. They'd tell us where to go.'

Ben opened his laptop again, but his hands were shaking. 'I'd better check something,' he said. 'I've had an idea – this is crazy, but wait a minute . . .' He fished in his pocket, and pulled out a piece of plastic. He loaded it into a port, and tapped various keys.

'Are you still online?' said Edgar.

'Yes. I'm online all the time, day and night.'

He hit return, and we saw various folders open. I could hear the sharp intakes of breath as he opened more, and I saw his fingers hammer at the keys.

'It's impossible,' he said quietly. 'They've gone.'

'What have?'

'The stuff I put up. I saved the documents – I put every single folder on the web, and . . . I can't find them. I've been hacked.'

'Try again,' said Stagger. 'Go slow – you're panicking.'

'I'm not, it's blocking me. Christ, I can't even get email.

They've locked me out, Stag. They've found me. It's me they're after, and they're tracking me!'

Edgar said: 'Guys, I think we should move.'

Ben stood up, and we heard his phone ring. 'They're tracking me!' he cried. 'GPS. Oh God, this is bad.'

In his effort to grab his phone, he dropped it. He went back to the laptop, trying to cut its signal – and that's when we heard the murmer of a car. It didn't stop, either: it came over the grass straight towards us. Edgar turned around, looking at options, and we were all on our feet. Eleanor's dog went berserk then, barking and growling – and Edgar made up his mind.

'Run!' he said – and this time nobody asked questions. We piled after him the way we'd come, skidding in the mud. He pushed through a hedge, past bins, round the back of people's houses, and we ended up cowering behind a shed.

'Is it off?' said Stagger.

'Yes,' said Ben.

'Closed down, totally?'

'Yes! Honest! Let's go . . .'

Ben was white-faced and near to tears. We moved forward, cautiously, in single file and at last we found the street. There were shops and people, and best of all – at that very moment – a bus, turning a corner towards us. Edgar sprinted to the stop waving at it, and two minutes later we were up on the top deck, huddled onto two seats at the back, nobody saying anything. We kept our heads down, letting the bus roll us across town into some huge estate we didn't know, letting ourselves get more and more lost. It was a while before we sat up again, at the very end of the line. We looked out onto a wasteland of trees and rubbish, and the driver got out to have a smoke. He let us stay on board, and we sat there until Edgar said the obvious thing.

'What do we do?'

'Jamie's dying, isn't he?' said Eleanor.

Ben nodded. 'Yes.'

'Then what *can* we do?' said Stagger. 'Is he still in Africa?'

'No,' said Ben. 'He's in England, but I can't remember where. There's more files, I can take a look. It's Manchester, I think – he had a relative there, and they flew him over. But the Lockson people won't see him – that's the point. They're denying everything, and . . . oh God – there was something I didn't show you. It's an email, you've got to see the email . . .'

'An email to who?'

'It's from your boss, Vicky. Helen Lockson – I backed it up. It's on a memory stick, here. Jamie got to England, and they've written letters, sent photographs. They've begged for help, but – wait.'

His laptop was on again, and we saw a handful of icons.

'You're sure you're offline?' said Stagger.

'Positive, yes. Look.'

It took him a moment to find the document, and a moment to enlarge it. When he turned the screen around, we saw the familiar font of a standard company email, and it was short and to the point. We sat there reading and re-reading, as the letters burned themselves onto our retinas, and Edgar started saying every vile, obscene swear word that he knew – and he knew a lot.

Mrs Lockson had sent the message. The word 'confidential' stood out in the heading, underlined – and the message was simple:

> **From:** Helen Lockson
> **Sent:** Wednesday 11 June, 2014 11.38
> **CONFIDENTIAL**
>
> Jamie Song will be dead this week – he can't last without treatment, and only I have his records. Ignore all calls, refer correspondence upwards. We will bury him. Literally.

The date was today, and from the timing – 11.38 a.m. –
I realized it was the very message Mrs Lockson had sent just
before her lunch break. Just before she'd left me alone in
the boardroom.

# Leela

## 12.36
## The mortuary

The mortuary was in the basement.

We went through double doors into a white room. Mr Ahsan was out of breath, and I watched him lean on a chair, wincing again.

'Wait,' he said. 'I'm too old, aren't I?'

'Are you?'

'Breaking down, Leela.'

'Can I get you anything?' I said. 'A glass of water, maybe?'

'Thank you. No.' He laughed. 'I'll survive. This is my last week: you realize that?'

'Oh,' I said. 'No.'

'I'm retiring on Friday. Give me your pass.'

He took it, and moved to a hatch in the wall. There was a book laid open on the shelf, and he filled in my details. Then he turned to me again.

'I'm from Pakistan, Leela. I went there last summer, as

a matter of fact, and . . . and a friend of a friend had passed on, so I went to the funeral. Do you know what they did with the body in that hot, hot place?'

'No.'

'They dressed it in its finest clothes,' he said.

'Oh.'

'The man had been a taxi driver, and they dressed him in his smartest suit and sat him in a chair. They carried the chair into the garden, and set him under his favourite tree. Then all his friends, all the neighbours, all the local children, Leela: they all came to see this dead man and shake his hand. At one point he toppled forward, so hard did they shake his arm. They had to sit him back up again! And someone said, "Ah, already? – the bugger's drunk!" He was a popular chap, you see – father of nine, and I thought, That's the way to do it, eh? That's the way to deal with death: you take the mystery away. Take away the hocus-pocus and the scary, religious clap-trap. Eh?' He came towards me, and peered up into my eyes. 'Do you know what I mean?'

I said: 'Not really.'

'Not really? No . . . that's a good answer. Could you wash your hands, please.'

There were two basins against the wall, so we washed together.

He said: 'If you don't like what you see, my dear, you let me know.'

'Is this another test?' I said.

'Of course.'

'I want to pass.'

'I'm sure you do, Leela. And there are many ways to fail.'

Someone came to meet us – a woman in a white coat. She swiped a card, and opened another door. I felt light, as if I hadn't eaten, and I was taking shallow breaths. I knew enough about hospitals to know that the mortuary is where bodies are kept, for identification or for post-mortem, or simply for collection.

'This is Valerie,' said Mr Ahsan. 'She's a technician here.'

'Hello,' I said.

'She makes the body presentable,' he said. 'That's important. It's often the last time you see the one you love, so it's a tender, vulnerable time. They say there is often nothing harder than this last saying of goodbye.' He turned to Valerie. 'I'd like to see Miss Cotter, please.'

'With your guest, Mr Ahsan?'

'I've signed her in.'

'She's underage, sir.'

'I know. That's why she's here.'

Valerie nodded, and I was more frightened than ever. I wasn't sure where to put my eyes, because I'd noticed an enormous sink, and next to it was a slab-like table made of metal, with a groove running all the way round it. I knew the groove was for liquids other than just water, and my imagination was taking me to dark places.

'This is not morbid, Leela,' said Mr Ahsan. 'This is necessary. I want you to see death so you can understand what life is, because it's life that's important.'

I nodded, but it was hard to listen to, or understand, what he said.

He continued, 'The woman you're about to meet had heart disease, and underwent two operations – I didn't perform them. They were successful enough, but any further intervention was going to be difficult.'

We were by a set of drawers in the wall now, and I honestly thought they'd be full of files. I thought it was an enormous set of filing cabinets, and we were going to study the woman's medical history.

'Open the drawer,' he said.

'This one?'

'Yes.'

I pulled the handle, and as it rolled out easily, I saw two white, human feet. There was a label attached to the big toe on the right. I pulled a little harder, and the feet were sliding past me just beneath my chest, for the drawer was a long, narrow compartment on levers and wheels, and there was a very old lady in it, who appeared to be fast asleep.

We stood together, looking at her.

'She was a missionary,' said Mr Ahsan. He spoke very

quietly. 'I never met her in Asia, though she worked quite close to where my family live. She worked in an orphanage, in fact. We did our best for her, but . . . it's a strange thing, Leela, to know that someone is slipping away and there's nothing you can do. You never, ever get used to that feeling.'

I looked at her more closely then, and I saw how pale the woman was. She lay there as if she'd recently been bathed, though the skin was very old and quite grey. Her eyes were closed, her mouth was closed and her cheeks were slightly sucked in. Her head was tilted back a little, so her sleep looked deep. She was 'undisturbable' – that was the only word I could think of.

'What are you thinking?' said Mr Ahsan. He was talking so quietly, as if we might wake her.

'Just that she's so . . . she's so still.'

'Yes.'

'She's so dead.'

'Yes.'

'So . . . gone.'

'She's so dead, Leela. And yes, Miss Cotter is gone from us. That's what I see too – and I don't ever get used to it. Maybe some of my colleagues do, but what I think is, *Oh God, give me life*. And this woman had a blessed life.'

'Did she?' I was waiting for her to open her eyes because we were talking about her. We were so close: she couldn't *not* be aware of us.

'She saved lives, this woman. She educated people.'

'How old was she?'

'Seventy-nine.'

I said, 'Can I ask you something, please?'

'Of course.'

I didn't know why I needed to know, but I said: 'What is it like? The actual moment someone dies?'

He thought hard, and I wondered if he was going to answer. 'It is different every time,' he said, at last. 'The same result, obviously – the body goes cold, in an instant. You feel it. The warmth is lost, and you know it will never come back. And the person that was there – as you said, just now – becomes so dead, and is gone. Oh, sometimes they fight, and are frightened. Sometimes they look forward to sleep, and sometimes – until the last moment – they are distracted. Sometimes they know nothing, of course. I was with a child last week – younger than you. And, Leela – the anger, and the injustice, that all the years the child should have were being denied him.'

'The child died?'

'Yes.'

'You couldn't do anything?'

He shook his head. 'Nothing at all, and he slipped away from us. It was those around him – those left – who fought. And they're left with pain that won't ever, ever go away. An agony reborn each morning, and from time to time all through the day infecting even your dreams. Hell can be no worse, surely.'

He smiled.

'I can accept Miss Cotter's death. I hope I will accept my own. When a child dies, it feels like somebody is shaking the world, smashing at it. That is another thing I never, ever get used to.' His pager was bleeping gently. 'Because there's nothing as dead as death, and that's what I wanted you to see . . .'

He unlocked his phone, and made a call - he spoke so quietly.

'Maurice,' he said. 'Do you need me?' He was silent for a moment, listening. 'I'll be up in five minutes. Can I bring a friend? She's thirteen.'

There was a pause.

'Thank you, Maurice.'

He clipped the phone away, and he said: 'Appendix, just come in, with possible complications - he wants support. Would you like to join me, or rest?'

'I'd like to come,' I said. But to be honest I also wanted to cry, and sit, and think, and be alone.

'Are you sure?'

'Yes.'

'Good.'

We looked down at Miss Cotter again, and he lifted his hand as if to bless her. 'Look at the miracle,' he said softly.

'I can raise my hand – look. I can move my fingers, stiff as they are. We say goodbye, Leela. We walk away. Doesn't it amaze you? We are alive, and can walk to the door – we should be thanking God every moment, no? Just for the gift of walking back into the world.' He was staring at me again, and it was so hard to look at him. He said: 'Do you believe in God?'

I said, 'I don't know.'

'The coward's response.'

'No,' I said. 'Sometimes I do. I'm still waiting.'

'Good.' He was silent for a moment. 'Miss Cotter was convinced,' he said. 'She had unshakable faith. We would argue and she'd tell me I was an ignorant heathen. I'm an atheist, you see, and I told her that God is incompatible with medicine – a myth for the gullible, and a comfort to the stupid.'

He chuckled, and I smelled cigarettes.

'She told me she'd wait for me in heaven. She couldn't wait to see my face . . .' He wiped his eyes. 'Oh, she could make me laugh, Leela. This dear, dead, cold, old person . . . she made me laugh so much.'

# THURSDAY

# Vicky

## 17.00
## The cinema complex

For twenty-four hours we did our best to play it cool.

We had to, hard as it was. If we just carried on as normal, what could the Lockson people actually do? Kidnap us? Stagger argued that all they'd been trying to do was scare us. They'd tracked Ben not to wipe him out but to show him he was in a dangerous place – it was no more than a warning. The poor boy didn't dare go home, though – the thought of being alone was too terrifying, so he spent Wednesday night with Edgar, who gave up his box-carrying at the gym so as to spend the next day at the flower shop.

I had to go back to school, first of all. I'd been formally sacked, so I had to face the school authorities and explain myself to Mr Millington. He had already phoned my dad, of course, and told him how disgracefully I'd behaved, so I had to report to the head teacher at ten to nine. Nobody wanted to hear my side of the story, and perhaps that was lucky. If I'd told them about the laptop and the files, what would they have said or done? – they'd have probably got straight on to Mrs Lockson. All Mr Millington wanted to do was make a speech about my flagrant disregard for rules, and how I couldn't be trusted. Everyone agreed that I'd undermined the school's reputation, and should be ashamed of myself.

All the time they talked I held a piece of paper in my pocket, tightly folded. It was the printout of Jamie Song – the photo of him playing basketball, in the best of health, and I clenched it in my fist and said nothing. My penance, they decided, was to join a junior year group for the rest of the week and clean up after it.

So I spent my Thursday with a load of Egyptians.

The Year Sevens were doing a history project, and had come to school dressed up as Pharaohs and slaves. I was soon helping with the papyrus-making, lost among tombs and pyramids. There was a big map on the wall, and I let myself sail down the Nile, right through the Sudan, until I got to Kenya: Jamie's home.

I found Mombasa, but Tiwi was too small. I unfolded my photo then, and there they all were: the boys and girls in Liquidator T-shirts, posing for the cameras, so full of trust. At break time I noticed how many kids had the drink in their bags – there were special snack-size cans and nobody could read the ingredients list even if they wanted to, because the type was so small. Some kids even carried Liquidator backpacks, which were shaped like fruit – all you needed was to scan a code off the cans and mail it. Yesterday I would have said the backpacks were cool, and I would have been swigging back the 'Tropical' with everyone else, getting higher and not thinking about my teeth or my arteries. Now the bags had a sinister, predatory look, and when a kid slung one on, it looked like the thing was clutching him round the neck, sucking his blood.

When I cleared up at the end of the day, I threw fifty-one Liquidator cans in the recycling bin. I breathed in the perfume, and was immediately thirsty.

That evening, we met at a cinema.

We'd been texting each other, and Edgar chose the place at the last minute. He led us to the side, and slipped behind a curtain. It was his secret way in, when he couldn't afford the entrance fee, and we followed him straight out again through a hidden door. We found ourselves in a corridor that led back to one of the public areas – a floor full of video games and fast food. It was noisy, crowded and dark – and the point was that if any of the Lockson gang had tailed us, they'd assume we were still sitting in the cinema.

Edgar was carrying a rucksack. 'Ben and me are going

north,' he said. 'It's the obvious thing to do, and we're leaving tonight.'

'North?' said Stagger. 'Why?'

'To find Jamie - or his family.'

'Edgar,' I said. 'That's not practical. I thought we were here to discuss the situation—'

'No. I discussed it. I've been talking all day.'

Ben said, 'Look, I'm still not sure—'

'Then I'm going alone,' said Edgar. 'We can't waste any more time - we've wasted today. What else is there to do?'

'The police,' said Ben.

Edgar swore. 'They're going to laugh at you, man - we've been through this. What we have to do is find the boy, and get his records to the right people. His medical records. We've been through this, Ben! - I thought you were coming.'

'But what if we can't find him?' said Ben - and he looked sick with fear.

'Do we still have his records?' I said. I'd slightly lost track of what was on Ben's laptop and what wasn't.

Ben nodded, but he still looked desolate. 'I backed everything up, soon as I decoded it. I do it all the time, it's an instinct. So, yes - I've got the stuff, and I've got his whole medical history—'

'Which is what the family needs,' said Edgar. 'We've got the records of the tests they did - there's pages of them.'

'So you could email them to someone,' said Stagger. 'Find out who his doctor is, perhaps—'

'But that's the point,' said Edgar. 'We don't even know if he's in hospital. We're going to spend days faffing about, and we need to find him fast.'

A silence fell.

'Look,' said Edgar, at last. 'You can do what you want. I'm not asking you to come, guys – really, I'm not. You can stay at my house, Ben, till it all blows over. But I am not living with myself if that message comes true. They are not burying Jamie Song – not while I'm alive.'

I said: 'Good. I'm with you.'

'Hang on, Vicky,' said Stagger. 'This needs thinking about—'

'I've thought,' I said. 'I'm not going back to school, not while this is going on.'

'I'm not saying we shouldn't do something,' said Ben. 'I'm not saying forget it, or ignore it – I'm just saying there must be better ways.'

'But you haven't thought of any,' said Edgar.

'A newspaper,' said Ben. 'Your dad, Vicky – he was a journalist. He'd publish this, wouldn't he?'

Stagger shook his head. 'He's unemployed, Ben.'

'Then the twins, at the *Gazette*. This could be a real exclusive—'

'I'm going,' said Edgar. 'Let's see the picture again –

come on.' He turned to Stagger. 'We've been looking at this all day – the last photograph, yes?'

I'd kept the picture of Jamie when he was healthy. Ben had the one from the back of the folder, and when he laid it on the table I'm afraid I had tears in my eyes, instantly. It reminded me of every famine, every war zone and even those awful death camps we have to learn about – Jamie's eyes followed you, wherever you put yourself, and I knew Edgar was right. We all stared at the face, and the sign under his chin:

'When are you leaving?' I said.

'Now.'

'OK. But Stagger? – you're going to have to stay here. With Dad.'

Stagger nodded. 'I'll talk to the twins, too – there might be something they can do.'

Ben nodded. 'I thought Eleanor could do some dog-walking, out at the Lockson place. Get some photographs of whoever comes and goes, because we'll need the papers, in the end.'

'Easy,' said Eleanor. 'I've got a new camera – I can do that, and I'll be careful.'

'Do you have an address?' I said. 'For Jamie?'

Ben nodded. 'I know where the letters came from. They wrote to Locksons, three times a week. And, oh – another thing. Every file is backed up on a memory stick, and the memory stick's in the flower shop. A blue and white pot, with a rosebush – it's display only, and we put it on the top shelf behind the till. That's what we bargain with, if things get nasty.'

'What time's our train?' I said.

'We're hitchhiking,' said Edgar. 'What money we have, we want to save. So you need to get your stuff, Vicky. We'll give you one hour. Meet at the bus station, and we can get a bus to the ring-road.'

# Vicky

## Evening
## M1 North

George behaved well.

We puttered into the bus station just before ten o'clock, and the boys were there already. I hugged Stagger, and he told me to be careful. We put on our coats because it was just starting to rain, and Ben checked the map and worked out the route. Half an hour later we were by a petrol garage with a nice, long slip-road, where the cars could stop easily. The plan was to get a ride with any vehicle heading to the motorway. Edgar did the first stint of thumbing, with Ben and me sitting on a low barrier just behind him. The rain got worse.

Edgar looked small, and even frail in his bomber jacket, so it occurred to me how weird it must look to see three kids trying to hitch a lift. If a police car passed, they'd have to take us in, and that would lead to all kinds of complications – it would end the whole campaign before it had started. Luckily, we only had to wait five minutes and a Range Rover stopped for us: the driver was a concerned mum, with a little kid in the baby seat. We told her some story about visiting Edgar's pregnant sister, and after another half-hour she dropped us on another long slip-road, where the northbound traffic gathered speed. She tried to give us twenty pounds, but Edgar refused.

Ben, I found out later, had withdrawn all his birthday money: we had a hundred pounds.

Almost at once we had another stroke of luck – this one, monumental. A lorry came hurtling towards us, with huge, high shoulders. Its lights were blinding, and it let rip a deafening fart of horns – the road actually shook beneath our feet. Ben thumbed at it even as we leaped out of its way, and none of us believed it was stopping. It lurched in on top of us, however, squealing, hissing, and pouring steam, and we heard the gears grinding as the driver fought to control it. The rain had turned torrential, so what a relief it was to climb into a massive, comfortable cabin.

At the wheel sat a kind of elf.

He was only a little bigger than Ben, and he introduced himself in a high-pitched voice as Colin. 'Keep It Cool, Colin!' had been emblazoned all down the side of his truck, and we found out almost at once, before we set off, that he'd been in the business for thirty-two years, driving refrigerated vehicles across the UK. We would soon discover he had friends steaming down just about every main road in the country, and he could chat to them all on the short-wave radio that dangled over his head.

'Where you going then?' he said as shunted forwards. He had a breathy, Midlands accent and a manic smile. 'Starting a bit late, eh? No?'

His head never stopped moving as he pulled out into the storm. It was clicking left and right all the time, checking mirrors and dials. He had skinny arms, I noticed, and he leaned across the controls the way I imagined a sea captain would take the wheel of a galleon. The cab was clearly his home: it had a bed behind, a fridge to the side, a sound-system all around and fairy lights over the ceiling. He had a little dog curled up on the dashboard, which I thought was one of those fake, nodding-dogs at first, until it yawned.

'So then, where to?' he repeated.

'Manchester,' we said.

'Oh, no!' said Colin. '*Manchester?*'

'Yes,' said Edgar. 'What's wrong?'

'Rudgwick,' said Ben. '*Near* Manchester.'

'Oh dear, no,' said Colin. He seemed anxious. 'Oh-dear-oh-dear, you shouldn't be starting from here!' he muttered. 'You should have started from Tuckers Cross, taken the A1. Loads o' traffic up through Hatfield, takes you straight in on the Northampton bypass – brings you in through, oh . . .' His face twisted with concentration, and he clicked a switch, gazing into a wing mirror. '*Corby*, that's the best bet, and then Rudgwick's out by the estuary. The only thing you've got to watch, though – when you go through Wythenshaw –

that's the low road above Mac, cos if you get stuck on that it's a bottleneck, night and day. Why take the motorway?'

'We thought it would be best for hitching,' said Ben.

'Well, you've got a point there, but . . . oh dear. You don't want be on this road, really.'

'How far are *you* going?' I said.

'Up to the M5, got a drop in Duncton . . . Pick up in Leicester, then it's overland to the viaduct near Stoke. You been there? Resurfacing all the way to exit twenty-two, but we'll miss the worst of it. I can drop you . . . ooooh . . .'

He paused, and peered at the road. He flicked a switch, and *crunch* went the gears. He accelerated hard into the next lane, hauling the truck into a wave of black water. The windscreen wipers came on faster, huge and noisy. He clicked his lights then checked his mirrors again, and at last the engine found an easier gear.

'I know,' he said. 'Easy. I can drop you by the Boddington Paper Mill, and I've got a mate who goes by there early mornings, four o'clock-ish. I'll give him a call . . .'

'Great,' I said.'

'Thanks,' said Ben.

Colin talked to us then, almost without stopping. The monologue lasted for over a hundred miles, and we learned about his driver friends and what they carried. We heard about those who'd been delayed because of crazy diversions, and he laughed about misleading signposts. There were road surfaces so bad you could lose your tyres, he said, and then he swore and told us a long story about a foolish cyclist who'd failed to signal, and had caused a twelve-car pile-up.

At three o'clock in the morning he took us off the motorway onto some kind of derelict bombsite, where he slammed to a halt. He then reversed, fast, through a spaghetti of ducts and pipes so as to change trailers. His hands were a constant blur, and his knees went up and down until I started to think of him as a mad, talking puppet. When he finally pulled in to our destination, we'd become firm friends, and he pressed a business card onto each one of us: '*Keep It Cool, Colin – Inspiration With Refrigeration*'. Then he radioed the mate again, who was heading to Manchester with a delivery of early-morning flowers. Where was he, and how long would he take to fetch us?

Ben and Edgar got tense thinking about their flower-shop experience, but I was grinning with sheer wonder. We waved goodbye to Colin as the rain turned to sleet, and in five minutes our next vehicle arrived. Soon we saw signs for Rudgwick Port, and then Rudgwick itself. The driver dropped us damp and steaming right in the town centre, and by four fifty-five we were drinking hot chocolate in an all-night diner.

I phoned Colin to say thank you, and I could hear him yelling happily over the engine noise, 'He got you there, did he? Good stuff! Just let me know when you're done . . .'

'We're about to have breakfast—'

'You stay safe, pet. You're on a mission, aren't you?'

'Kind of, but—'

'Don't tell me. But if you need a ride south, darling: get on the phone.'

'You've really helped,' I said.

'Good luck to you!'

We dozed for an hour, and then we were woken by the smell of bacon butties. When it was light enough to see, we set off into the gloom. We didn't talk about Jamie, and we hadn't much idea about what we'd do when we found his house. Looking back, we were all avoiding the one, big obvious question – because none of us wanted to deal with it.

Was he even alive?

That awful email was burned into our memories. We didn't need to get the paper out. We could see it, in black and white:

---

**From:** Helen Lockson
**Sent:** Wednesday 11 June, 2014 11.38
**CONFIDENTIAL**

Jamie Song will be dead this week – he can't last without treatment, and only I have his records. Ignore all calls, refer correspondence upwards. We will bury him. Literally.

# FRIDAY

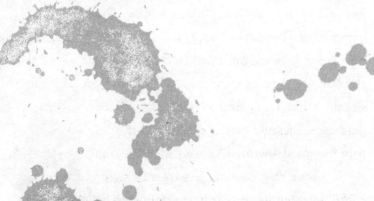

# Polly & Molly

## 12.58
## The *Gazette*

Mr Bickersdyke, our editor, rejected every idea we offered him.

We were beginning to realize that despite running a newspaper, he didn't actually like news. It took up too much time. What he liked was advertising, which brought in large amounts of money very quickly. For that reason, Saturday's *Gazette* was going to be dominated by advertisements for Liquidator. Liquidator, you'll remember, was the main sponsor of the 'Africa's Weeping!' gig, so the parent-company had bought up space on almost every page. There were going to be cut-out Liquidator coupons, and a special children's competition inviting them to complete the slogan: 'I like Liquidator because . . .' There was even a double-page feature on the special-healthy-freshness of the fruit they used – written, of course, by the company.

It wasn't easy working within such tight commercial constraints, but we were still determined to be journalists.

I – this is Polly – had spent the previous day working alongside a police liaison officer, while I (Molly), had visited a food bank and a traveller community that was in conflict with a local landowner. We'd cancelled another gym class, which we hated doing – but it meant we could work till midnight again. The articles we created were both topical and challenging: we were determined to see them in print.

When Friday morning came round, however, Mr Bickersdyke didn't even show.

How lucky that I – Polly – had realized we'd need keys of our own, and that I (Molly) had got the set we'd borrowed duplicated at a nearby store. We let ourselves into the office, and pressed on. We phoned our boss just before lunch, and took him through our lead stories – there was even a new piece, about a dog attack outside a local law firm.

'No,' he said nervously. 'It's too controversial.'

'What is?' I said – I being Polly.

'All of it.'

'All of it?'

'Everything.'

He sounded almost tearful, and hung up abruptly. Then the other phone rang, and before I (Molly) could say, '*Gazette*, good afternoon?' – we heard a voice say, 'Who's that?'

The voice sounded serious.

'Molly Tuttle,' I said. 'Assistant Editor.'

'Hi.'

'Hello.'

There was a pause. 'What's on your front page this Saturday?' said the voice.

'Who's calling?' I said.

'I can't say,' replied the voice. 'But I've got something sensational for you. When can we meet?'

I looked at Polly. 'We need your name, please. We're pretty busy, so we can't meet unless—'

'I can't give it,' said the voice.

'Why not?' we asked together.

'Because it's top secret, and it's big, and I could get myself killed.'

That's when we lost patience, I'm afraid. We jumped to the obvious conclusion: it was someone from school, wasting our time. We put the phone down, and got straight back to work.

# Stagger

## 12.58
## The street

I wasn't wasting time.

All right, maybe I should have got to the point quicker but the fact was, I was getting scared again. I'd delivered four pizzas that morning, George behaving well (despite the throttle delay, which is a fuel-pipe problem). Four pizza deliveries I'd made, and each time I got back on the bike, I saw the same car going slowly past me. Two guys inside, pretending not to look, and OK, it wasn't the big silver thing we'd seen before – it was a little blue Fiat, in fact – but it was always there, just when I looked up. Either they'd hacked my phone, or they were in touch with my manager, or . . . I couldn't think of anything else.

I phoned Vicky's dad, and he was at the library. I told him to stay there. Then I parked up, checking I was safe, and that's when I called the Tuttles. There was no sign of the car.

When I called again, I said my name straight away: 'It's Stagger,' I said. 'And this isn't a hoax.'

'Stagger?' said Polly. 'Vicky's friend?'

'Yes,' I said. 'I need to see you as soon as possible, please. We've got something big.'

# Polly & Molly

## 12.59
## The *Gazette*

'We're actually quite stretched at the moment,' I said – this being Polly (on the extension). I didn't want to be rude, but the fact was we had so much copy to check we had no time for anything else.

Molly said: 'What's the story? Can you tell us on the phone?'

'No,' said Stagger.

'Why not?'

'I'd rather meet. Do you know that Indian restaurant, on . . . Magdalen Street?'

We did, but I thought he still sounded suspiciously melodramatic, so I looked at Polly, and she was just about to say, 'How about tomorrow?' when we heard a terrified gasp and the sound of screeching brakes. After that came a cry of either pain or fear, and a car horn blasted, long and loud. Finally, there was a sickening crunch, as if the phone had been smashed with a hammer.

'Hello?' I said – me being Molly.

'Stagger?'

All we could hear was interference, like static.

'Stagger?' we said together. 'What's happened?'

But nobody answered, and then the phone died completely.

# Stagger

How stupid can a person be?

I was right out in the open, but I still didn't see it coming. You can tell yourself to be careful, and you tell other people, and then you make big, stupid mistakes as if you haven't a brain in your head.

The guys were watching, and they saw me on the phone. Maybe they were even tuning in? I never found out. What I do know is that the car charged at me out of nowhere, coming right across the traffic and accelerating fast. I heard it, and swung round just in time: I grabbed the bike and dived forward.

If I hadn't moved, I would have been mown down, legs broken. It was all instinct, heaving George out of the way. A convenient tree meant the car skidded straight past, braking hard as a door opened and the passenger jumped out. I pressed ignition, and he started, first time. I revved hard, and George forgot his fuel problems because this really was life or death.

I only just got a leg over, and we zoomed off over the grass like a bolting horse, straight onto the pavement and down the kerb. I yanked the throttle open, clattering and juddering, and I couldn't use the mirror because it was shaking so hard. My helmet was back there on the ground, and my phone had gone: I just had to ride like the wind because when I did look round I could see the car had reversed backwards and was coming right after me.

What do you do? You don't even think.

I skidded through bollards onto the opposite pavement, where some woman with a pram jumped out of my way, too scared to scream. There was a one-way street, and I took it, wrong direction. That would mean they couldn't follow, but I should have known better. Horns blasting, tyres screeching – they were behind me again, and I thought they were going to run me down, but I stayed ahead by inches.

There was a zebra crossing then, and this will haunt me for ever! A whole line of kids walking over it in those high-visibility tunic-things, as if that's going to save them, just because they're visible – I had no brakes even if I wanted to brake, so I yelled out, loud as I could, and the line broke apart and let me through. I glimpsed a teacher pluck a couple of little ones to safety because the car came crashing through straight after me, and I was praying, not to God, but to the bike: 'Come on, George,' I was saying. 'We can do this! Don't stop! Don't even think about mechanical failure . . .'

I turned up an alleyway, too narrow for a car.

'. . . if you get me through I will polish you and cherish you!' Stupid stuff, I know, but it kept me from dying out of sheer total, brain-frying terror.

Dead end.

Stuck! Just a fence in front of me, with a car park beyond. I looked behind, and what did I see? The passenger, again – black jacket, black jeans – and he was racing towards me, head down, sprinting. I think I actually screamed because I had twenty seconds, max. I revved, but suddenly there was no power – then it came, delayed, motor screaming louder than I was. The fence wasn't strong, and one panel was giving way, so I aimed George straight at it, and somehow we battered our way through. I was stamping and kicking, and bending low under nails which tore my coat half off and cut me deep on the shoulder. I got by, though, and we burst across the tarmac, skidding round skips and bins, and there was a long, concrete drive that let me push George up to thirty again, and we were skimming towards the exit, racing to safety.

The man chasing me gave up, and half a minute later I found the road. I got to some roundabout, and took an exit into a housing estate where I went left, then right, then left, then left again, and kept turning randomly, deep into the centre of the maze, until I found this little scrubby bunch of trees and I nursed George in among them, and sat there shaking, and – I don't mind admitting it – sobbing. I had blood all down my arm and face and I could actually feel my heart battering away like it had come loose in my chest.

Oh God.

No phone any more. No helmet, no papers . . .

I didn't know what to do. I sat there until the adrenaline storm passed and I felt a bit calmer. I thought, I'll find a phone box. Take it easy. Get Dad, Vicky's dad, to safety – wherever safety is . . . we can't go home any more. Warn the others. Call up the Tuttles again, and tell them the whole thing without bullshit, because the sooner the world knows about this the better, because if those men come for me again I won't be so lucky . . .

I had a vision, then, of what they would have done to me if they'd caught me, and I'm afraid I was sick on the grass.

I sat there for about twenty minutes, just me and George. Then I went to start him. You won't believe this, but it's true: he was as dead as a doornail, not even a peep. The battery was totally, utterly flat, and if that had happened earlier – if he'd let me down – I would not be writing this. I'd be on my back in a shallow grave. Dirt in my face, every bone broken.

# Eleanor

## 12.59
## Lockson & Lockson car park

I did not set the dogs on Mrs Lockson.

She'd actually been quite rude to me, telling me to get away from her car even though I'd looked at the map and discovered a public right of way running right past her building – and she should have known about that, being a lawyer. I told her so too, and she went pink under her tan, which was obviously fake, and said: 'Just get those horrible dogs under control.'

Horrible, they were not. Boisterous – yes. But lovely.

This is what I say to people who live in flats and are thinking about getting major pets: think harder, and get a goldfish. Do not get a pair of beautiful, playful german shepherds who only want wide-open spaces and fences to jump – they will be difficult. But people are a lot more stupid than dogs, and – I have to say it – rather more selfish.

My favourite of the two was called Lightning, and the other was Thunder. I'd been warned that they were over-familiar, so I was totally unemotional with them.

That was Mrs Lockson's big mistake: when she got excited, she released a certain pheromone, which made the dogs think she wanted attention, and was even up for a bit of flirtation. They responded. When she tried to push them off, they thought – quite naturally – that it was part of the game and wanted more. I can't remember who grabbed at her skirt, whether it was Thunder or Lightning or both of them together, but I would swear on a whole house full of Bibles and Qur'ans that to the dogs it was a harmless bit of horseplay.

If Mrs Lockson hadn't screamed she would have been fine. The scream released even more pheromones – a whole storm of them, in fact, and when some security man appeared, waving his arms and releasing more – well, the dogs thought it was party time. They just overdosed on sheer, doggy excitement, and off came the skirt, ripped to pieces, and poor Mrs Lockson ended up on her bottom.

They didn't see me taking photos.

I'd hidden my brand-new digital camera in a Donald Duck lunchbox that I'd pinched off my baby sister. The lens was poked through a hole I'd cut, and I could get my finger in and click away in total secret.

So, yes, I did send the best one to Polly and Molly, really hoping they'd plaster it all over everywhere . . . but knowing they probably couldn't, or she'd sue them like the cruel devil she clearly was.

# Vicky

## 12.59
## Up North

Meanwhile, we'd caught another bus. And then another.

We had Jamie's address, where the family's last letters had come from, so after a few false starts it wasn't hard to find a map and work out where to go. We got down by some boarded-up shops, and made our way into a square of bleak-looking tower blocks.

'This is the place,' said Ben. He was hunched over his laptop, and a gale was blasting between buildings. 'We want one called . . . Hyacinth.'

There was no one to ask.

The only person we could see, even in the distance, was fighting with an empty shopping trolley, heaving it into the wind. I remembered another children's play area, totally deserted, with swings that looked like gallows: the chains were clinking and twisting, and it was raining harder. We found the right entrance, though, and stopped at the elevator. Its doors were wide open, but the inside was black from fire damage.

'Stairs,' said Edgar. 'What level?'

'Six,' said Ben. 'You think this is home?'

'Must be.'

'What a shock,' I said. 'Imagine this, after a little village by the sea.'

We climbed six flights of stairs, Edgar leading. I could see he was tense, but we didn't pass a soul. The walkway took us past a dozen identical front doors, and we could see we were getting close from the numbers. You can imagine our surprise, then, when we came round the corner and found our path blocked by a huge metal grille. It sealed the passage from floor to ceiling, and we gazed through it onto a pyramid of rubble. The far side of the block had collapsed.

'I hope he isn't under that,' I said.

'It's condemned,' said Ben. 'This whole estate, by the look of it—'

'What you lookin' for?' said a sharp voice. We swung round together, backs to the mesh.

'Nothing,' I said.

'What you doing then?'

A girl was standing by one of the doors, with something furry drawn around her shoulders. Her legs were stick-thin in high boots, and her nose looked as if it had been sharpened to a point. The hair was a mass of intricate braids, and her eyes were big, unblinking things, which made me think of a cartoon bird or bug. She was fierce rather than funny, though.

'Do you know a kid called Jamie?' said Edgar. 'Number six hundred and thirty-one: Jamie Song.'

'Jamie Song?'

'Yes.'

'How d'you know him?' She spoke quickly, and the words ran into one another. '*Howjenoim?*'

'We don't,' I said. 'But we need to talk to his family.'

'What about?'

'We've got news,' said Ben.

'Good or bad? They was waiting for that.'

'Mixed,' I said, after a pause. 'But very, very important.'

The girl just gazed at us, and Edgar stared back. 'Do you know him or not?' he said. 'We've got a picture – d'you want to see it?'

'No.'

'Why not?'

'He's the little sick kid, isn't he? Arrived a few weeks ago.'

'Do you know where he went?' said Ben.

'I know the family a bit – everyone does. I know where they probably went to, but I don't know for sure.'

'Where?'

'Stowno,' she said. 'That's where they all go.'

'He needs emergency treatment,' said Ben, and Edgar was unfolding the photograph. 'Is he in hospital? – because he should be.'

The girl laughed at that, but I couldn't see why. I couldn't work out how old she was, either – it was between ten and twenty-five. She came closer, and I caught a whiff of perfume. She looked at the picture, and I saw her wince.

'Where d'you get that?' she said.

'We found it,' said Ben. 'And we think we can help him. We need to see his doctor.'

'He won't have a doctor,' she said. 'What's wrong with him, anyway? – some bug, some virus?'

'No,' said Edgar. 'Worse than that, but we've got all his records. We know everything, and it's *not* a virus.'

'And you got money? Because I'm working.'

'We've got some.'

'Show me.'

'No,' said Edgar. 'We've got nothing spare, and we need to see him, now. Do you know him or not? What's your name?'

'They're all illegal, you know – you do know that?'

'Illegal, how?' I said.

'No papers. No hospital.'

'Can you take us to him, or–?'

'I can take you to Stowno, but it's twenty for the taxi.

Twenty for the time. I was living there too – it's a bad place. Dangerous. And my name's Tilda.'

She led us back the way we'd come, and over a bridge. It was wired in like a rat trap, to prevent suicides, I imagined. Then, after several more twists and turns she hammered on a door that flapped wide open, its lock smashed and splintered. A man appeared, and called for a boy, who led us – with Tilda – all the way down to ground level again, where a line of cars sat in a forlorn, dented, punctured, rain-soaked row.

'That's the taxi,' said Tilda. It was a mini, at the end of the line.

The engine cranked into life, and the wipers cleared a tiny patch for the boy to see through. Soon he was struggling through narrow streets, then down into the unexpected darkness of an underpass. Rudgwick oozed into an even wetter, greyer wasteland, and some miles later I saw a sign:

'They all stay there,' she said. 'Came out weeks ago. Have you seen him, Chucky? The little sick kid – Jamie?'

'Jamie who?'

'Song,' said Ben, and Edgar showed the photograph.

'Shit,' said our driver, glancing at it. 'What's he got?'

'Nobody knows,' said Tilda. 'Did you see him?'

'No.'

'You think he's alive, still? He's half-dead there, isn't he? – when was that taken?'

We said nothing, but I saw Edgar's fists clench. We drove through more endless rain, and at last we reached a river. Along its bank stood a line of warehouses, and I could see dump-trucks shifting piles of stone from the torn-up road. Cranes reared up into the sky, but were motionless now, thick with rust. The tarmac turned to gravel, which gave out into mud.

Our driver didn't park; he just rolled to a slimy halt by a jumble of high sheds and skips. He led us to a door, and when it closed behind us we realized the inside was colder than the outside. The walls were wood, the floor and ceiling were wood – and the wood was rotting.

Ben was nervous. 'Why are we here?' he said.

'It's where they come.'

'What, you mean people stay here?' I said. 'Jamie's family came here?'

'Probably,' said the girl.

'Why?'

'Why what?'

'Why would anyone come here?'

Tilda laughed, and the answer was soon all too obvious. People stayed here because they had no place else to go.

We walked along a passage in single file, past an old man, unconscious on a stool. We were led up some stairs, which corkscrewed to a dark landing where every window was boarded up. The rooms off that had no doors, and we could see bunk beds lit up by dangling bulbs. A woman crouched by a saucepan, mixing something on a tiny, hissing gas stove. Next to her, a half-naked child sat flapping at the smoke, and as my eyes got used to the gloom I saw more and more people, squatting and sprawling on mattresses. We picked our way through them. Some were asleep, and some were playing cards. I could hear a television, babbling in a foreign language, and over it all I could hear the rain again, rattling on the roof.

'You really think Jamie's here?' said Edgar. 'He can't be.'

'I don't know,' said Tilda. 'Wait.'

'Can you ask someone? It's urgent.'

'You said that.'

'I meant it.'

She spoke to a man, and it was a language I'd never heard before. He pointed to a woman, who pointed to a door. We went through it into a longer, narrower room, lined with more mattresses, and Tilda asked again. A young girl nodded at a curtain, and we filed through it towards a

space that might once have once been a cupboard or store-
room. Now, it was a tiny home and a woman stood up at
once and took Tilda's hands. The conversation erupted in
the same, soft language.

Edgar, Ben and I stood there, staring about us – and
Edgar had the photograph ready. We knew, though: we were
standing in the very place it had been taken. We recognized
the bunk bed, and the shadowy patches showing damp.
The room was cut in half by a washing line that sagged with
shirts and underwear, and there were toys strewn across
a mat.

The two beds were empty.

'He's gone,' said Tilda.

'Gone?' said Edgar – and I think all our stomachs
lurched. 'Gone where?'

'I don't know – that's what I'm asking.'

'To the hospital,' said the woman slowly.

'That's good, thank God,' said Ben, and I could hear
the relief in his voice.

'What's the name of it?' said Edgar. 'Who took him?'

Again, the language crackled back and forth.

Behind us, a man in an overcoat appeared, and he had
a baby in his arms. We were pressed further into the cell
and the rain beat even louder over our heads.

'She doesn't know its name,' said Tilda. 'She says it's
the big one.'

'Who's he with?' I said.

'I don't know – I'm trying to find out.'

'Look,' said Ben. 'We need to find him, Tilda – it's why we're here. There can't be that many hospitals—'

'There can,' I said. 'It's a big city.'

'Wait,' said Tilda. 'Have some tea. Everyone's watching, so sit down a minute. We'll find out.'

I turned, and saw what she meant. Half a dozen children had crept up to the doorway, and were gazing at us, solemn-eyed. I saw another flaming stove, and I saw a kettle – all I could think about was what would happen if the place caught fire. Edgar was crouching, looking at the empty bunk, and I saw tears in his eyes.

'Jamie lived here?' he said, and the woman nodded.

There was a toy rabbit on the pillow. Next to that was an old, battered book of fairy tales, and against the wall a basketball.

'Is that his ball?' he said.

The woman nodded. 'Jamie,' she said. 'Very sick now.'

'Very sick,' said the man. 'Very sick, so . . . problem.'

The washing line was unhooked and coiled in a corner. There was the rattle of crockery, and one of the children stepped close, and opened a box of biscuits. Crates and chairs were produced, and we sat in a circle together, sipping our drinks. That's when I saw that the man was holding a piece of paper. I also noticed that his hand was mutilated – he'd lost three fingers, so unfolding it was a delicate business. But he opened it onto his knee, and the letterhead jumped out at us, black and bold: 'Lockson & Lockson'.

Someone gave him a box then, and it was full of similar papers – there were envelopes too. We saw receipts, all paper-clipped together, and I knew at once what it was. It was the whole time-wasting correspondence as the lawyers stalled and wasted time. The one he showed us was short, and urged the recipient to *send the child's medical records as soon as possible, so further checks could be swiftly carried out*'.

'And they had them,' whispered Ben. He was near to tears, as well. 'She had them, on her laptop. They just want him dead.'

'Which hospital is he in?' asked Edgar again. 'That's the important thing – that's all we want to know.'

'Jew,' said the man.

'St Jew,' said Tilda. 'St Julian's?'

He nodded. He had a soft, gentle voice, and he smiled at me. 'Saint Jew,' he said. 'He is my nephew.'

'Jamie Song?'

He smiled, and nodded. 'Half-brother boy. My. Nephew.' Then he shook his finger and thumb. 'Very sick. *Ve-ry* sick!'

'We know what's wrong with him,' said Ben. 'We'll talk to the doctors, OK? They can still treat him.'

'*Eyes*. No good now.'

I looked at the little bed again, and for a moment I saw Jamie there on the mattress.

'You find him,' said the man quietly. 'You help him, yes?'

'How long's he been in hospital?' I said.

Tilda translated.

'Oh,' said the man. 'Maybe . . . last night?'

'What? Only last night?'

'That's not good,' said Ben.

The man spoke in his own language, but at last Tilda looked up at us. 'Late last night,' she said. 'He . . . he wasn't breathing right. And his eyes, his sight – there was something wrong with his eyes.'

Edgar cursed quietly. 'How bad? Tell us.'

She spoke again in the foreign language, and both adults nodded. I saw the woman cross herself, and some of the children watching did the same.

'He was going blind,' said Tilda. She hunted for the right words. 'They don't know, but . . . there was blood too.'

Ben stood up then, and he was really polite. He said, 'Thanks for the tea. We have to go.'

'I'll come with you,' said Tilda.

'We're going to find him,' I said to the man, and we all shook hands.

He took his sad little tin box then, and closed the lid. Then he took my hand again, and kissed it.

Tilda said, 'Look at that. He's relying on you now.'

'We'll do our best, tell him.'

'He thinks you're his saviour. People like you . . . you can work miracles, yeah? What's your name?'

'Vicky.'

'You're going to have to work one now, Vicky. Don't let him down.'

Edgar looked away, and shook his head. 'They think you're rich,' he said. He spoke quietly still, but I could hear the fury in his voice as he said it. I saw the bitterness in his eyes too, which were still wet – and he wouldn't look at me. 'They think you can sort it all out, Vicky. Wave a magic wand, and save his life.'

Chucky dropped us at a bus stop – he wouldn't drive into town because, like Stagger, he had no licence or tax. We waited a long time, but when the bus came we saw it was going right to the hospital – that was its final stop. Everyone got off there, and a great river of people trudged up a ramp towards its big glass doors.

What did we see, staring down at us? A giant billboard fixed to the hospital wall, with a young boy grinning at us in triumph. He was gleaming with perspiration, for he'd just won some tournament. He was a blond, white, spiky-haired god, bursting with health, and there was lightning around his shoulders. The word *Liquidator* shrieked over his head. Underneath that was the all-too-familiar slogan:

'. . . ONLY FOR WINNERS . . .'

We stood under it, feeling sick and afraid.

Nobody would say it, but we knew there was every chance we'd come too late. It took real courage to walk in and up to the desk, because now we feared the worst.

What if Jamie hadn't won? What if the whole game was over, and Jamie Song had lost?

# Leela

## 12.59
## East Dean hospital

Mr Ahsan drank a glass of water with me. The appendectomy hadn't been complicated after all, and the little girl was recovering on the ward, calm and comfortable.

'My last few days,' he said. 'I've given my life to this place.'

'Are you retiring completely?'

'Yes.'

'Is that good?'

'No. What will I do? Smoke and drink and die.'

We stood in silence, and at last he said: 'I wanted to meet one more student, Leela. A genuine novice. I wanted to glimpse the future, and remember the past. I think I wanted to remember what it was like to be truly amazed.'

'Will you go back to Pakistan?'

'No.'

'You're not old, though.'

'I can't work any more, my fingers are stiffening. You have, how long? Once you're qualified, eh? Thirty to forty years, to heal the world – and I hope you will . . . Where will you start, I wonder? Everywhere, people will need you. We're easy to ruin, Leela. We're hard to restore, that's the simple truth of it. And I've seen such things, such suffering – and I talk far too much, I know that.'

'You don't.'

'Today I finish.' He laughed. 'A lifetime's work, and I give up my badge today and walk out for the last time – there was going to be a party. I said, "For what? You think I'm celebrating?" I always wanted to work, and I read your letter, you see. You sounded just like me – you sounded hungry, so I thought, *To hell with the rule book! Let's watch her fly* . . . This is sentimental nonsense, I know that . . . but I had a dream, and the dream recurs. A child, who needs me – whom only I can help. I had to be ready, always – for that special child.'

We sat in silence.

'There are so many children, aren't there? And I still wait to meet the one in my dream.'

I said, 'I don't quite understand—'

'I thought it was you,' he said.

'Who?'

'The child I could help. But now I know it's not because – well, with respect – you don't need anyone.'

# Vicky

## 14.18
## St Julian's hospital

They'd never heard of him.

Nobody knew who Jamie Song was, and the first receptionist sent us straight to 'outpatients'. The nurse there sent us to somewhere called 'toxicology' because of the things Ben was saying – he had his laptop open, with all the medical records on it, and we showed the dreadful photograph. The toxicology man sent us to an annexe, which seemed designed mainly to house long, looping queues. You couldn't be sure how they worked because there were standing lines, and sitting areas where people took numbers from a little machine and waited to be called. There were queues to join queues, and when we got to a little window, the person there was dealing with three different things at once. She was on the phone, and then someone in a white coat came bustling in to ask her about forms, and meanwhile the phones would start ringing again, so when she looked up at us she'd lost the thread of where we'd got to.

We showed her our photograph, but she just stared at it, glassy-eyed with tiredness. It did no good at all.

'Jamie *Song*?' she said.

'Yes.'

'S - O - N - G? That's the family name?'

'Yes,' said the Tilda. 'That's what they use, we think.'

'And he arrived last night . . .'

'That's what we were told,' I said.

'Who's his doctor?'

'We don't know,' said Edgar.

'He had an appointment? He'd been referred, or—?'

'No,' said Ben. 'We don't think so. And he probably doesn't speak English – look at him.'

'But he *is* a UK citizen?'

'No.'

'Oh.'

We watched as the nurse scrolled down a computer screen, and then her mobile started bleeping.

'There's nothing here,' she said at last, clicking the phone. 'Hello? Try the duty nurse in A & E – people often get in that way. Hello? Yes, I've got it, I'll be with you . . .'

As she spoke, someone was leaning in behind us with a fistful of prescriptions, crushing me against the windowsill. I snatched the photograph back, and we found a table in a horrible cafeteria, where Ben lost a pound to a drinks machine that swallowed coins and gave us nothing. There were Liquidator bottles all along the bottom shelf, and another poster, this one with an exquisite elfin girl who'd just won a gleaming silver trophy. I wanted that drink more badly than ever, and I could see Edgar did too.

'I used to have five a day, sometimes,' he said. 'Two to start with, and then it went up.'

'You don't know the half of it,' said Ben.

'What?'

'Hook them while they're young. They're bringing out a version aimed at toddlers next year. Then it's baby food – you can read all about it, it's all in the files—'

'Look, what do we do?' I said. 'We have to find Jamie.'

'Try the morgue,' said Tilda.

Edgar slammed the table. 'Shut your mouth!' he cried. He stood up, walked away, and then he came back to us. 'We split up,' he hissed. 'We do a proper search, all right? We go in different directions . . . ask everyone we see. Eight-year-old kid from Kenya – we show his picture. Someone might know, and we meet back in here in half an hour. If we haven't found him, we . . . I don't know. We think of something else.'

Ben shook his head. 'But they must have records!' he said. 'There must be a more efficient way – who's he with? Who brought him here?'

'They might have just left him,' said Tilda. 'They do that sometimes, or there's too many questions.'

'So he's on his own?' I said.

'He might be.'

We parted, and for thirty minutes I explored corridors, and got lifts up onto wards full of sad-looking people. I lost myself totally, and what was strange was that nobody seemed to notice me. I never got challenged. I just wandered, saying the same thing: 'I'm looking for Jamie.' I showed the photograph, knowing it bore little resemblance to how he looked now – but it got people's attention. 'He's a little Kenyan boy,' I said. 'He arrived last night – have you seen him?'

Nobody could help. 'Have you tried Admissions?'

'Yes,' I said. 'They sent me up here.'

'Who's his doctor? What's his second name?'

'Song. Jamie Song.'

Some people just said no. Some people asked me what was wrong with him, and most ended up telling me to try the hospital Reception again because I was wasting my time otherwise. I ended up turning round and trying the next ward, or the next long corridor until I was lost all over again, and tired of my own voice asking the same, dumb question. I met Tilda by a pharmacy, and she was more exhausted than I was, and a lot more irritable. Walking amongst the sick is enough to make you sick, and I'd seen things I didn't want to see – life-stopping illnesses – and it made me so glad I was well. But it made me much more frightened for Jamie.

'I need food,' said Tilda. 'I haven't eaten today.'

'Why not?'

'I was working.'

'What do you do?'

'Can't you guess?'

'No.'

'I'm not gonna tell you then. And here's your friend.'

Ben was waiting for us, by the drinks machine that had cheated him. You could see by his face he'd got nowhere, and was too tired to talk. The text came in just as we sat down, from Edgar. Two words only:

> GOT HIM

Ben texted back, and we huddled round waiting for the response. It arrived at once:

> radiology corridor e5
> left side come quick

# Vicky

## Continued ▶

We started walking, and then we were running. We got lost, then saw a sign, and we were running faster than ever. Suddenly we were there: E5, and Edgar was waving at us. We pushed through a cluster of trolleys, and the one in the centre carried a sick, lost, frightened child, and Edgar held the rail as if he'd never let it go.

The patient was Jamie, and he was alone. We'd looked at the face so many times, but it was still a shock to see it there in reality – the face we'd come all this way to find. Jamie Song was alive, and breathing, and he would not – *could* not – die now. Death was unthinkable.

But his breathing was uneven . . .

They'd wrapped him in a hospital gown. Tilda went straight to his side and took his hand, and he stared up at her, utterly bewildered. A faint smile flickered – he must have been so glad to see someone – but it disappeared almost at once, and his eyes closed. He didn't take up much space on the trolley – he looked like bones, to be honest, that had got mixed up in a sheet. We could see his chest rising and falling as he struggled for breath.

'Hi, Jamie,' I said.

I remember I said it really softly, and his lips twitched again as if he so wanted to smile. One eye opened wide, but it was glazed and dim.

'Hi,' he said.

'We're your friends, OK?'

'Friends . . .' He swallowed. 'Good.'

'We're going to help you. Who's with you?'

Ben was looking at a clipboard. 'Jamie St John . . . Otieno,' he said. He had trouble with the last name. 'That's the family name then. Not "Song" at all.'

'Never heard it,' said Tilda. 'What's he waiting here for? What's radiology?'

Jamie had shut his eyes again, and I saw the effort it took to re-open them. His tongue passed over his lips, and he tried to speak. 'Thank you,' he said, at last, in halting English. Then he smiled one quick, dazzling smile before his whole face was creased in pain.

I found his other hand – the one Tilda wasn't holding. I lifted it up and, oh God, it was a bunch of twigs on the end of a light little stick of a wrist. 'Jamie,' I said, but I started to cry. Edgar had turned away, and I could see he was broken, struggling not to crack wide open. I put the little hand against my cheek, and said: 'We'll find your doctor, OK? We've got your records now, and . . .'

'Do you need something?' said a voice.

It was one of those teacher-type voices, and we all swung round. A man in a white coat had emerged from a nearby cubicle, stethoscope swinging. He had the same tired look I'd noticed in the receptionist we'd spoken to, but he was cross and impatient.

'Do you know this boy?' he said.

I said, 'Yes. We're family.'

'Well, where have you been? You're not going to help him by crowding round – you'd be much better off getting him registered—'

'He's an emergency,' said Edgar softly. 'Why's he in a corridor?'

The doctor turned away. I could hear someone shouting, and then I heard a crash of steel pans dropping on the floor. He waited for quiet, and said: 'We're investigating, all right? We've been trying to contact his parents, and if we knew what was wrong we'd be a lot further forward. So at the moment—'

'Why is he waiting here, though?' I said.

'There's nowhere else,' said the doctor. 'He'll be through as quickly as possible, and we'll at least get him

X-rayed.'

'Haven't you done that?' said Edgar.

'No. We're a machine down at the moment—'

'We've got his records,' said Ben. 'Could you look at them, please?'

The doctor pinched his nose, and when he looked up he had the same trouble focusing that Jamie had. He was drunk with fatigue, and I could see him struggling to stay calm.

'We'll X-ray him first,' he said.

'But we've got what you need,' cried Ben. 'It's all on my laptop – right here. X-rays too – everything.'

The doctor laughed a short, hard cough of a laugh. 'You've got his patient records?' he said.

'Yes.'

'I can't take records off a laptop. Medical records have to be transferred to us by his GP, and they have to be verified. We're going through a process—'

'He's diabetic,' said Ben. 'Did you know that?'

'I don't need to know that—'

'He's been poisoned, and it's urgent. His kidneys are damaged, and look . . .' He dropped his voice to an urgent whisper: 'He's not got long to live – you can see it. We've got lists of what he drank and how it affected him. There was a breakdown in sugar levels caused by an overdose of . . . I can't remember all the names, but they're here on my laptop. He got sick in Kenya, and the people who have his records are deliberately withholding them – that's why you haven't seen them.'

The doctor didn't speak for a moment. 'OK,' he said, floundering. His pager or mobile phone started bleeping. 'Why don't you . . . the best thing I can suggest is that you go to Reception, and ask for a form—'

'But we've been there, dammit!' shouted Edgar.

'I can't stand here discussing it—'

'Why not?' I said. 'Why can't you discuss it?'

'Because . . .' The doctor wiped his face, and he looked desperate. Then he said, more aggressively: 'Because I'm not qualified to do so. I'm a duty radiologist, and I've got about twenty people to see! Look out, there's a trolley . . .'

We heard a sudden, urgent clattering, and sure enough a team of medics was hurrying along the corridor, straight towards us. They were wheeling a trolley with a patient attached to a drip, and we had to leap to the side to avoid being run down. In that moment the radiologist side-stepped away, through a curtain, and was gone.

'We have to get help,' I said.

'How?' said Tilda. 'What do you mean?'

Edgar said, 'He can't stay here – he'll die. Someone has to see him, and do something.'

Looking back, we must have been mad.

But nobody argued, and ridiculous as it was, we sprang

straight into action. We had half a plan, I suppose: we'd get him out of the corridor and into a taxi. I'd speak to Colin – who'd promised to help. We'd talk to Leela on the way, and get *her* advice. The important thing was to find someone who'd treat him immediately, for every minute that passed was leaving him weaker.

Tilda stayed with Jamie, while Ben ran ahead to hunt down a cab. Edgar followed with me, but we weren't fast enough – because that was the moment Lockson and Lockson made their move.

# Edgar

**Continued ▶**

I'd say they were after all of us, but Ben was the main target.

Whether they'd got a tip-off from someone inside the hospital, or had the place staked out and saw us, I don't know, and I never heard. They jumped us as we hit the street because the first thing I saw was a silver car coming fast, doors opening as it came, and two guys getting out who didn't look like friends.

They went for Ben together, and as the car skidded up on the kerb, the first one slammed him with his fist, and tripped him onto the pavement. The second man grabbed his bag and wrenched it from his shoulder. This was kidnap, so they yanked him up and round to the car, where someone else was waiting to haul him inside. Ben just had time to shout as he was pulled in by his hair.

One second it takes, and your mind's made up – then it's all about doing it. I went in feet first, and I got the first guy hard in the mouth with every kilo of my weight. He should have seen me, but he was still grabbing at Ben so he ended up flat on his back and I saw his head slam down so hard on the pavement I thought I'd killed him.

I stayed upright, turning with the elbow, going in for the next guy because, believe me, I wanted to do someone, badly – I wanted to break bones. A blow to the face can miss, because your instinct is to flinch away. The throat, though: that's much harder to defend, and I caught the bastard full under the chin, right in the jugular. He got his knee up and we pushed off each other leaving Ben half on the road, and me to defend him now, hands up for when they came.

I wanted more.

They were too stunned, though, and the guy on the ground was only half-conscious. I could hear the driver yelling, and the car horn going – and I should have crippled them both, but I was very aware of Ben. Everything's still, all around us, like the whole place is frozen – and I'm trying to look left and right as the man I floored struggles to sit up. I thought, *What's in his pocket?* Because you never know – a knife changes everything. So I got in front of Ben properly, and now Vicky's screaming something, and the guy with the smashed-up throat's hurt too, but half on his feet. He's having problems breathing, and he staggers to his mate while the guy in the back shouts, 'Get in! Get in!' – over and over.

It was all too public, I suppose – they didn't want to risk it – and at least they had the bag, so they had the laptop. That was why they piled back into the car, and were gone.

Ben was bleeding badly.

He was holding his arm too, where they'd jerked his rucksack off. Worst of all, we're surrounded by well-meaning people who do nothing when you need them, but now want to take charge and show how much they care.

You can hear: 'Oh my word, look at his face!'

'Call the police!'

'I got the car number – did you film it?'

A fat woman kneels down by Ben, but he pushes her away, and I'm trying to lift him.

'It's all right, lovey,' she says. 'What's your name? – let's call your mum.'

I said to Vicky, 'They know where we are.'

'Yes,' she said. 'So they know where Jamie is too.'

'You're right. Let's go.'

'Edgar,' she says, 'They'll kill him!'

'That's what I'm saying!' I shouted. 'Go. Now.'

There was a traffic warden trying to get us to the side, getting all-important with a radio. Someone said, 'I've called the police – they're on their way' – and all I could think was how we had to be faster than ever and get back to Tilda. I got Ben on his feet, but some idiot old man had grabbed his arm, and I came close to decking him.

'What school do you go to?' he said. 'What school?'

I swore in his face.

'No need for that!' he said, and there's phones snapping us and people closing in. I thought how any minute we'd be having to explain the impossible, and if we did say the truth you can bet by the time they'd understood – if they listened, even – Jamie would be gone from that corridor, and we'd never see him again. So I just pushed through, holding Ben so I was almost carrying him, Vicky ahead of us, saying, 'It's OK – we're fine, thank you, we're fine . . .'

We're getting through the scrum, back to the hospital doors and Ben says: 'They got my laptop.'

'I know.'

'And my phone.'

I said: 'So we don't have his records?'

'Not any more. We don't have anything, Edgar.'

But we did, and I said so, right in his ear. 'We found Jamie,' I said. 'He's alive, Ben, and that's what matters. We're getting him out.'

'Am I a mess?' he said, trying to wipe his face.

I tried to laugh. 'You're fine,' I said – but he wasn't; he was badly cut and there was an awful lot of blood. I felt dreadful then, when I looked at him, because I should have been in front, and I should have seen them coming. I should have known it was on the cards, and I should have protected the boy a lot better than I did. That was my job, for God's sake – it was why I was there. I hugged him tight. 'Sorry,' I said.

'What for?'

He was starting to shake, and you could see he was in deep shock. I think he was realizing just how lucky he'd been, because if they'd got him . . . if I'd stayed with Jamie, for example, and he'd been out there on his own – if they'd got Ben in the car . . . I hugged him even tighter, and he was crying, and we moved as quick as we could back to radiology.

Tilda was waiting with the trolley. 'Someone's been asking for him,' she said. 'Questions.'

'Who?'

'Some big guy in a suit. Asking if anyone knew where Jamie Song was. He went off that way, but–' She saw Ben's face then, and I saw her mouth drop open.

'Move,' said Vicky. 'We're leaving.'

And without waiting for permission or arguments or any paperwork crap, we dragged that trolley straight down the corridor, shoving through crowds. I lifted Jamie up then, and carried him in my arms – and how much did he weigh? It was like picking up a tiny little doll, or a puppet, and Vicky put her coat over him so no one could see. I felt his arms go round my neck, just like Rio at his bedtime, just like little Rio, and if anyone had even tried to stop us they would've been dead – simple as that. We put our heads down, and lost ourselves in corridors till we found a window, and Vicky jumps out first. I hand Jamie to her, and we're all out, walking fast. Then, so lucky (looking back), we see a taxi that had just dropped someone, and five seconds later we're inside it. Vicky's phoning Colin again and we push out into the traffic.

'Where to?' says the driver.

'Out of town,' I said. 'Ring-road, please – can you get us to the motorway?'

'Northbound, or south?'

'South.'

Colin got straight back to us, and yes, he said – he could help. Vicky told him what we'd done and what we wanted, and yes, he said: no problem. He knew a guy close by who could fetch us, no questions asked. He spoke to our driver and told us where to go and then Vicky told him more about Jamie, and his condition, with Ben trying to remember all the stuff he'd read on his laptop. Then she tried to call Leela, but her phone was switched off, so we texted instead, and there was nothing more to be done.

I just sat there, with the kid back safe in my arms. All I knew was that it really was a race now – a race against time, for life or death.

Nobody spoke.

We just sat there, all thinking the same thing: *Come on, driver: go faster. Don't stop for anything. We don't know what we're doing, but we're doing it.*

# Polly & Molly

## 15.05
## The Gate of India restaurant

We met at 'The Gate of India', at exactly three o'clock.

Stagger was with Vicky's father, and he – Mr Stockinger – had the largest glass of whisky we'd ever seen served, and looked distinctly shaky. Then again (this is Polly) – so did Stagger, whose jacket and T-shirt were torn and bloody. He kept looking around the restaurant as if he was worried someone was after him, and it was quite clear he was in trouble. It was also clear he had important things to tell us.

When he'd finished I'd jotted so many questions onto my pad that I didn't know where to start. Polly came in first with the most important: 'Where's the evidence?'

'We've got all the files,' said Stagger. 'They're safe.'

'Can we see?' I said.

'Not at the moment, no.'

'Why not?' We said that together.

'They're hidden,' said Stagger. 'And we need to work

out what we're going to do with them, because if they get lost or stolen . . . we're back to square one.'

It seemed strange to come to a meeting empty-handed. Stagger had convened it, after all, so the onus was on him to offer information if he wanted to be taken seriously.

Mr Stockinger raised his head at that point, and I – Polly – wasn't intending to count the number of drinks he was consuming, but it's hard not to notice when somebody orders one. He was on his third whisky and soda, and his hands were unsteady.

'I'm not sure these girls believe us,' said Mr Stockinger. There was a definite slur in his voice. He took another sip, and the liquid spilled down his chin. 'It's what I've always said, you know. People can't take too much truth.'

'We can,' I said – this being Polly.

'Good,' said Mr Stockinger. 'Because these Lockson scum are scared. You don't send out the dogs unless you've got an awful lot to hide.' He smiled. 'And we've met their dogs. Twice, now.'

'That may be so,' I said – this being Molly. 'But in the end, it's not simply about believing you, is it? We have a Liquidator advertisement on our front page tomorrow. The company you want us to expose has bought up half the paper, so it won't be easy running a story that accuses it of corruption.'

'You want it to be easy?' said Mr Stockinger.

'No,' we said together.

'Because it never is,' he said.

'But it has to be done,' said Stagger.

'You realize the timing, of course?' I said – this being Molly, still. 'It's the eve of the "Africa's Weeping!" concert. The story would be an international sensation.'

Mr Stockinger nodded. 'Exactly.' And we got a gust of alcoholic breath.

'That's the reason it's so urgent,' said Stagger.

'And I know your editor,' said Mr Stockinger.

That surprised us.

'I worked with him, for a very short time. Has he inspired you?'

'Not really,' I said.

'No?'

'No.'

'We've been trying to freshen up the paper,' I said (Polly). 'We want to be journalists, but he hasn't been very enthusiastic about our ideas. We've made a few changes, so Saturday's edition might be a bit better—'

'It won't,' said Mr Stockinger.

'Why not? We've put in a bit more news.'

Mr Stockinger drank again. 'That's what he won't allow,' he said. His eyes drilled into Polly first, and then they turned on me. 'He won't let you change a goddamned thing, and you know that. Why are you wasting time?'

'He's looking at our latest ideas now, actually—'

'You're wasting your time, girls. *He's* wasting it, and he hasn't the guts to tell you. The *Gazette* exists to do one thing, and one thing only. It sells us things that we don't want and don't need, to generate profit for its owner.'

'That's a little harsh.'

'The truth is.'

'Then if you're right,' I said – this being Polly again – 'how can you possibly hope to break this amazing story through us? Surely you should be talking to a national paper – or doing something on the web, or—'

'No,' said Stagger. 'Wait.'

'We haven't told you our plan,' said Mr Stockinger. 'Or why we summoned you.'

A silence descended, and we were determined not to break it. A waiter came over and topped up our drinks, and still we simply looked at one another.

'We're not interested in the *Gazette*,' said Stagger, at last. 'We want to use the building, though. We want to print our own paper, and to do that, we need your help.'

Again, we said nothing.

'We want you to get us into the basement.'

'When?'

'Today. Copy the keys—'

'We have done,' I said (this being Molly).

'Really? Why?'

'We had to, just to get into our office—'

'Good. Then get us in there as well, when everyone's gone home, and let us down to the cellar,' Stagger said.

Mr Stockinger leaned forward. 'Have you been down there? Did he let you down into the junk room?'

We both nodded, remembering our trip on the very first morning.

'You saw all the rubbish?' he said.

We nodded again.

'There's something special, at the bottom. Something I wouldn't let him dispose of, partly because it's an antique. Partly because I learned my trade on it. And it's a printing press, girls – all ready to go. I even put a cover over it to keep it clean: it's called a Pipshum 5000. One of the most reliable presses in the world, and you don't even need power, if you haven't got it. I've printed stuff in war zones, overnight . . . We'd use bicycles to turn the plates if we had to, and write by candlelight. She's the revolution-aries' friend.'

'You want to print your own paper?' I said (this being Polly). They both nodded.

'But what would you do with it? How would you sell it?'

'We'd give it away,' said Stagger.

'How long would this take? How many pages?'

'Four' said Mr Stockinger. 'All the facts they're trying

to hide. All the letters and emails, eh, Stagger? All the photographs . . .'

Stagger was smiling. 'We print it tonight – that's the plan. Work overnight. Then we get a van, and take it to the "Africa's Weeping!" gig, tomorrow. Walk into the crowd . . . hand them out, free of charge.'

'This is your chance,' said Mr Stockinger. 'Why are you wasting time with Bickersdyke? You said you wanted to be journalists – that's what you told me. Why not risk an exclusive? Why not change the world?'

We were back at the *Gazette* building soon after four o'clock, and it was deserted. We let ourselves in, and climbed quietly up to the office, and I swear at that stage all we wanted to do was sit down quietly and think – our heads were spinning.

The door was locked.

A heavy strip of steel had been bolted to it, and there was an indestructible-looking padlock sealing us out. Above it was a postcard, pinned to the wood, and we read the message with total disbelief and fury:

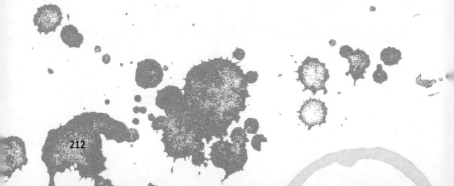

Dear Polly and Molly,

Thank you so much for your hard work this week – I know you've done your best. I have been advised, however, that our advertisers are concerned about the changes you propose and they have asked me to terminate your employment with immediate effect.

Please leave all keys on the mat, as your services are no longer required.

Sincerely,

Cyril Bickersdyke

# Stagger

## 16.11
## Street

I'd gone straight off to call Ben and get the backups.

I'd borrowed Molly's phone, and I thought I'd misdialled at first, because the voice that answered was deep.

'Hi,' it said. 'Who's this?'

'Stagger,' I said. 'Is this Ben's number? Ben Gallagher?'

'Sure. How are you, Stagger?'

'I'm fine. Where's Ben?'

'Indisposed, old buddy.'

'Oh. Who is this, please? I need to talk to him.'

There was a silence then, and I could hear other voices.

'Hello?' I said.

'Is this your new number, Stagger?' said the man.

'What? No. Who is this, please?'

'We've met before.'

'Where's Ben?'

'You don't remember?'

'No—'

'It was in your house, and we warned you very clearly—'

'Where's Ben?'

'He's on the run, Stag – you understand? He's running for his life, and so should you be. So should you all. We're coming for you, and I'd better tell you something, before you hang up . . . You listening? We know where you are, and we know what you're doing. I'm on my way, in person—'

I managed to cut the call, but my hands were shaking and my mouth had gone dry as dust. I thought I was going to fall over, but I stood there, dead still, and of course the phone rang so I nearly dropped it, and I tried to turn it off, but I couldn't work out how! So I had to hold it as it buzzed louder and louder – I was totally paralysed . . .

I found the off switch at last and killed it. Then I started walking. They had the twins' number now, so what did that mean? – could they really trace us? I remembered the giant in our kitchen, in his smart suit and tie – his massive hands. Then I thought about Ben and the others, and where they were and what was happening – and what, if anything, I could do to help.

There are times you can't answer a single one of the questions that's coming at you, so you just walk in the hope that your head might clear. I thought, *Get the memory stick.* That's the one practical thing now: at least do that. It's what

Ben said: it's something to bargain with, if everything's lost. If we were caught, or in danger, we might just bargain our way out and save our skins.

I started running, and I got to the flower shop just before it closed.

# Vicky

## 16.11
## Motorway south

We were in big trouble.

We'd been picked up by Colin's mate, and crammed together in a van for more than an hour. Tilda was close to breaking point. She'd taken Jamie from Edgar, and could feel him getting weaker.

Ben said: 'How is he?'

'He's alive,' Tilda said. 'What are you doing though, guys? This is kidnap.'

'Nobody's been kidnapped,' hissed Edgar. 'People were after him, you saw that—'

'But what's your plan? What mess are you in, anyway?'

'Trust us,' I said. 'We're going to meet up with another driver. He knows what's happening, and he'll get us to a decent hospital.'

'We need a doctor,' said Tilda. 'You shouldn't have moved him.'

'Shut up,' said Ben. 'Please shut up! We had to.'

'Why?'

'Because bad people want him dead!'

I leaned over and pushed Jamie's blanket back. A pair of big, black eyes looked out at me, and I saw the awful craters of the sockets. There was pain behind them, and his breath was soft and feathery.

'Hey,' he said. He just managed to whisper it – one word – and the smile appeared for a moment, before the pain removed it.

'Jamie,' I said. 'You hold on, all right?'

'I'm . . . OK. Just . . .'

'What?'

'I don't know.'

He whispered something to Tilda, and she hugged him harder. She whispered back in his own language, and rocked him.

'We're taking you somewhere,' said Edgar. 'We're going to get you sorted, promise.'

'Is he hungry?' said Ben.

'No.'

'Thirsty?'

'He's sick, all right!' cried Tilda. 'Don't you understand that?'

I watched Jamie blink, and I could see it was an effort for him just to stay conscious. Tilda adjusted his position, drawing him back onto her lap, and in a moment he was dozing again and there was a trail of spit down his chin. I tried to call Leela again, but her phone was still switched off.

Ben said: 'Look. If they've got my phone, then they have all our numbers. They could be working out where we are, from the calls we're making.'

'Can they do that?' said Edgar.

'I don't know, but it's possible.'

'So what about when I phoned Colin?' I said. 'Or texted Leela? Are you saying they can home in on that? Is that how it works?'

'I'm saying they might,' said Ben. 'There may be a way of working out where our signal is coming from, what mast is receiving it. I don't know, Vicky – I'm not an expert, am I? I'm just scared.'

'Me too.'

When my phone bleeped, I almost dropped it. I actually cursed aloud when I saw that yet again it was Spud telling me what a wild time he was having in the drains. Five minutes later Katkat called, and as she was the last person I wanted to hear from I didn't take it. I texted Leela instead, wondering if my messages had been hacked, and if we were running straight into the most dreadful, deadly trap.

She didn't reply.

Minutes later, Jamie had a fit.

We weren't prepared, and it was horrible. It started

with the most awful retching – I saw him twist like a fish, straight out of Tilda's arms. She tried to lift him, but the poor boy writhed and twitched again, his fingers like claws. Tilda cried out, for the spasms were taking hold. Our driver cursed, and swung off the motorway, blasting his horn. We'd reached the service station, at last – just in time – and the first truck we saw, thank God, was Colin's: 'Inspiration with Refrigeration!' It was waiting for us in the car park, lights blazing. We tumbled straight out onto the tarmac, and Jamie was half carried and half dragged towards it.

'He's dying!' said Tilda. 'Get an ambulance!'

Edgar was holding him now, and the poor little boy was gasping. The blanket was off, and we could all see his awful, skeletal frame. I could see the whites of his eyes too, which were rolling back in his skull.

'In the cab,' said Colin, who had rushed to meet us.

'We need doctors!' cried Tilda. She was sobbing now, and didn't want to let go of the boy's arm. 'He needs help! We shouldn't have moved him—'

'I know what he needs,' said Colin. 'Give him to me.'

Somehow, we got him up to the cab, which seemed even higher this time. The engine was thundering, and Colin clambered onto his seat so that he could lean down and take the patient from us. We swarmed in after him, and within ten seconds Jamie was laid out on the bed behind the driving seat. I saw Colin check his airway and pull his eyelids back. I saw him feel the pulse in his neck, while Jamie lay there, horribly still.

'Get the box,' Colin said to me.

'Which one?'

'Above your head. The red one.'

Edgar grabbed it, and in a moment Colin was holding it open.

It was a first-aid kit, full of bottles, instruments and tubes. Jamie's eyes had reopened, but they looked glassy and unfocused to me, and I think everyone could see how ragged his breathing was. There was a new sound too – a rattling in his throat – and we heard a soft yelp. Colin's little dog was there, standing rigid on the dashboard.

'Hypodermic,' said Colin. 'Quick as you can.'

'Where?' said Edgar.

'Blue and white packet. Top left.'

I got to it first, and tore the wrapper open.

'Careful. Now do exactly what I say,' said Colin, and he looked at Tilda. 'What's your name, love?'

'Tilda.'

'Go to the garage, and buy sugar.'

'I'm not leaving him. I promised—'

'Go now. They'll have packets of sugar, so get me a big one.'

Tilda nodded. 'OK. Now?'

'Yes. I'm going to get insulin inside him, all right?

Then we're going to feed him, and he's going to be OK.'

'Is he dying?'

'He'll be fine if you're quick. Go!'

'And you know what you're doing?' Tilda whispered.

Colin was nodding. He'd unwrapped the hypodermic, and plucked a small jar from the case. Seconds later, he'd plunged the needle through the lid, and was drawing fluid into the chamber.

'Are you a doctor, Colin?' I said.

'T.A.'

'You're a soldier?' said Edgar.

'Territorial. I can patch people up, and I don't travel without the kit. Give me the bottle – the little one.' He transferred liquid to cotton wool, swabbed Jamie's arm. 'Awful, what you see,' he said. 'What you pass on the road – turn him now. Get his knee up, nice and tight. I'll test his blood, OK? Someone open that thermos, please.'

I'd never seen anything like it. It was battlefield stuff, designed for war zones and car wrecks, and the truck was the perfect workstation. It was warm, and the bed was hard. There were spotlights over the roof, which were bright on Jamie's skin. Colin felt for the muscle, then injected so, so slowly. He took a droplet of blood, and ran it through what looked like a calculator, and by the time he was done Tilda was knocking on the window.

She clambered in, and set the packet down.

'What's his name? Jamie?'

'Yes.'

'Sit him up. Can you drink, Jamie?' said Colin softly. 'Can you drink something for me?'

The little boy squirmed, but there was already colour coming back into his grey, wasted face. He winced, and turned away. Colin held him gently.

'Mix sugar into the flask,' he said. 'A third of the packet, and shake it.'

Tilda did so, and Colin took it from her.

'Adrenaline first. That was easy, so . . . come on, kiddo. Let's drink something.' He put the flask to his lips.

'Drink it!' said Tilda. '*Kunywa, mpenzi . . .*'

'Go on, love,' said Colin.

'He can't.'

'Yes he can. When was he fed?'

'We don't know,' said Ben.

'He's starving,' said Colin. 'Swallow it down – good boy. Let it in, nice and slow. You can do it.'

A hush fell, and we simply watched. I could see Jamie struggling: his throat was so frail and narrow, and the muscles stood out waxy with sweat. Colin put his arm round the tiny shoulders, drawing him close, and twice Jamie tried to get away, groaning. Tilda was talking softly to him, all the time, in his own language. The rest of us were willing the liquid into him, gazing in silence.

'Is he better?' I said at last – knowing it was a stupid question.

'Better than he was,' said Colin.

'He'll be all right then?'

'No.'

'He needs an ambulance,' said Tilda. 'Why won't you call one?'

'Because I'm faster,' said Colin. 'We nearly lost him, didn't we? He's a fighter though, this one. He's not giving in yet.'

'He'll be all right?' said Tilda.

'You his sister?'

'No. But I promised his uncle . . . he can't die!'

'I'm not going to lie to you,' said Colin. 'He's a long way from all right, but we can help him. This is a layman's diagnosis, but I'd say he needs a full-on blood transfusion. His kidneys are down, aren't they? That's the real problem.'

'But we have got time,' said Ben. 'I mean . . . he's stable now. We can find a hospital?'

Colin took the bottle away, and I suddenly realized he was angry. He couldn't speak for a moment. He felt Jamie's pulse again, shaking his head.

'How old is he?'

'Eight.'

'Eight years old? And he was *in* a hospital, yes? That's where you found him?'

'And they wouldn't look at him,' I said. 'They were just going to X-ray him, and—'

'He doesn't need a bloody X-ray,' cried Colin. 'He needs surgery, fast. Now. Tonight—'

'Colin,' said Edgar.

'What?'

'We need to move. Look . . .'

The dog had started to growl. Edgar was standing, and I saw him point through the windscreen. We followed his gaze, and his finger, and I'm afraid I screamed in pure and total terror.

A silver car had pulled up close to Colin's truck, blocking our path. All four doors were opening, and the men we'd met before were getting out. Worst of all, it was the man – the man who'd sat in our kitchen, but he was bigger than ever, standing back and talking into a phone while the other three came towards us. Another car was approaching too – flashing its lights. We were cornered, and the men knew it. There was something almost leisurely about the way they strolled up to the cab. The first man jumped up to the door, and Colin's dog went crazy.

'Who's this?' he said, but yet again it was Edgar who saved us. He dived across to the door-lock, and slammed it down in time.

'Oh God,' gasped Ben. 'Drive, Colin. Please.'

The cab was shaking.

'They're after Jamie!' I yelled – and I felt the air as the other door opened.

Tilda screamed, and tried to close it, as Edgar leaped again, right across our knees. He kicked the door so hard that the man swung backwards, and was forced down onto the tarmac. A third leaped straight into his place, though, and grabbed Edgar's shirt. Ben gouged at his face, while Tilda punched and clawed. They rolled him out together, on top of his friend, and Colin slid, cursing, back into the driving seat. We hauled Edgar back in, and seconds later, the lorry was in gear.

That's when I saw the gun. It was a kind of slow motion, because your eyes don't believe it. All I could think was, *No – it's a film . . .* And I watched the big man lift his weapon, and point it – and the windscreen exploded in a blizzard of glass. Colin shunted the truck forwards, revving hard. The man fired again – but still we advanced, and I saw mouths open as we came straight for the whole lot of them. One rolled sideways as we smashed into the car, and that scattered the others. Ben got the door closed, somehow, and I pressed what I thought must be the horn, deafening everyone.

There was another crunch as silver metal buckled under our bumper. Colin scraped the first vehicle right across the tarmac, then stamped hard on his brakes. He reversed immediately, leaving it smashed and rocking, its roof caved in where we'd ridden half over it. Then, as the men regrouped, he hauled the wheel round to the left and we were thundering into them a second time. Our trailer caught the second car, turning it in a spray of sparks, and moments later we were rolling across the car park.

'They're doing my tyres,' said Colin.

'What?'

'They're shooting at the wheels!' he cried, and he tried to weave left and right.

He was staring into his wing-mirror, and second gear went up to third – the engine was screaming. There were horns all around us as other vehicles screeched to a halt, and I could feel us leaning lopsidedly as the tyres burst and Colin wrestled for control. He bumped us over an island, and flattened a road sign. At last we were skidding down the slip-road, back onto the motorway, faster and faster. Colin clicked his lights, and checked his mirrors again – then swung us out to the middle lane, ignoring the hammering of our ruined wheels. I blasted the horn again, and watched the speed indicator rise, up and up – forty, then fifty, then trembling and jolting up to sixty.

The wind poured through our broken windscreen, and pressed us into our seats.

'See what I mean?' shouted Colin. 'I'm faster than an ambulance.'

We were all too shocked to speak, and I didn't hear my phone. I sat there in the gale, and became aware of it as it juddered in my pocket. Somehow I fumbled it up to my ear.

It was Leela: at last.

'Oh God! Leela!' I had to scream over the noise.

'What? Vicky–?'

'Can you hear me?'

'Yes! What's wrong? I got your texts–'

I interrupted her. 'Leela, I need the biggest favour I've ever asked anyone.'

'Where are you, Vicky? Are you–'

'Are you at the hospital?' I yelled.

'Yes, but–'

'What?'

'Yes! About to go home – what's the matter?'

'You can't leave,' I cried. 'Stay there! I need directions! I need to speak to that doctor – that surgeon. Can you put him on, Leela? This is life or death!'

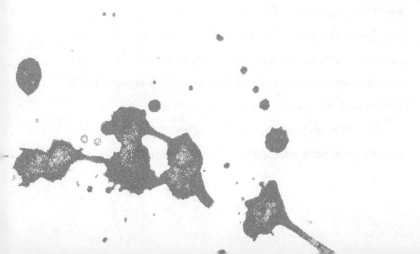

# Ben

## Continued ▶

I'll take this next bit because I remember every detail, and unlike Vicky, I wasn't hysterical. I was furious and scared, thinking *How long before we're stopped? How long before the wheels give out?*

Colin was manic. Outside lane, lights flashing, horn blasting! – every other vehicle was scattering out of our path. Vicky was babbling on to Leela still, while Edgar held Jamie. I thought, Just talk to the surgeon – get him on the line!

Of course, when she got him, she passed him to me. That meant I was trying to remember everything I'd read about the kid's treatment and symptoms, and the doctor was asking me questions I couldn't answer, using words I'd never heard. We so needed the medical records!

Then: a new disaster.

The motorway was blocked, and we were slowing right

down. Other drivers were waving at us, some of them on their phones – Colin changed right back through the gears now, and soon we were crawling. We came round a bend and it was one of those great long rivers of red: tail-lights for miles, and we just sat there in silence. Reception had gone, and the phone was dead.

'*LONG DELAYS*' said a sign, in case we hadn't noticed.

I had a look at Colin's navigation system, which was fine on direction and useless for up-to-the minute information like traffic flow – there was no way you could get detail from it, so suddenly we were at a complete, total standstill with no prospect of movement.

Edgar said: 'What do we do?'

Dumb question, because the answer was obvious. There was nothing we *could* do.

'This is my fault,' says Colin.

'How?' I said.

'I should have gone off at Luton,' he says. 'I should have known about this. It's that blasted, bloody concert.'

He meant 'Africa's Weeping!', of course. It was happening the next day, so North London was already gridlocked.

'You could reverse,' said Vicky. 'It was only a mile or two—'

'You don't reverse on a motorway!' said Tilda. 'We're going to kill someone if we're not careful.'

'I can be careful,' said Colin.

He put his indicators on then, and as soon as there was a gap he slammed the truck into it. All down the line there were these toots of protest, but he didn't give a damn – he pushed and pushed, and we watched cars squeeze off to the side . . . he was coming through, unstoppable. Suddenly we were on the hard shoulder, and I thought he'd change his mind and go forward. When he put us in reverse Vicky ended up on the dashboard, half on the dog – she literally jumped out of her seat with the shock of it, because he was seriously going to roll us backwards, to the junction he'd missed.

Soon – unbelievably – we were on a slip-road heading for a roundabout, still in reverse. We fishtailed across it, screeching, because I think half our wheels were down to bare metal, and we saw a sign saying: LONDON 33.

'Where's the hospital?' said Tilda.

'Miles away.'

That's when I thought of the only real solution. I said, 'Edgar. Give me your phone.'

'Who are you calling?'

'A friend.'

I didn't want to jinx the idea by telling him.

The traffic was worse than ever, and on top of that, the police had to be on their way. We'd been lucky so far, but how many laws had we broken? I'd seen people filming us, and I bet they'd been reporting us too. Colin would be arrested, obviously, and that would be the end: we'd be stuck on the roadside talking to idiots, and how many hours did Jamie have left? I didn't want to think – none of us did. There was one person who could help, and that was my buddy in the Emergency Call Centre: Michael Blake. That was my big idea.

His phone rang, but he didn't pick up.

# Michael

## 17.15
## Brisley Control Centre

I didn't pick up because my phone was at the bottom of my briefcase, and I'd only turned it on again a few minutes earlier to text my dad to say I'd finished my shift. I didn't really like to take a personal call, but I didn't recognize the number, so I thought – in the end – I ought to, just in case there was a problem.

I said, 'Hello? Who is this, please?'

A voice said: 'Mike. It's Ben.'

'Ben?'

'Ben.'

'Hi.'

'Where are you?' he said.

I told him I was still at work, but only just. And I was about to tell him about the program we used to track police cars, but he interrupted me.

He said: 'Shut up, Mike. I need a favour.'

'Oh,' I said. 'What?'

'How do you feel about being a hero, and saving someone's life? How brave are you, buddy?'

There was a bit of a silence then because I'm really not very brave at all. I would never volunteer for anything heroic, and I could sense something dangerous was about to happen.

'It's a bit tricky at the moment,' I said.

'Why?'

'Well . . .'

'What's wrong?'

'Could we talk on Monday, maybe? – back at school?'

That's when he swore, so I just stood there and listened.

# Ben

## 17.16
## Motorway junction

'I need a helicopter,' I said.

He didn't reply.

'Mike? Are you there?'

'Yes.'

'Did you hear me?'

'Er . . . yes.'

'An air ambulance, Mike. I need you to call one up now, and get it straight to us - no questions asked. Can you do it?'

There was another long silence - I could hear him breathing.

'I'd like to, Ben,' he said. 'But I'm about to be picked up. Do you want to speak to my dad when he comes?'

'No.'

'I bet he can help you—'

'It's you that's got to help us. I want you to get back to

your workstation, and call up the heliport. I want you to say the magic words, and scramble us a helicopter.'

'Oh God,' he said, at last. 'You don't understand. You need official clearance, and a special code. Then it depends on priority—'

'Can you get all that? Jump the queue?'

'No!'

'Why not?'

'I'm not authorized! I don't have access!'

'Mike,' I said, 'you have to get it. Go back to your desk, and tell me when you're there - we're going to do this together, you and me. Hurry up, please.'

Time passed and I thought for an awful minute that he'd put the phone down and legged it.

# Michael

## 17.16
## Brisley Control Centre

I wanted to run.

It was so difficult though because Ben had done me a lot of favours in the past, and there was something dead scary in his voice – I knew he wasn't mucking about, or daring me – I could tell it was serious. So I put my briefcase down, and went back to the computer I'd been using. It was next to my supervisor, but she was on a break.

'I'm back where I was,' I said. My voice was trembling again, like it had been all morning. 'Listen, Ben, I need to ask special permission, you see—'

'Not today.'

'No?'

'No. Where are we, Colin?'

I heard a voice then: 'Dunstable turn-off,' it said. 'Needs widening, look at it.'

'OK, Mike?' said Ben. 'You're doing well. Just scan in

the A54, and find that intersection on your screen – you got it? There's a cinema complex.'

'Yes, I've got you,' I said. My fingers were shaky, but the maps are very responsive. In any case, we'd just sent two police cars to the area because of a lorry driving dangerously – the calls had been flooding in, and both units were close.

'Call us a helicopter,' said Ben. 'We need it in the cinema car park, five minutes ago.'

'Ben,' I said – and I had to brace myself for this. 'Ben. Please. I can't just scramble you a helicopter!'

'You can, Michael,' said Ben. 'We've got a very sick kid, and a hospital waiting to receive him. We need an air ambulance – this is what they're for, isn't it?'

'I'm not allowed, Ben!'

'Why not?'

'I told you, you need the code, and that means being a manager. They'll know it's a kid . . . I'd be sued – and so could you!'

'You have a supervisor,' said Ben. 'What codes did she use?'

I nearly fainted when he said that. 'Oh God, no,' I said. 'That's forbidden! – you're not allowed to use other people's codes, Ben – ever. They explained that to me, it's the golden rule—'

'Come on, Mike!'

'But you're not listening, Ben! You're not!'

'No, Mike, *you* listen!' he said, and he was trying to keep his voice down. 'We're breaking rules today. I would dearly love to be at school right now – I really would. We'd be sitting in a classroom together, putting our hands up, asking the teachers . . . But that's not life. I'm out here, in the real world, and so are you–'

'Oh, Ben!' I was nearly in tears. 'You don't know what you're asking–'

'I do!' he said. 'I know exactly what I'm asking, and I'm not asking again. You're going to put this phone down – leave it switched on. And you're going to hack in with the boss's codes, and you're going to do your bit. I'm not threatening you, OK? You're one of my best friends, and I wouldn't ever do that. But if you let me down now, you will feel bad for the rest of your life, and you may end up killing yourself. Do you hear me?'

'Yes.'

'This isn't a game, mate. It's the world. So put the phone down, and make the call.'

# Vicky

## 17.17
## Motorway junction

The truck had come to a standstill, and we were all huddled round the phone.

I don't think any of us were breathing at this point – I know I wasn't. Even the truck's engine was quiet, and we heard the clunk of the mobile on Michael's desk as he did what Ben had told him to do. We shunted forward, two metres at the most, but the cinema complex was coming into view – and it had the perfect landing zone.

Moments later, Michael was back.

He cleared his throat, and we heard some bleeping. 'Priority, please,' he said, and his voice was unusually high. I realized he was being smart – he was impersonating his supervisor, taking action! 'Priority requested,' he said. 'This is a, er . . . ten-one-one from Centre Oscar Lima. Priority please, requesting . . . airborne unit. Extreme medical emergency. Over.'

There was a burst of static, and we heard the reply: 'You're through, Oscar Lima. Identify please, over.'

Michael gulped. 'Seven Tiger,' he said.

'Tiger? Over.'

'I mean Terror. No! – *Tango*. Sorry. Over.'

'Receiving and . . . cross-check. Enter your code, please.'

We heard tapping. Oh God, we could see him there, headset on, staring at the screen – so brave . . . Ben held the phone up, and we strained our ears.

'Thank you,' said the voice, at last. 'You have clearance to proceed. Go ahead, please: standing by for a ten-one-one, and checking, over.'

'Thank you,' said Michael – but his voice was cracking. 'Hello, hi. I'm requesting, um . . . airborne unit, medical emergency at road intersection. Coordinates as follows: Delta . . . um, oh God . . . B . . . brave, Tango—'

'Be brave?'

'I'm . . . getting confused. Bravo, thank you. Delta Bravo Tango—'

'Delta Bravo?'

'Yes. Over. Zero-zero-four. Whisky . . . Foxtrot. Over!'

'Received and checking . . .'

We could hear the clicking, and it must have been ten long seconds before the same voice said: 'Unit available, over.'

'Really?' said Michael.

'Delta Bravo Tango, Zero-zero-four Whisky Foxtrot – affirmative. ETA seventeen twenty-nine, dispatching. Over.'

'Confirmed,' said Michael. 'That's appreciated, over.'

'Requesting police backup for location landing – divert units, and . . .' There was another pause, and we could hear fingers hammering on keys. 'Airborne unit dispatched. Ground contact close . . . Over and out.'

'It's on its way,' said Ben – and I kissed him, hard on the cheek.

At that very instant, Colin saw a break in the traffic and he jammed his way into it. He heaved us over the kerb, straight through a hedge. Suddenly we were in the car park and there was a stretch of ground in front of some fast-food store that had closed down, and – thank God – there wasn't a vehicle in sight.

Moments later, Tilda and Edgar were lifting Jamie down, and we heard the sirens. Two police Land Rovers hurtled up to us, blue lights flashing. They weren't there to cause problems, or slap us in handcuffs – no. They were there to tape off a landing site and offer immediate and unconditional assistance. And I will never forget the next sound, as long as I live: it was the most magical noise in the world . . . it was the sound of distant rotor blades.

We looked up. We saw the lights. The police were organizing cones, and seconds later one of them was guiding the pilot down with a pair of bright red fire-sticks.

Edgar was shouting into the phone, and he pushed it into Ben's hand again. It was one of the medics on board, and the poor boy had to go through it all again – everything he could remember about Jamie's condition. I gave them the hospital name and address, but I had to scream it at the top of my voice because the helicopter was landing.

We had touchdown, and the door opened. Someone took in Jamie like he was a special, precious parcel, and Tilda climbed in behind him – there was her face at a window as she was belted into her seat. Almost at once the machine was rising again – it was as if it had hardly landed. Up it went, and we watched it until it was just a tiny point of light, and we stood there together as it crossed the sky.

Ben, Edgar, Colin and me . . . we watched, holding each other, until it disappeared and the sky was empty.

Colin said: 'You've got more to do, haven't you?'

We nodded.

'Go, then. Fast.'

'They'll arrest you, Colin,' I said.

'Who cares?'

'They're looking at the truck. Oh, Colin, look at your wheels!' I think each one had been shredded. The cab had no windscreen, and the policemen were open-mouthed.

'Don't waste time,' said Colin. 'Go, love – go on, all of you. I'll deal with the law.'

We knew thank you wasn't enough – but what could we say? There was no time for speeches, and he was dead right – there was still so much to do. Most importantly, we had to get Ben's memory stick, and get the Jamie files copied over to Leela. Then we had to find Stagger, and work out our next move. We had to be cleverer than ever, because the Locksons would still be right behind us.

We shook hands, and hugged, and then Edgar led us across the road. He'd spotted an approaching train, for it turned out we were right by a station.

I took the fatal call as we reached the platform.

'Vicky,' said a voice. 'It's Stagger.'

'I thought it was Molly,' I said. 'Where—?'

'I'm using her phone.'

'Why?'

'Are you all right? Let me talk to Ben, please.'

Ben grabbed the phone. 'It's me,' he said.

'You're OK?'

'I'm fine – what's the problem?'

'Ben,' said Stagger, 'I'm outside Stems and Petals, that flower shop—'

'Good. Have you got the backups?'

'That's what I'm calling about. Blue pot, on a top shelf?'

'Yes. You can't miss it.'

'It's gone, Ben. I just spoke to the owner.' He paused, and gulped. 'She sold it, two hours ago.'

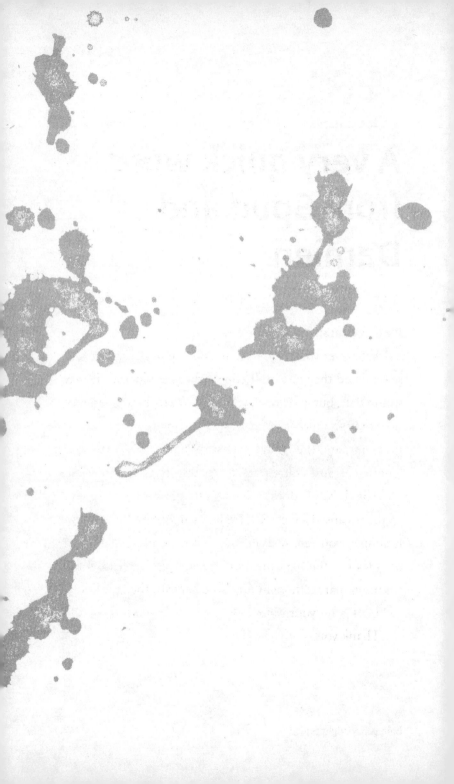

# A very quick word from Spud and Damien

Please be careful with your waterworks.

Whatever you pour away all ends up in the drains and sewers, and they just can't cope – they get blocked. It may sound daft, but we can tell you from two nights' experience now that so much time is wasted sorting out floods, and problems, and they lead to electrical faults and worse, and it's often because of irresponsible people who just don't think.

The E.N.S.* does nothing but answer alarms, half of them caused by carelessness or stupidity. Our mission is simple, you see: to keep the sewers running smoothly. So, please – the next time you burst a pipe or leave a tap running, spare a thought for those beneath the ground.

Look after your water.

Thank you.

* Emergency Night Squad

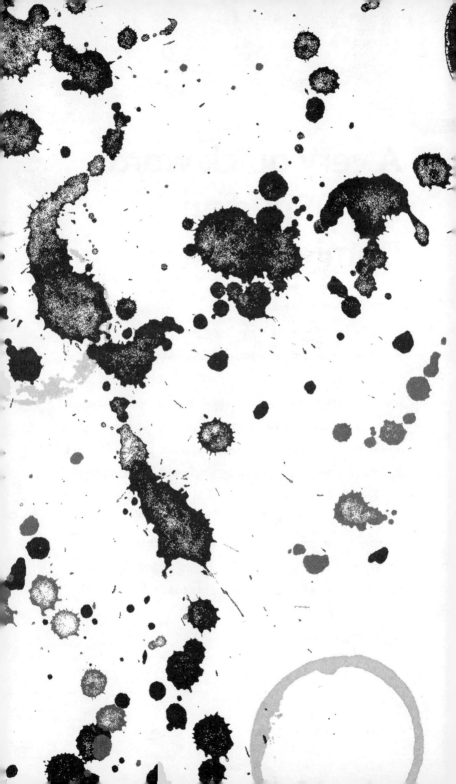

# FRIDAY
# NIGHT

# Vicky

## 00.23
## The *Gazette*

Katkat called me again, not long after midnight.

Where were we? Huddled on the steps outside the Tuttle twins' padlocked office, wondering what to do next, and wondering if we'd ever see our homes again. We were hungry, exhausted and irritable. We were still alive, which was a blessing, and we'd managed to re-group – us and Stagger – which was amazing considering the danger . . . Best of all, Jamie was in a proper hospital – though we had no idea what Leela's surgeon could do without his records. The newspaper idea was now dead in the water, as we had no files, no proof and no evidence. On top of all that we knew the Lockson people had to be lurking somewhere, ready for their next assault. They'd got the memory stick, somehow – it was the only plausible explanation. We had absolutely nothing.

I took the call, just to get rid of her.

'Katkat,' I said, 'I can't talk. I'm waiting for the hospital to ring—'

'Oh no! Are you ill, Vicky?'

'I'm not, it's a friend—'

'I've been trying for ages – you didn't pick up!'

'Look,' I said, 'we've had some pretty bad news. I can't tell you the details, but we've got major problems—'

'I wish you were here, Vee! I wish we could have a proper catch-up, because – oh, wow . . . I've got so much to tell you, I don't know where to start – things have been crazy out here too, totally amazing. We're on a ten-minute break, OK? – so I can't stay long. He just works all night! But, Vicky – listen. You've got to keep this to yourself, OK? – but you were right! I'm in the Snowy band, singing . . . can you believe it?'

She paused, to let it sink in.

'It's happened, Vee!' she cried. 'You said it would, remember? – and it did, almost straight away. I'll get you a ticket for the gig, because you have to come, that's the first thing – I'll get you backstage if I can.'

'How?' I said.

I was totally stunned, as were the others. Everyone was listening in, leaning forward to hear.

'She's lying,' said Ben.

Stagger shushed him, and I turned the phone to speaker.

'It was just the most amazingly incredible piece of super luck,' said Katkat.

'Are you serious? You're singing, with Snowy?'

'Yes! That's what I'm saying.'

We sat there, dumbstruck, as she explained the appendicitis emergency and her lightning audition. It had been nonstop rehearsals ever since, she said, with no end in sight. 'It's going to be such a concert, Vicky. Everyone's wired up, and Snowy . . . oh! I've fallen in love!'

'Katkat, how? Who with?'

'With him! He's just like a little boy. I mean, he's a superstar – yes? – and I was so scared at first, but oh, wow . . . he's the most approachable, ordinary, down-to-earth *sweet* guy you've ever met. He's so nervous, you know. He's frightened!'

'What of?' I said.

'Oh, *people*,' said Katkat. 'The world, you know? He says people are so hard to get to know – they're the scariest thing of all, and we go through life just wanting to be *loved*. And whether you're a singer or . . . just a sandwich maker, like you – or even a geeky little freak, like Ben—'

'Katkat,' I said. 'Listen—'

'Even if you're fat, like Eleanor – it's the same for *everyone*, isn't it?' she cried. 'We're like lonely little boats, says Snowy, looking for harbours. We get scared, and the waves keep us apart.'

Ben leaned in and turned the volume up to max.

'He's so sad!' she said – and her voice filled the stairwell. 'Why?'

'This is confidential, OK? – but Snowy finds it genuinely hard to *trust* anyone. People lie to him, and use him – that's why he never speaks to the audience, ever. Just plays the music. That's what he told me, anyway – he seems to really like me for some reason, I don't know why. What's there to like?'

'Not a lot,' said Edgar softly.

'What?' said Katkat.

'Katkat,' I said, 'I'll call you back—'

'Everyone *wants* something, you know? Which is how I feel, about kids at school. I was never accepted – that's why I got ill . . . but who cares now? I'm not ever going back to that dump: I'm a singer now, Vee – this is my life! Can I play you something?'

'Katkat, no—'

'You know "Tell the Truth", don't you?'

'Yes, of course—'

'Well, guess who's doing the solo, right in the middle?'

'Who? Not you! – are you joking?'

'Listen – shh! I recorded the whole session . . .'

We huddled even closer, and there were bleeps and clicks as Katkat found the right file. We heard the throb of a keyboard, and a bass guitar. Over both, deep and

magical, rose the unmistakable voice of Snowy himself –
and we all knew the melody. Molly scrabbled for a lead,
and seconds later she'd amplified it through her laptop.
The voice poured out, gravelly and rich, and the words
were too familiar:

> 'It can be a pressure, yeah? – like a weight on your heart.
> No one does it for you, girl, cos no one plays your part . . .'

'Katkat,' I said, 'is that you in the background?'

'Yes!'

'You're singing with him . . .'

'I told you, Vee – I'm right next to him. I'm doing the
big solo, listen!'

'She's joking!' hissed Edgar.

'Katkat, this can't be real . . .'

The song continued, and Katkat whispered over the
top of it, 'It was the first rehearsal, OK? He heard me sing
it then, but last night we all went down to the lake and he
asked me in front of everyone. He'd just got back from
seeing Rosie–'

'You're doing the solo?'

'Yes! It was going to be his daughter, but she's still in
hospital, thank God. So he had to ask her permission,
because – well – you know it's always sung by a child?
That's traditional, right?'

'Sure . . .'

'So Rosie said yes, and he begged me to do it. What could I say?'

We were all staring at each other, speechless.

Everyone knew the song because it had become Snowy's anthem. He'd written it for the '*Capitalism Sucks*' tour five years previously, and it had since become the highest-earning single of all time, forcing Snowy out of the country for a while as a tax-exile. The start is magical: traditional Latin rhythms shift to African, and then a huge children's choir sweeps in over everything. The choir is amazing enough, but when it reaches crescendo it launches what critics call 'the ultimate solo in musical history'.

That's what Katkat was referring to, and that's what we heard – her voice soared upwards, pure as bubbling spring water. It was only a practice, obviously, but we still had tears in our eyes. The song is famous for making people cry! Drivers have to pull in if it comes on the radio – it's too raw, too moving. And someone we knew as a classmate – Katkat Madamba – was going to walk out on stage the very next day and perform it to a round-the-world audience of a trillion people.

We sat there, and the solo faded to silence.

'Wow,' said Stagger quietly. 'That's too much.'

The twins were open-mouthed.

'Incredible,' said Ben.

'You don't think I'm up to it, do you?' said Katkat softly.

I was jerked back to reality. 'What?' I said.

'You think I'll fail.'

'Katkat, no – of course not – why *would* you fail?'

'Oh God, Vee. I should have told him. I should have just said no!' Suddenly she was crying. 'Oh, what's the point? I should go, look – I shouldn't have called, should I?'

'Katkat,' I said. 'You don't sound happy—'

'I'm not,' she wailed. 'How can I be?'

'But it's going so well for you! What's wrong?'

'Oh God, Vee! I'm throwing up, and we're starting again – there's so much pressure—'

'Katkat, listen – you have to rest!'

'You don't know what pressure is, Vicky! – do you? Your life's so easy, so . . . predictable – always has been, while mine . . . Sometimes I just want to kill myself! I tried, last year . . .'

There was an ear-splitting crunch as she wept, and I thought she was smashing up her phone. 'Katkat!' I cried. 'Stop!'

'. . . what's the point?' she mumbled. 'Vicky? – what's that noise?'

'Where?'

'It's terrible . . .'

'Isn't it you?'

'No!'

We were all on our feet, because the sound wasn't at her end at all – it was right underneath us. Edgar had rolled to the nearest window, and the twins looked terrified. Somebody was beating at the *Gazette* front door, far below us, blow after blow – and the whole building shuddered. Then the doorbell rang: a long, shrill scream that filled the stairway.

'Katkat,' I hissed. 'Wait there!'

The hammering started again, slow but regular, and we all jumped to the only possible conclusion: we'd been traced, yet again – because of Katkat's call. It was the Lockson thugs, and any minute they'd smash the door from its hinges to make an end of us. Edgar had his face pressed to the glass, peering downwards. Everyone else moved up to the top landing, cornered and helpless.

'Christ,' hissed Edgar. 'I can't see anything!'

'Is it them?' said Stagger.

'I don't know. Is there a back way out?'

The bell screamed louder, howling like a fire alarm.

'No,' said Polly. 'We're trapped. It's over . . .'

# Eleanor

## 00.43
### Front door – The *Gazette*

All I knew was I had to see them at once.

I'd run right across town, and I had no phone to call anyone, so I just stood there trembling, thinking, *There's a light on at the top! They're inside, still – thank God! Why won't they answer the door?*

It was the twins I was after, of course, so I got the shock of my life when Edgar opened up and stood there, ready to fight me to the death – and you should have seen his face! He just goggled at me – so I said the obvious thing:

'Edgar,' I said. 'I've got a world exclusive.'

And he didn't even nod, or smile, or say a word – he was like a statue, with his mouth open.

'I need to see Polly,' I said. 'Molly too – can I come in?'

He came to life at last, and dragged me inside. He slammed the door, and checked the lock, swearing his head off – and I set off up the stairs, three floors at least so

I was out of puff when I got there. They were all huddled together at the top, scared out of their wits – and again, nobody spoke.

'I've brought you something amazing,' I said. I had my laptop under my arm. I'd transferred the photos and I just prayed they wouldn't be corrupted or lost, because no one would ever believe me if they were.

There was still no sound from anyone, and I think it was Ben who finally said, in a whisper: 'Eleanor?'

'Yes,' I said.

'What are you doing here?'

I just smiled at him, and opened up the screen. 'I've run away from home,' I said.

'Why?'

'To bring you this! For the front page . . .'

I turned the laptop round, and of course I couldn't get the keys to work at first because my fingers were shaking. They were staring at me still, which made me more nervous – but in the end I pulled up the right folder, and opened it. The first photo blasted up, and I enlarged it to maximum.

'I was there,' I said. 'Just as he arrived. Total, total miracle!'

'What is it?' said Polly, squinting at the screen.

'The first one's a bit blurry,' I said. 'But you wait . . .'

I clicked over to the next shot, which was better. It showed the car, and him getting out of it. The big bodyguard was just behind him, and I'd stepped back to get them in focus.

'Can you see?' I said.

'Is it Snowy?' said Vicky.

'Yes!'

'Where?'

'At the hospital!'

'When?' said the twins.

'Just a few hours ago!'

I was grinning like an idiot, and I clicked up number three, which was a gorgeous close-up. We were in the lift by this time, and I'd managed to squeeze the camera under his nose. It was still in the lunchbox, don't forget – down by my waist, so I aimed upwards as he looked down, and I got his craggy old face in dark glasses, and the big scarf he has wrapped round his shoulders. And that shot really did the trick! They all huddled closer, and gasped!

'My God,' said Stagger. 'We've just been listening to him.'

'How did you get in?' asked Edgar.

'It was the private entrance,' I said. 'Right round the back – I'd just returned a dog to a nurse, and there he was—'

'You followed him?' said Molly. 'He hates photographers!'

'I know!' I said. 'They thought I was just a little kid, I suppose, visiting someone – same as them.'

'Oh God, that's beautiful,' said Molly – and she inched closer, so her nose was almost touching the screen. Ben pulled her back, and Vicky pushed in as well. Edgar had come underneath, so he had a good view – and I clicked to number four then five. They were looking at a corridor now, with all these nurses lined up, smiling and waving as Snowy walked through, looking just like Jesus.

'It's where his daughter was!' I said. 'The bed at the end. He'd come all this way to see her, and sing her a song.'

'And what did he sing?' said Polly.

'"Roses"!' I said. 'Just for her. Do you want to hear it? I recorded it . . .'

They went silent again when I said that – they just stared at the laptop, and then at me.

'We've just heard "Tell the Truth",' said Stagger. 'You didn't get "Roses", did you?'

'Yes,' I said. 'I *filmed* the whole thing, start to finish.'

It was totally illegal, and we all knew it. People have been sued for recording Snowy – but it was so dead easy, so how could I resist? All I'd had to do was flick a switch.

I pressed play, and there was the prettiest little tinkling sound, from Snowy's mandolin – he always carries one, wherever he goes. And he'd perched on the bed, next to his little girl, and we all watched together as he picked out the intro. 'Roses' was written not just for her, of course, but all children of the world, especially those less fortunate – and, oh! – it takes you to a different stratosphere. We saw little Rosie stir as he played, like a fairy-tale princess, and

I'd zoomed in a bit to catch her as she turned her head – eyes closed – smiling in her sleep. Snowy bent forward, and sang the first verse:

> *'The roses grow wild for you . . .*
> *Monsters, they turn mild for you . . .*
> *How did we make the right choice?'*

There was a tiny squeal from one of the nurses, which everyone shushed. Snowy smiled, and stopped – and you could have heard a pin drop. He picked out the tune a bit – and that's when we saw Rosie open her eyes and smile . . .

> *'When did we see that world had gone crazy?*
> *Spinning in space that is misty and hazy?*
>   *Turn me around round, baby,*
>   *Let me be found, baby.*
> *Roses grow wild at the sound of your voice . . .'*

He stopped again, because Rosie was lying there with tears in her eyes – she must have thought she was waking up in heaven. Then Jun came forward with some real, actual flowers, and Snowy took them from him. It was just the most perfect scene, because it was a little tiny rosebush! – and he put it in Rosie's hands, and strummed another chord. He was so happy to see her, I suppose –

and nobody could speak because it was too moving. She smelled the roses, and smiled again, and he was about to sing the second verse when Ben suddenly – without a word – twisted the laptop out of my hands and made a kind of screeching noise.

I went to grab it back, but missed, and it was like Ben didn't even notice me – so I really went for him because I thought he might damage it. Edgar grabbed me and Vicky screamed! – everyone was suddenly on their feet, but Ben was just stuck rigid, not moving a muscle as Snowy kept singing. He was gazing at the screen still – but something was wrong because he was white as a ghost, and whimpering.

'What?' I said, because I was scared now. 'What is it, Ben? – what's the matter?'

'Nothing,' said Vicky. 'Be quiet.'

'Why?'

I saw then that everyone's face had changed. They'd all gone dead serious, and the smiles weren't there any more, and they weren't in the magical land that Snowy's song had taken us to. They'd come back down to earth.

'It's not possible,' said Ben – and he was so quiet I went cold.

He scrolled back a bit, and the others clustered around him. He pressed play, and fiddled with the zoom. Then he paused again.

'We've found it,' he said.

# Edgar

**Continued ▶**

I saw it at the same moment Ben did, but he got there first.

I knew what it was, at once, but I didn't do or say anything because not having physically held it with my own hands, and only heard about it . . . I couldn't be sure it was really THE ONE, so I just stood there blinking, while Stagger . . .

# Stagger

## Continued ▶

. . . was blinking as well, even as Ben snatched the laptop.

Like Eleanor says, Jun had just handed the thing over – it was there, like an apparition, sitting on the bed while Snowy got ready for the next verse. The kid held it, with all the blooms waving – exactly what we'd been looking for.

But I couldn't speak. I grabbed at Ben because he'd gone completely white, but he twisted away from me, and as he tried to get down the stairs he tripped right over Molly's feet, because he was still staring at the laptop. He fell down the stairs, and didn't even notice. He rolled over backwards, and landed upside down, with the laptop safe – holding it up, still gazing at it . . . and we watched him bring it down to his lips, and kiss the screen.

'Eleanor,' he said, 'I love you.'

# Ben

## Continued ▶

Because it was the answer to our prayers.

I was looking at my very own rosebush in my very own pot. He'd bought it, for the girl. My rosebush, with the stem I'd pushed down so its roots were in the soil, all in a blue and white pot which I'd put up on the top shelf so as to be safe from customers. And in that soil – no doubt about it – was my memory stick. So I just lay there on my back on the landing, and I didn't need to enlarge the image any more because it was so, so clear.

I thought it had to be a dream, and I looked at them all looking down at me, thinking, Are we all having the same one? Why aren't any of us waking up? This cannot be real . . .

We don't have words for it.

I have words for when I'm angry, but when I'm in a state of complete, total joy and wonder, I just go numb.

Vicky snapped me out of it. She grabbed Polly's phone

and was straight on to Leela. Leela picked up at once, and didn't waste a second – she raced over to the ward. She called us back five minutes later, and she was in it, looking for Rosie's bed. We all sat there, listening, as her shoes clicked over the floor.

I had the phone.

'OK,' she said. 'She's fast asleep.'

'And the pot?'

'On the table.'

'So take it! Steal it.'

'I've got it here. Wait.'

'It's definitely the one?' I said, seconds later.

'It's a small rosebush,' she said. 'Blue and white pot. I'm taking it outside . . .'

'It's at the bottom, Leela. Look in the earth.'

I shut my eyes, so I could hear better. Her footsteps again, and a door opening, and then what was probably a bathroom door, and the clinking sound as she put it down. Then rustling, and more clinking – and, oh God, the agony! I couldn't keep still – I was like a little kid.

'Have you found it?' I said. 'Please, Leela – is it there?'

'Wait!' she said.

'I can't. Is it there or not?'

'There's something. A kind of lump.'

'I wrapped it in tape–'

'I know. I can't get it out.'

Silence.

'Got it.'

Then we all heard her unwrapping the plastic, and there was no doubt. The memory stick was in her hands, and we had everything back! We had Jamie's records. We had the photos and the files, which meant every shred of evidence. We could bring the Locksons down, still, because we were back in the game with a paper to print.

# Leela

## 01.05
## East Dean hospital

There was a problem, though.

The medical records were on the memory stick, of course, just as Ben had promised. I emailed everything else over to Polly and Molly, and then turned my attention to the Jamie files: that was the priority. I printed his case notes, and Mr Ahsan studied them.

It was soon obvious things were far worse than he'd thought. Nobody had realized what that child had endured. His kidneys had been almost wrecked, and the barrage of sugar had caused catastrophic damage. There was a risk now of permanent blindness, and his heart had been under severe strain for days. We had him on a ventilator, and when we went to see him the big question was whether he could endure the interventions that would either save his life, or kill him.

He was so small on the bed, and Tilda was next to him

holding his hand. I watched his chest rising and falling, and Mr Ahsan looked grave. You'd have to get permission, normally, from the parents. Without consent you shouldn't do anything – but that night 'nothing' would have been fatal.

Mr Ahsan said: 'You believe in God now, Leela?'

I said, 'You asked me that.'

'Have you made up your mind?'

'No.'

'Then pray,' he said. 'I'm an atheist, as you know. And I'm going to.'

That's when he simply threw away the rule book. Officially, he didn't even work at the hospital any more, but I heard him requisitioning the theatre, and calling in his team. By one-fifteen we were scrubbed up and ready to go, and everybody knew it was fifty-fifty at best.

'You need to speak to him,' said Mr Ahsan. He was looking at Tilda.

'What should I say?'

'You tell him the truth.'

Tilda said nothing.

'You understand what we're doing,' said Mr Ahsan. 'The child does not. This is the chance you have to say whatever it is you wish to say. What he needs to hear – you understand?'

I saw Tilda nod, and I saw her move back to Jamie's side. His eyes were wide open, but I don't know if he could see her. I saw her whisper in his ear, and touch his face, and I saw him smile and clutch her hand.

'OK,' he said – such a soft voice, from dry, tired lips. 'Thank you.'

And she kissed him goodbye.

# Polly & Molly

## 01.05
## The *Gazette* basement

Meanwhile, we were in a hurry.

Edgar took as long a run as he could get and launched himself at the office door, kicking hard. One, two, three shattering blows and he'd splintered a panel. The padlock would never give, but he soon had a hole wide enough for Ben to squeeze through. I (Polly) told him where to find the key to the basement.

Would we really find a printing press down there? Could we hope to get it working if we did? We just had to believe, for it was now another race against time. We found the trap door, and hauled it open.

I (Molly) led the way, using my phone as a torch – we couldn't even find the light switch at first. When Stagger located it, a chain of dim bulbs flickered on, and the cellar looked even gloomier than it had on our first morning. The floor was made of cobbles, and there were islands of cracked cement where machines must once have stood. The walls around us were raw brick. There were low archways supporting an oppressively low ceiling: most of them were blocked in and sealed, so it really was like being in a dungeon. There was also an intermittent stink of drains, gusting up from somewhere, and the piles of junk seemed higher than we remembered, and far more jumbled. Edgar pointed to a pile of mangled typewriters – and I remembered what Vicky's dad had said about covering the machine: we could see a tarpaulin under the debris, and it was concealing something huge.

'That's it,' said Vicky. 'It has to be.'

Stagger said, 'Let's go.'

We formed a human chain. Five minutes later we'd uncovered a contraption spiky with levers – this is Polly again – and there were several sets of rollers. Six claw feet kept it steady on the floor, and there were a number of trays housed in its belly, with belts winding above and below. Wires emerged from the heart, and tapered into what looked like a small television set. It wasn't: it was an ancient computer.

We ran a lead up to the nearest socket, and Ben pressed buttons. To everyone's amazement, the screen came slowly to life. Lights blinked, and the glass turned a very soft green. Underneath, a motor tried to chug, and Stagger identified a battery. We spent the next ten minutes racing up and down stairs, running more leads and cannibalizing cables. We were desperate for a soldering iron, but Edgar's penknife and a candle had to do so that when Stagger threw the main switch we cowered back waiting for an explosion. Instead, the machine shook itself, like a giant insect that had been buried in the dark and was finally awake again. Arms rose into the air, as if was stretching.

How we wished Mr Stockinger was with us.

On the other hand, he was safer where he was. Vicky had spoken to him on the phone and persuaded him to check into his clinic, so I (Molly) made Stagger call him again. His voice sounded groggy, but he talked us through the set-up, and the Pipshum 5000 was soon ready to go. That, in a way, was the easy bit. The real job was still ahead of us: the writing and editing of a paper that would change the world.

'*Poison!*' said Ben. 'That's our headline, with a skull and crossbones.'

I (Polly) rejected it at once because to me it sounded like a tedious health warning. 'We need something less conventional,' I said – and it was Vicky who grabbed a pencil and thought fastest.

'You're forgetting the point,' she said.

'The point,' I replied, 'is simply to get the paper *read*.'

'But this is about Jamie,' said Vicky. 'It always was. It's about what happened to him.' She mocked up a front page and put two large squares in the centre. 'Whatever we do, we've got to link the drink to that boy's face.'

'That's good,' I said – this being Molly again. 'So we use the before and after photos—'

'And the email,' said Edgar. 'Hit them hard with that . . .'

Stagger agreed. 'We make the central accusation clear – that Liquidator's addictive. It was tested on innocent children . . . then, shhh!' – he had to really fight to make us listen – 'once we've got people's attention we move on to the more complicated stuff.'

'Which means a science page,' said Ben.

'Exactly.'

'We can show how it hooks you—'

'Show the marketing plan too,' said Vicky. 'How they'll raise the price and reduce can sizes. People need to know everything . . .'

We worked together. Stagger got under the Pipshum and was busy with rags and an oil can. Eleanor worked with Ben on the visual layout, while Edgar devised headings and sub-headings. That left me and Polly to do the main text with Vicky. We had another meeting, and dosed ourselves with coffee. Then we tweaked and tucked, cut and pasted, and it all slowly came together.

'Are we ready?' I said. It was four o'clock in the morning. 'Stagger? How are you doing?'

He was stripped to the waist, damp with perspiration. The Pipshum was gleaming, and when he flicked the switch the printing plates swung out ready. Ben sent the data – and there was a hush as we waited for the first, trial copy.

A black bar travelled across the computer screen.

There was a silence then, and we heard paper unfold and rustle. We gathered round, and saw the rollers turn. Off went the first page, through slots and chambers. It folded and reversed, and the plates came down to kiss it. At last, our front page emerged, cut, folded and gleaming with ink . . .

The headline looked ferocious.

# 'LIQUIDATOR KILLS!'

That was our statement, in the simplest font we could find – the letters sharp as knives. Under it, Jamie's eyes stared into ours – two of him, side by side. To the left, he was well, and bursting with health. To the right was the picture we'd come to know so well: a dying child, gazing at you – begging for help. Our own eyes flickered between the two images, for you couldn't turn away.

A few words of graphic explanation followed, and across the bottom Edgar had stretched Helen Lockson's hideous email, with date and sender's name:

---

**From:** Helen Lockson
**Sent:** Wednesday 11 June, 2014 11.38
**CONFIDENTIAL**

Jamie Song will be dead this week – he can't last without treatment, and only I have his records. Ignore all calls, refer correspondence upwards. We will bury him. Literally.

---

'We've done it,' said Eleanor.

And I remember the next part so vividly, because Stagger made for the stairs to get the next roll of paper – and we thought nothing could go wrong. Me and Polly were right behind him, just as he put his hand on the rail. That's when the lights went out – *click* – and the Pipshum died. We were plunged into a darkness so black it was like blindness, and there was nothing to do but stand absolutely still and silent, ready for trouble . . .

# Edgar

## Continued ▶

So I got my phone out, and switched to flashlight.

I wondered first if we'd tripped a fuse somewhere, since the place was so old – but it was soon clear we hadn't because there were noises above our heads. There were footsteps on the floor, so you didn't need to be a genius to work out someone had unplugged us.

I stopped breathing, and stood ready.

'Who's got keys?' said Ben. His voice was a teeny little whisper, and Polly says back: 'Only our boss. That's the editor.'

Molly cuts in: 'It won't be him. He wouldn't be in this early—'

'Shh!'

I went up the steps a bit – and I'm not into spookiness, ever – but my shadow was like some big black goblin on the wall, and I got about five paces at the most, and the trap door lifts up and there's torchlight, powerful and blinding, right in my face. Under it, I can just make out a pair of boots – and I knew who'd come to call. I wondered how we'd ever forgotten them.

The guy was even bigger than I remembered, and he looked dog-tired and sick to death: we were in his way again, and all he wanted was to get the job done, once and for all. He had two backups behind, with torches of their own – so I stepped back down and we all eased into a kind of huddle, not holding hands but close together. A woman came next, in awkward heels. Behind her was a little fat suit in specs, who looked as scared as we were . . .

Five long seconds of silence, then, 'Dear oh dear,' says the fat guy. 'Molly. Polly – I . . . told you to go home. Mrs Lockson, they've let me down – shall I call the police?'

'We don't need the police,' says the woman.

'Don't we?'

'No.'

'I'll be on to their school first thing. It's the most extraordinary abuse of trust.'

Mrs Lockson ignores him, and talks to her team. 'Take everything, please,' she says. 'Let's get this over with.'

'Let's have the technology first,' says the big guy. He sounded oh so civilized and polite, but wary too – and he stares around the basement checking out each one of us. 'Vicky?' he says.

'Yes?'

'You told me a lie.'

'Because what you're doing is unfair!'

'Is it? Really?'

'Yes!'

He seemed thoughtful for a moment, and we saw him nod slowly. 'Maybe you're right,' he said. 'But as of now, we have to protect ourselves – and that means closing things down.'

That's when they started work. They were like some super-efficient clean-up company, and they went for our phones and laptops first. Leads were yanked out of sockets, and the dusty old computer Ben had been working on was wrenched up so hard its base split and shattered. They dumped everything in bags, and the boots went up and down while the torches swung . . . I saw more men up on the steps, heaving it all up and out, so we just stood in silence.

They broke up the Pipshum, and the twins' old boss was still on the stairs, shouting over the noise – but nobody took any notice. They laid into it that machine with hammers till it was just a mess of rollers and tubes. Then they got bolt-cutters, and chewed through its cable – and that was the moment Eleanor made her move, and did something brave. She'd hidden a phone somehow – I don't know whose – and now she grabbed it like a gun, pressing the digits fast, desperate to contact someone, I guess. The nearest thug snatched at her wrist, jerking her up off her feet, so I couldn't stop myself and went it hard from the side, cutting his legs from under him and slamming him hard on his back. I would have stomped on his bollocks if Stagger hadn't grabbed me.

'Don't, Edgar!' shouted Vicky. 'Please . . .'

'It's over,' says Stagger. 'OK?'

'It's not over for him,' said the giant, looking at me – and I smiled at him again, meeting his eyes. What I wanted was a fair fight, just the two of us. He was three times my weight, but I knew I could have got under his guard and put his nose bone into his brain – one movement.

'Hey,' said one of the other men quietly. He was looking hard at Ben, who'd shifted or scratched his nose. 'Don't anyone move again, all right?' Ben put his hands by his side, and I saw then that the guy talking was the one I'd caught full in the mouth. His face was so mangled it looked melted, and when he looked at me I smiled.

'Leave them alone,' said Mrs Lockson. 'I want no bruises. Check the pockets, and don't leave a mark.'

They frisked us hard. Out came our wallets, purses, sticks of gum, and they bagged it all up in silence. Someone took our carefully printed newspaper, and handed it up to the woman. I remember her eyes bulging as she read it, and her mouth like a slash of blood-red lipstick, gleaming in the torchlight.

Eleanor tried again then, bless her. 'What you're doing

is wrong, and you know it!' she said. Everyone turned to look at her. 'Jamie Song could have died.'

'Is he not dead already?' said Mrs Lockson.

'No!'

'Are you sure?' She was quiet for a moment, staring down at us. 'Where have you hidden him, I wonder? He won't live, you know—'

'He will!' said Vicky, and the woman's eyes turned to her.

'He can't,' she said. 'We'll pay for the funeral, of course. We'll send a wreath, even. One of several.'

Polly said, 'Look. Please. You've got everything – can we just go home now? Our father's going to be worried, he's probably trying to call us—'

'I doubt it.'

'Mr Bickersdyke, he's expecting us home—'

'But he's not,' said Mrs Lockson. 'You told your parents you were working all night, so nobody's going to worry about any of you for quite a few hours. And the concert starts soon, which is going to be quite a distraction.'

'You've brought this on yourselves,' said the editor. We could all see how frightened he was – he was rubbing his hands. 'You can't blame me – I told you to leave . . .'

'So what's happening?' said Molly. 'What are you going to do with us?'

Mrs Lockson was quiet again, 'Let's just say you're in

for an uncomfortable time,' she said, and they all started moving.

The torches swung around us, and the boots tramped up the stairs for the last time. The trap door slammed shut, and it was pitch-darkness again because we didn't have anything – not even a match – so this was a blackness right up against your face. We stood still, listening, as the footsteps clattered this way and that. We heard thumps and crashes, and then the front door slammed. We heard a car engine start, and then silence.

'Stay still,' said Stagger. 'Let's just listen. Check they're gone.'

We stood there for another long, empty minute.

'We're OK,' I said, at last. 'Let's keep calm, and work out how we can get out of here.'

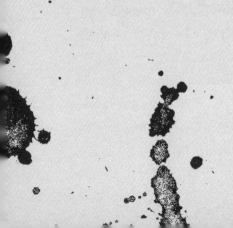

# Vicky, Stagger, Molly, Polly, Eleanor, Edgar & Ben

## Continued ▶

We were totally trapped, and they hadn't gone at all.

We stood there, wondering what to do, and all at once there was a thin light through the floorboards, right over our heads. There was a thump that made us all jump and grab hold of each other, and it sounded like something huge and heavy was being dragged into place. What was worse was a groaning sound, followed by a slow, even hammering.

'Stay calm,' said Stagger. 'There'll be another way out – there's bound to be.'

But we knew there wasn't because we could remember just how small the cellar was, and how deep. We heard a trickling sound then, as if someone had left a tap running,

and there was another noise like wrenching metal. There was a muttering, and – again – the sound of metal . . . but this time it was like someone had a saw.

'I can feel water,' said Eleanor.

'Where?'

'It's coming through the floor – what is it?'

We could all hear the splashing, and it got louder and louder. Suddenly the water was gushing and Polly screamed as it hit her. She stepped back, and we all tried to protect ourselves. Chairs turned over, and we tripped over them and clutched at each other. The downpour got worse, as if major pipes had been ripped apart.

'They're going to flood the place,' said Molly.

'We're locked in,' said Polly. 'They're going to let the basement fill up. They're going to drown us . . .'

It seemed crazy at first – it seemed ridiculous. But where would the water go? – we were already ankle deep. We tried to stay dry, of course – but in total darkness it was impossible. Edgar tried the trap door, and we listened to him hacking at it without success. We felt around the walls, trying so hard not to panic! We hunted for any kind of recess or gap . . . and within five minutes the water was up to our knees.

We clambered onto the stairs, and sat there shivering.

'Look,' said Stagger. 'It's a punishment, that's all . . . it's just to frighten us.'

'No,' said Polly. 'They want us dead. They'll say it was an accident – what better way of keeping the secret?'

Just then, there was a sudden flash of electrical blue. A bolt of lightning went from floor to ceiling, and it was followed by a horrible hissing and the stink of scorched metal. The flash had illuminated the cascading water, and our own frightened faces. We sat there, helpless and bewildered, waiting to be drowned or electrocuted. The water level rose, and all we could do was wait for the next explosion.

Stagger and Edgar did what they had to do: they tried the trap door again, hammering, screaming and shouting. They gave up out of sheer exhaustion, and we were quiet again, listening to the gurgling. The next flash of blue showed us what we already knew: the water was up to our chests.

We sat there, too frightened to speak. We squeezed up to the top steps, so our heads were pressed against the wooden boards, and soon the water came to our necks. We didn't cry, because we were so busy imagining what it might be like to drown, and it couldn't and wouldn't happen – how there had to be something we could do. The water would force us up to the ceiling, though – it was obvious what would happen. We would gulp that last mouthful of air, and our lungs would be fighting for the next. That's when we'd take in the first mouthful, and cough it out again. That's when the spluttering would begin, and we'd be forced to swallow. Do you swallow and keep swallowing? What else can you do, for the cold, black water is unlimited, and soon we'd all be spinning and struggling amongst the bubbles – that really would be the end of us. We'd be pressed against the boards until our bodies filled and sank. Seven of us, turning slowly in the darkness, while nobody came to save us, and nobody noticed we were gone . . .

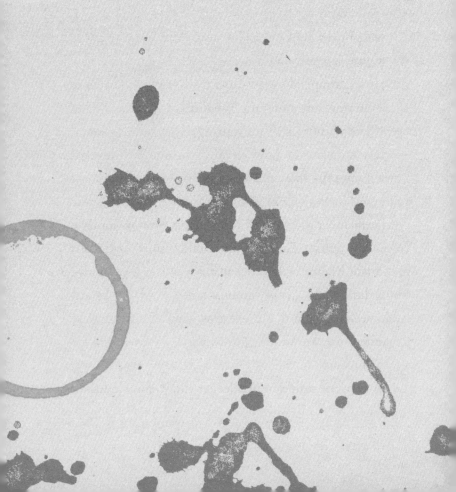

# Leela

**04.49**
East Dean hospital – in theatre

We were fighting for life too – but the life we were trying to save was Jamie's.

He was wrapped in gauze and cloth, with one patch of flesh showing, just under his little ribcage, right side. That was where we now had to cut to reach his kidneys. It was emergency dialysis, and the surgery couldn't wait. The light burned onto the skin, and when the scalpel went in I was there to clear the wound and hold back the muscle.

I remember the clink of instruments on trays and the rush of the pumps. There was a constant throb of monitors, and a word here, a muttered instruction or suggestion – but so little said – as the minutes rolled slowly by. Even I could see that Jamie's pulse was slowing. His lungs were exhausted, and we were fighting. We'd been fighting for nearly three hours . . .

In went the scalpel again, deeper and wider. Mr Ahsan

probed, and I could see the painstaking connection of the frayed blood vessels. I could also see and feel the failure, as the tiny veins slipped and came apart, and once again we had to go deeper. He turned Jamie on the table, and at first I didn't know why. Then I realized: he wanted his patient facing east, for what I'd felt in the room was death. Death was coming closer, and the child was slipping away.

Why the east? I know now, but I didn't know then. To face east is to be in the eye of God, and if God saw – if God could only be made to see – then He might grant the child a little more life. It sounds crazy, but why not? When life is in the balance, I think we do anything to cheat and steal a little more of it. So I had to watch, helpless, as Jamie's pulse slowed and his little heart gave up.

He couldn't go on – and the machines recorded it. Again, Mr Ahsan took the threads of his arteries, and reconnected. Again, he cauterized, as another milligram of hormone dripped into the child's battered system. I remembered the corpse he'd shown me – old Mrs Cotter – and the terrible truth about the body: 'Easy to ruin. Hard to restore.' I could stand and move and think, and I was warm . . . but the warmth was leaving Jamie's thin body, as water runs through your fingers, dripping into the dust.

We all watched the monitors, and the master-surgeon worked, and prayed. Again, I didn't know it then, but it was a prayer you hear across the world, when a parent begs for the life of a stricken child:

'Spare him, God, for this is a life unlived.'

Mr Ahsan said the words aloud. He cut, and I saw the blood run, warm no more.

'There are great things to be done,' he said. 'Dear God, there are great things to be achieved by this Your servant. Grant us time. Together. Still, that the sun may shine upon this face, that he will honour You for longer, in the days that are Yours to grant. For this child is special . . .'

I could not close my eyes to pray with him, but I started to repeat what he said, aloud – and so did the others.

'For this child is special,' he said, and we said it too. 'As *all* Your children are special,' whispered Mr Ahsan.

We whispered it too, because all children are special – I knew that as a truth I'll never unlearn.

'*All* of them are hungry for life, dear God – and we beg Your mercy for him, knowing Your will . . .'

The pulse slowed further, and the monitor sounded its sad, hopeless alarm.

'Knowing that Your will must be done . . . Spare him, please, for this is a life unlived . . .'

And Jamie Song died on the operating table at 05:57:32.

# Katkat

## 05.57
## Out in the garden . . .

I tried to phone Vicky again, but she didn't pick up.

Perhaps I'm misremembering now. All I can do is say what I saw, and if I've got confused then you can understand why . . . we'd been working through the night, snatching sleep when we needed it, and waking ourselves to work on. Snowy said that energy was easy to destroy and hard to create, so if we felt it we should use it.

All at once, I wasn't tired.

I can still see his shape, and the way he moved. I remember what he said, of course – but most of all I remember his eyes.

# Leela

## 05.58
## East Dean hospital – in theatre

When the heart stops, there are times it's foolish to resuscitate – sometimes there's no point trying. Mr Ahsan stepped back, and there was no hope – because Jamie had left us. To pound him with electricity, that would have been useless. His poor, battered body had taken more than it could take, and I will never forget the feeling of failure, and worse than that, the feeling of shame.

# Katkat

## 05.58
## Out in the garden, still . . .

We were round the lodestone, that's the epicentre of the whole place, where all the force comes right up through the ground. It's a big slice of granite set over an ancient well, and Snowy often sits there to get special inspiration.

He said: 'Ready again?'

We nodded, and someone said, 'Sure.'

'Go for it.'

'Ready here.'

Then a bird started to sing, and we paused, because Snowy held up his hand. It was the first of the morning chorus, and we sat there and waited. It was an interruption, in a way – and then another one joined in – skylarks, or blackbirds . . . maybe a thrush? I've never known my birds. But they were in harmony, and we caught the first glimpse of the rising sun – that ghostly pink over the horizon . . . it was like the whole garden was tilting, and I felt cold.

Snowy said, 'Use it, guys. Use the birds.'

He meant to make it part of the song, though I didn't know how – he often said things that you didn't understand, but you had to trust. The guitar started, very soft, and the birds got louder, in my head and outside it. I remember looking up and the sky was glowing brighter right in my eyes. The pink was easing into red – a great blush as a new day started, and I thought, *Oh my, this is for me! 'Africa's Weeping!' The gig is rolling in as the earth turns – my own, big, special occasion, and I will never be the same after this . . .*

Then Snowy started to sing:

> '*A stone in your shoe and a stone in your fist*
> *A stone in your throat when you ask for a kiss*
> *So we walk up the hill and we notice it's cold*
> *For this is the grave where the stone has been rolled.*'

I came in on the last line, backing him:

> '*This is the grave where the stone has been rolled.*'

I got it right! The harmony worked for the first time, and everyone smiled.

> '*Let the water flow, now –*

> *Let's see what's in our soul, now.*
> *Crack the world in two or get it moving, let it roll.*
> *Because I'm frightened of the morning,*
> *As I never know what's dawning,*
> *And I want to do what's right, but I'm too cold.'*

That's when he stopped, dead – and I didn't even notice at first, because my job was to back the chorus:

> 'I'm so frightened of the morning . . .'

– that's what we were all singing, and there were chimes still ringing. I think the birds were calling extra loud, and some of them had taken flight, because I do remember a beating of wings, close to me. Anyway – all I can do is say what I saw as the silence fell, and Snowy froze. That's all I can say.

A tiny figure had appeared in the circle, and was looking straight at me.

He was completely naked, I think.

He was thin too, and he stood absolutely still – and my first crazy thought was that he was a Snowy-fan who'd broken in, though he was way too young, so next I wondered if it might be someone's little boy, sleepwalking? *But how could he have walked to the very centre of our space without being seen?* Those were the thoughts tumbling through my mind as he came closer to mine. That's when I saw two dead-looking, hollow, black eyes and that's when I saw the skull under the skin. I realized, then, that the body wasn't thin – it was skeletal – and that his right hand was reaching out as if to touch me. The mouth opened, but it was as if speaking was hard, and I knew he'd come a long, long way to tell me something important . . .

And he said, simply: 'Tell the truth.'

Such a soft voice.

Almost nothing – just a whisper – but I heard exactly what he said, and I could not look away. Three words only, and even the birds were hushed, and as he said them the sun rose suddenly, and the first rays hit us like a spotlight.

They hit the lodestone, turning it crimson. The shadow fell right on me so the little boy turned to silhouette. I tried to get up, but couldn't – not until he touched me, and honestly in all my life I have never felt a colder touch. It was just a finger, on my forehead, but suddenly there was ice through my veins, and I tried to cry out, but couldn't make a sound. Worse than that, worst of all, his eyes reflected mine and I knew for absolutely certain he was dead. I saw eyes I'd never forget, and at the moment he touched me the rock beneath us cracked wide open, splitting between his feet. Every mirror in the house shattered, and the strings burst on their instruments.

The garden was suddenly full of screeching, and Snowy cried out. The band leaped up and Jun lunged forward.

I remember getting tangled in the silk, trying to back away, and I remember turning but the boy was there again, reaching out for me. I turned the other way, but he was in front of me, closer than ever, and whichever I went, there he was, with his hands up, trying to speak, trying to talk to me!

I swear everyone was yelling, most of all me, and the intruder alarms sounded, howling over the whole estate, and that's when I simply passed out in someone's arms, and fell straight down into the darkness.

# Leela

## 05.58
## East Dean hospital – in theatre


Forty-two seconds passed . . . and then his heart started again.

Jamie's heart started again, but it was nothing to do with us. He'd gone, and he returned because he chose to. We didn't move, and nobody spoke. The pulse was weak, but it stabilized and then suddenly it strengthened – and still we did nothing. We could only watch, for there was a power at work beyond all our understanding. The monitors flashed. The ventilator gasped – it had been stilled, but now the boy's lungs filled with oxygen and life flowed back into him. I watched it return, and when I touched him, he was warm.

One hour later he was in intensive care, and Tilda sat beside him, keeping vigil. She watched over him as the day grew bright, and I saw the red sun rise higher and higher, until the horizon was a sheet of flame.

# Spud & Damien

## 05.59
## City sewers


We got the call just as were knocking off, and the computer was registering a T.S.O., which means 'Total Short-out.' All we knew at that point was a system above ground had lost pressure, so it was up to us to do the A.I. (Advance Inspection) – and by rights we shouldn't have gone, because we'd been on twelve hours. We were dead keen to see an Electrical Fault, though – both of us – because we'd read so much about them. We persuaded the boss, and got a location-fix, and off we sailed. It was under some rotten old warehouse, which had caused problems before.

Anyway, we got there in five and closed down the central spigot. It was a question then of logging the fractured main, and making it safe. Then we'd hand over to the day staff, who'd do the A&R (Assess and Report).

It was a wide stretch of sewer, so we tied in to the side, and threw up an access tower – that's two minutes' work if you know what you're doing. We scrambled up together and got the power-lock on the most likely-looking manhole – one that was dripping steadily, just asking for attention. She swung down easily enough, but wow! – what a waterfall! It damn near took us with it. We were roped together, though, so it was a question of clinging on tight as the excess came past us – gallons of the stuff that had filled up the basement areas and covered the fuse boxes. We went in together, flashlights on.

Well! We saw immediately that it was anything but routine, because the space we'd climbed into was a mess of smashed-up furniture and old industrial wreckage. There was a spiral staircase that had been torn from its moorings, and the vortex had wrenched out some of the brickwork.

We did not expect to find people, and all I can say is we'd arrived in the nick of time. We counted three, first off. When we pulled back an old tarpaulin, we found two more, so that's when the rest of the crew came in with us and scoured the place. The head-count reached seven! The poor things were soaked to the skin, and I genuinely thought they were goners. It was Spud who turned one over, and heard a sort of retching, coughing, gulping belch – so we got all of them into recovery, and that's was when they started sitting up, one by one. They were covered in silt and filth – they looked like swamp-creatures, really . . . so when one of them spoke, I thought I was hearing things.

'Spud,' it said – just faintly. We both rushed over to it.

I got my handkerchief out, and washed the mud from the eyes. Oh lord, it was a girl – and she was reaching up, as if to see if I was real – reaching out, so I put my arms right round her, as she was obviously in shock.

'Spud,' she said – and of course I recognized her then. It was Vicky. We turned round, and that's when we saw Ben behind her, and then Eleanor. One of them had dragged himself to his feet, and we recognized Edgar – then Stagger, Polly and Molly all gazing at us as if we were ghosts. The last of the water had run out by now, and the electrics were off. We just stared at each other, realizing that we'd been about sixty seconds from the most terrible, unthinkable tragedy.

Getting them out wasn't easy.

We had to sling up a rope-harness and drop them gently, one by one. We got them into the boat safe and sound, and they sat there together in a line, bobbing quietly. We filed an online S.E.R. (Site Exit Report), and sailed back to base. Half an hour it took, and it was very obvious what they needed: a hot shower, dry clothes, and then a celebration breakfast.

It was S.S. all the way, then: Slow and Steady. Our friends were out of danger, and I suppose, well . . . in a way, we'd saved their lives.

# Edgar

## 06.31
## In the sewer tunnels

I don't know how the call got through to us because we were way underground. Maybe Spud and Damien had special phones, with special reception? – but anyway, Vicky was too weak to hold the phone, so I had to put it against her ear.

'Leela?' she said.

And we heard Leela's voice, clear as a bell: 'Vicky, what's wrong? Where have you been?'

'What?'

'I've been trying everyone . . . Where on earth are you?'

'Leela,' said Vicky.

'Yes—'

'How's Jamie? You got the records, didn't you?'

'Ages ago, you know that. It's finished, Vee – it's all over.'

My heart stopped, and I closed my eyes. Everyone was listening – everyone could hear.

Leela's voice came again: 'He's come through,' she said. 'Through?' said Vicky.

'He's made it. He's in intensive care, but he's stable – Tilda's with him now. They're together, and he's stable.'

Vicky said nothing then. Nobody did.

'He's alive, Vicky,' said Leela. 'Do you understand me? He's going to need time, and care – more surgery, no doubt about it. But there's every chance now. Every chance, and it's looking good. He's . . . a warrior, isn't he? That boy wants to live.'

She was quiet for a moment, and we sailed on without speaking.

'You guys saved him,' she said, at last. 'You realize that? I don't know what happened to him, or how – or who's to blame. But you and the others . . . are you there?'

'Yes.'

'You saved his life.'

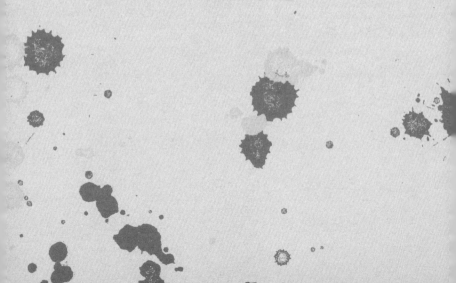

# INTERLUDE

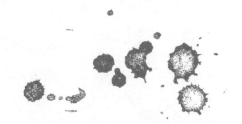

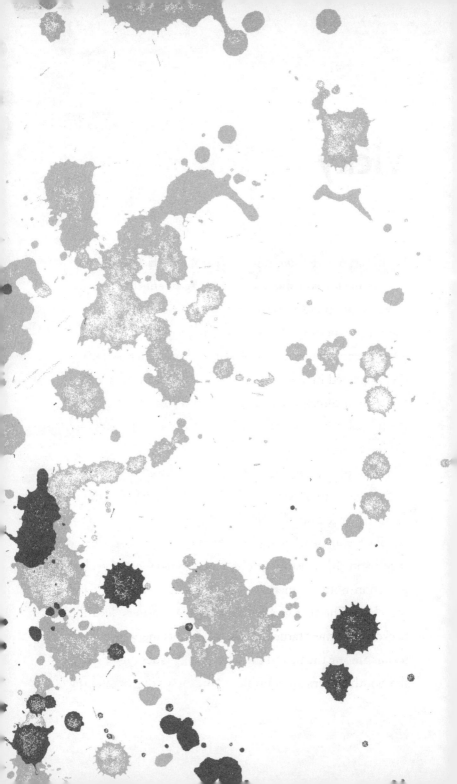

# Vicky

Let me stop here for a moment, before the last charge.

Let me tell you about a TV advertisement that received its world premiere at the 'Africa's Weeping!' concert. It was the most expensive commercial ever made, and it was, of course, for Liquidator. It's also the only commercial Snowy ever appeared in, and it was shot by a multi-award-winning Hollywood director whose fee was fifteen million dollars. He filmed it in twenty-two different countries spread over all five continents, with a cast of eight hundred and forty children under the age of fourteen. Satellites beamed the images into an estimated three billion eyeballs, half a minute before Snowy walked on stage.

First, you see what appears at to be a standard, ordinary rock band. It's blasting out an iconic Snowy number, but you soon notice something rather strange: each musician is a child. The first group you see are westerners, and the backdrop is the Statue of Liberty. The camera skids and zooms among them, and the whole thing fades quickly into the South American equivalent, and now you're watching two dozen kids hammering away on percussion in front of that Christ statue in Rio de Janeiro. This mixes to an Indian band in multi-coloured robes, and they're gyrating under the fountains of the Taj Mahal, before everything shifts to Inuits on an iceberg, and children in kimonos on the Great Wall of China . . . and on it goes. The cuts are so quick, and the cameras so mobile, that you'd swear it was the same band.

The countries keep changing, and the kids just get more beautiful.

It's 3D, so you move among them as they play. They're lean and fit, and their skins are smooth – in fact, they glow with health – and as the music rises to a crescendo, up and up, you close in tight on the vocalist, who is Snowy himself, in shades . . . You zoom right into his wise old, craggy old, prophet-like face and then the whole thing seems to freeze as the words wheel around you in a halo of lightning.

The children gather, holding hands, and there's a surf of froth rising up to their shoulders as the logo bubbles up in silver:

# LIQUIDATOR

The words are gasping at you, boiling, and you reach for that drink, knowing it's exactly what you need.

The children are in white, and they gaze at you. They are a super-race, with wide, clear, confident eyes. I remember thinking when I saw it, how simple the message is: if you buy our drink, you will be beautiful, and you will win. If you don't, you'll remain ugly, unlucky, un-special and un-loved. You'll be a loser, in other words – for ever – and you'll have no one to blame but your own, stupid self.

# SATURDAY MORNING

# VICKY

## 07.52
## Canteen

We docked by a flight of steps.

Spud and Damien led us up to a locker room, where there were benches and pegs, and an old lady gave us towels and soap. We filed into the showers, and hosed ourselves down in hot water. When we emerged from the steam we found overalls laid out ready, so we slipped them on and met in the canteen. Moments later, we had food piled high on our plates, and the only sound was the sound of our eating. It was some time later that Edgar put down his knife and fork.

'Ben,' he said.

We all looked up.

'What's the matter?'

Ben was sitting there, white-faced and still. He hadn't touched his food, and his hands rested on the table.

Eleanor touched his arm. 'Are you feeling sick?' she said. 'Do you want to go home?'

He shook his head.

Spud said, 'Do you want a drink? Shall I get you coffee?'

Ben shook his head again, and closed his eyes. We watched, because something strange was happening. His lips pursed, and relaxed again, and he moved his tongue. Now, you have to remember that Ben had taken quite a battering the previous day, so his face was a mess of bruises. The left side was badly swollen, so I wondered if he'd broken a tooth and needed a dentist. I was just about to ask when his eyes flicked open, wide and bright, and he opened his mouth, wide. Slowly, and carefully, he extended his tongue and we leaned in to look because there was something large and black resting on the tip. He balanced it there, so carefully, and we saw that it was a neat plastic case with a metal strip down its centre.

It was a little memory stick.

He took it between his finger and thumb, and wiped it with a napkin. Then he held it up again, and I think it was Stagger who asked the obvious question.

'Where did that come from?'

'The basement,' said Ben.

'What's on it?' said Polly.

Ben swallowed. 'Have a guess.'

'Not the files,' I said – and Ben nodded.

'Everything,' he said.

Nobody spoke, and nobody moved.

'Every file?' said Edgar, at last. 'You mean, all the stuff . . .'

'Yes,' said Ben. 'I did a backup, soon as the lights went out. I'd been doing it every ten minutes – it's a habit. I didn't want to lose our work.'

'In the dark?' I said. 'You backed up in darkness? – how?'

Ben looked at me. 'Vicky, when the power fails, that's what you do,' he said. 'It's total instinct. You pray the battery's kicked in, and it's the first thing you do—'

'But that means the whole paper's on it,' said Stagger.

'Yes.'

'What about the other material?' said Molly. 'Sorry, but the photographs, the evidence – the emails? Ben – are you saying every single document's on that stick, and you've had it in your mouth for . . . how long?'

'Ages.'

Eleanor said, 'But they searched us. I remember.'

'And they didn't check my mouth,' said Ben. 'I put it in when you went for the phone, Eleanor. The guy grabbed you, and Edgar kicked his arse for him, so that was the distraction. And I managed not to swallow it, I don't know how—'

'Oh God,' said Edgar. 'This means . . . I'm not quite sure what it means, but this is important, isn't it?'

Ben nodded. 'I'll tell you what it means,' he said. 'I think we have a decision to make, because this is serious, and things are far from finished. Now, we came as close as you can come to dying back there, didn't we? They were trying to murder us, and very nearly succeeded. That's how dangerous we are. They need us dead, and I said that right from the start. They'll be coming for us again soon – you can bet your life – because these files . . .' And he held the stick up again. 'These files will destroy them.'

'It's not over then,' I said.

'No way.'

'I thought it was,' said Eleanor. 'I thought we'd just go to the police now, and let them deal with it.'

'We could put everything online,' said Molly.

'No,' said Ben. 'They'll be ready for that. We've had this conversation before–'

'But we can't do any more,' I said. 'Look at us!'

'You want to give up?'

'No,' said Stagger. 'She doesn't mean that – that's not fair–'

'I tell you want I want,' said Ben – and his eyes were glittering. 'I want revenge, and I'm not leaving that to other people. Nor am I spending the rest of my life waiting to see if they come after me. I haven't been home yet, don't forget! – but I bet they've smashed up my stuff. They've got my laptop, and all our phones – they took everything. So I want to bring that company to its knees, and I want to see that woman in jail. I mean, sure, guys . . . if you're feeling tired, I can understand that. If you want to finish your food, get some sleep, that's your choice. But I don't think it's the right one. I think we stay together, as a team, and finish the job.

'How?' said the twins.

'I don't know.'

'But seriously, Ben,' said Stagger. 'What can we do now?'

'We can think,' said Ben. 'We can put our heads together, because where do you think Mrs Lockson is right now? With all the executives and company directors?'

'Where?' said Eleanor.

'They wouldn't be at home.'

'They're waiting to check on us,' I said. 'To make sure we—'

'No,' said Ben. 'They'll be at the concert. "Africa's Weeping!"'

'That's true,' said Edgar. 'The drink's the main sponsor.'

The twins were nodding. 'It's their main marketing event,' said Molly. 'It's the international launch, really—'

'You read the files,' said Ben. 'They're giving away trillions of cans, literally. Today that crap goes global for ever.' He smiled, for the first time in a long while. 'I want to ruin them.' He said. 'We can't go home and hide, can we? We've got to attack.'

# Edgar

**Continued** ▶

That's when I saw it.

It helped that there was a big TV on the far side of the hall, and they were showing pictures of the gig. London was getting ready, and that was the trigger: the plan just dropped down into my brain, and as I've said before my brain is a lot smaller than Ben's because I am so bad at planning, or thinking ahead, so I just *do* stuff, usually. This time, I sat there. I got a certain way with the idea, thinking it through – and I said, 'Spud, buddy?'

'What?'

'Damien. Can I ask you something? – both of you.'

'Sure,' said Damien. They'd been looking so confused because they had no idea what we'd been talking about, or why we were all so serious.

I said: 'The sewers. They go right under London, don't they?'

'Of course,' said Damien.

'They go for miles, everywhere,' said Spud.

'So you could get us to a certain place, could you? In one of those boats. We could sail off now, if we wanted to?'

Spud nodded. 'Easy.'

'But our shift's finished,' said Damien. 'We wouldn't be authorized, and the placement's over—'

'Doesn't matter,' said Spud.

'How come?'

He held up a piece of plastic. 'I've got my dad's pass.'

'OK,' I said, trying not to get excited – trying not to get ahead of myself. 'Wait a second, there. When we got to this certain place – *if* we got there . . .'

'Where?' said Polly. 'Where do we go?'

'Listen – I want to be sure of something. The drains are all connected, yes? So if we got to that stadium, for example – could we climb up out of the boat, and get inside it? Could you get us there, in the next two hours?'

'Yes,' said Spud.

'You sure?'

'We've got the laptop, we can navigate—'

'And Katkat's there, inside,' said Stagger. 'She's probably arriving right now.'

'But we don't have tickets,' said Eleanor. 'I tried for hours—'

'We won't need them,' I said.

'Of course we will!' said Eleanor. 'It's sold out!'

'No.'

'I want to watch it,' she cried. 'I want to watch it on TV – that's the next best thing!'

'Wait,' I said.

I stood up then, and one by one they stared up at me. It was dawning on us all, and I could see it in their eyes. Would our dear little star-struck friend Katkat stoop down to help us? Or would she be too wrapped up in herself? Oh God, there were questions, of course: how would we find her, and would she even talk to us, if we did? What would we say, what could she do? What did we really expect, hours before the biggest gig the planet's ever seen? – because it was like Ben said, an event going live, right around the world – and it started soon.

What could we really hope to do, even if we got there? – all those questions were good, sensible ones, and the only thing I knew for sure was that none of them had answers. Which was why we had to get up off our arses, and start moving.

Ben said: 'Let's go.'

# Spud & Damien

## 10.00
## Drain network

First, it was about health and safety.

We went to the locker room, and did a KRO6, which is a Kit Requisition Order for the full works: hard hats, flashlights, boots, goggles and gauntlets. By the time we got them all to the landing stage, they were twice their normal size, in high-visibility jackets with walkie-talkies strapped to their shoulders, and they'd doubled in weight. You can't go into the sewers unprotected, though – that's basic. We flashed the old pass, and were through the turnstile, to the jetty. There's six power boats in the fleet, and they were all sitting in dock, refuelled and ready.

'You want to be quick, right?' I said – this being Spud.

'Of course,' says Edgar.

'OK.' I stepped aboard the fastest. 'This is for emergencies – serious stuff. Goes like a bomb.'

I put my code in, and that's when I noticed the time:

ten o'clock, exactly. Ten in the morning, so the concert was starting at that moment, on live TV. We'd known the schedule for weeks: they'd be letting off the balloons first – two million of them, each one showing the face of some little African kid, and that meant the first band was on, and the whole world was watching.

Stagger said: 'Three hours, guys.'

Three hours, and the Snowy band would take the stage for his first appearance in years.

There was no need to synchronize watches: they're attached to the life jackets, radio-controlled. We made sure we shared the same frequency, though, and did a headset check, because the last thing you want is to be down here on your own, unable to communicate.

We were away from the quayside now, and the gate had lifted.

'Everyone ready?' I said.

'Go,' said Edgar. 'We're on a countdown.'

Damien opened the throttle, and we roared out into dark water.

# Edgar

## Continued ▶

That first tunnel was a long, low-ceilinged bullet hole. The water under us was oily, and the lamps on our helmets illuminated rusty metal walls. We came into a lagoon, and having spun in a complete circle, Spud leaned on the tiller and we were shot by a swift current into a narrow canal that took us off at a right angle. The boys had some kind of navigation-laptop, which they checked together, and we ducked under a spider's web of pipes, pausing just in time to let a waterbus sweep past. Then it was full throttle again, right through its wake.

I remember foul smells and a terrible bubbling from below. We weaved around whirlpools and plunged through waterfalls, and when we came into a vast chamber we felt rain on our faces. We bobbed there, under a patch of distant sky, while Damien double-checked the map. We turned back on ourselves, and found a new channel that took us, eventually, to a dead end of steps. We tied up, breathless and exhilarated.

'Are we there?' said Eleanor.

'No,' said Spud. 'Nowhere near.'

'What now then?' said Stagger.

'The laptop says change. Happens all the time, cos of the levels.'

We clambered up to a metal door. Spud swiped his magic pass, and led us onto a stone platform. There we found a line of canoes chained to iron rings. Stagger pulled them loose, and in a moment, we were pushing off – three in three. A waterslide dropped us into churning water, and the ceiling was lower than ever – we had to hunker down and paddle as best we could. We took a tributary off to the left, then battled upstream, our paddles ringing against stone as it got shallow.

That's when the water gave out completely.

'Dammit,' said Spud. 'She's dry.'

'We're stuck,' said Damien.

'So what do we do?' said Edgar.

'I don't know.'

Ben cursed. We were beached and helpless. 'Is there any other way?' he said. 'We can't just sit here.'

'We'll just have to go back,' said Spud. 'But it's a hell of a way round, and I didn't expect this.'

Damien checked the map again, and pointed. 'I say we walk it,' he said. 'We'll join up with Tributary Seven, and that water's rainwater – she should be full. We can go from there.'

'How far?' said Spud.

'Twenty minutes, give or take—'

'Good call. Get the ropes.'

The canoes were heavy, but we dragged them forward while Stagger and Damien unrolled cords from their backpacks. They knotted them, and minutes later, we were hauling all three boats together along the gulley, as rats darted over our boots. It was back-breaking work, but at last we were going downhill, and in the distance we heard the churning of rapids.

'Careful,' said Spud. 'This is illegal.'

'What isn't?'

'Mid-air launching. Toggle up, and go slow.'

We saw the torrent then, hurtling past a cliff-edge of concrete. We dropped the canoes in, and hooked ourselves together in pairs. We clambered down, one after another, and threw the ropes off, and then it was a mad paddle as we shot forwards. We found a calm spot further down, and spent a moment wiping the water from our faces. We came to another lagoon then, but this one was eerily green and still. In fact, the water seemed thick and stagnant, and algae-clad walls reared up over our heads in vast, gothic arches. It was a drowned cathedral, and we eased ourselves past statues, up to their waists in slime.

'Where on earth are we?' I whispered.

'St Peter's,' said Spud. 'Under the Thames, hopefully.'

'Look at it,' said Stagger, and his torch shifted from face to face – a whole row of gentle-eyed saints gazed down at us. There was a dull thudding, and I could see columns of dust floating down over their shoulders.

'That's a tube train,' said Damien.

'Good,' said Spud. 'Jubilee Line, I think. We're somewhere round Greenwich. Bit of a detour, but back on course.'

'Keep going,' said Edgar. 'We can do this.'

We paddled for another hour and came to a dock. Spud jumped onto it, and we tied off next to a ladder. That took us up into dark shadow, and again we felt rain on our faces. I saw pipes rising, with narrow gantries between them, and a peppering of tiny, winking lights.

'Is this it?' I said.

Damien nodded. 'I hope so.'

We crossed a bridge, and a spiral staircase rose up into pinpricks of light.

'Quite a climb,' said Polly.

'Why aren't there any signs?' said Stagger. 'I haven't seen a single name, or direction—'

'You're supposed to know,' said Spud. 'If you don't have the gear, you shouldn't be down here. Let's keep moving.'

I could feel vibrations in the hand-rail. Somewhere – not so very far away – we heard the thudding of distant drums. We reached the top landing at last, but a pair of steel doors blocked our way. Five words ran across them in huge red letters:

**STRICTLY PRIVATE: STADIUM PERSONNEL ONLY**

'Shall I phone her?' I said.

Edgar nodded. 'She told you to come. I heard her.'

Stagger laughed. 'We've come to get our tickets,' he said. 'She'll be delighted.'

I dialled, but the signal was so intermittent I texted instead. Meanwhile, Spud was requesting the coordinates of the electronic door-lock, firing off a message to Control. The sequence was scrambled back to him, and it took thirty seconds to tap it in. The doors swung open, and we found ourselves looking straight into the lens of a security camera.

Under it stood a uniformed guard, and he wasn't smiling.

# Stagger

**Continued ▶**

I remember Spud just standing there, and I thought, Oh God – this is it. What on earth were we thinking?

He said, 'Hi.'

No answer. The man just stared at us, fingering his radio.

'How are you doing?' said Spud.

'Not too well,' said the guard – and he spoke dead slow, and dead suspicious. 'What's going on?'

'Um . . . header tank,' said Damien. 'Are you the one that called?'

'Header tank? What's that mean?'

'CWW,' said Spud.

Damien opened the laptop then, while Spud held up his pass. 'City Water and Waste,' he said, and he managed to sound just a little impatient – like these delays were a real pain in the neck. 'Emergency callout,' he said. 'Access required for an SF-zero-one. That's a System Failure, priority. Who reported it?'

'Oh God, it's on a spur,' said Damien, under his breath. 'That's bad.'

'What is?'

'Right below your central spigot, by the look of it,' said Damien. He turned the laptop around, and showed it to the guard, who'd been joined by another. 'Runs through some of the, er . . . dressing rooms, I'd say. You must know where they are?'

'Hold on a sec . . . who called you?' His radio was crackling.

'No idea,' said Spud. 'But we were told it was urgent.'

'We're going to need clearance,' said the second man. 'CWW? Why's there so many of you?'

Damien looked at Spud and sighed. 'Look,' he said. 'All I know is the call came in fifteen minutes ago. Broke our backs getting here on time – are you saying someone's playing games?'

'I'm saying we don't know anything about a call, or a tank—'

'That's the problem then,' said Spud. 'Sounds like they haven't told the front line. But if your tank's down, buddy – that's going to short your electrics. We'll have to shut off your generators, and then it's full-on evacuation. Everyone out.'

'Would that stop the show? You can't do that!'

'We'd have to,' said Spud.

'Hang on, no—'

'But it's simple at the moment. If we don't waste time talking about it.'

'How long do you need?' said the guard.

'Twenty minutes,' said Damien, checking the time. 'Let's get to it, boss. Everyone ready?'

We moved forward, nodding, but the guard held up his hand.

'No,' he said, and we stopped dead. 'It's madness in there. Chaos. I'll get you an escort.'

Ninety seconds later, a thin kid on roller-blades appeared, with a security pass round her neck. There were explanations, and suddenly we were being led through more doors, into a long, curving passage. In the distance, we could hear cheering, and we started to run.

# Eleanor

## 12.12
## Stadium

It was a total madhouse!

It was wonderful, as well – the guide person went clattering down some stairs and doubled-back on herself, back the way we'd come, and it was hard to keep up in heavy boots and carrying all the gear. But we managed it, and found ourselves in the biggest lift I'd ever seen, which was crammed full of costume racks and trunks, with everyone shouting and the lift-gate clanging open and shut as we went up or possibly down – I couldn't work out which. In the end, we were led out into a tunnel, which was more like a race track, full of buggies zooming past with lights flashing, blasting their horns. We pressed into the walkway on the side, and were taken left and left again, until we'd gone in at least two circles, everyone we passed babbling on their phones:

'Where are you?'

'On the way!'

'Stand by entrance ten! Cue exit five!'

I was keeping my eyes peeled for the musicians, of course – just in case. Stupid, I know, but I'd never been backstage anywhere, not even at school because I never got a part in the play, ever, and I thought, *You just never know!* – *I might see Snowy!!*

But I didn't, and we got taken to a place called 'Sector C – waiting rooms', and there were enormous TVs there, in every corner showing what was happening on stage. Totally amazing! Cameras zooming around this great long line of drummers (which was one of the support acts, of course – not Snowy). Then they'd cut to the stadium crowd, and everyone was on their feet, howling and waving before the big 'L' of Liquidator spins round and you're back on-stage again. Not that we could stay and watch, because we had a new guide now and this one was a man who raced up stairs past queues of little kids, who were mainly Japanese, in kimonos, but then I saw a long line of little Asian girls in the most beautiful saris . . . then we get herded downstairs again into something called 'Red Zone', and the walls aren't white any more, but the colour of blood! There were big black arrows and numbers, and I remember 'CH1 to J1'. I was thinking, Don't get lost, Eleanor! – you'll never get out again! – and I was getting more and more nervous, because the next sign said:

– and that was our destination.

'OK, guys,' said our guide.

Phew! – we stopped for breath.

'This is a restricted area,' he said. 'We don't normally let anyone through here – not without special clearance.'

'Really?' said Edgar.

'Really. So I'm going to call security—'

Damien touched the boy's arm, ever so gently. 'Don't waste time, chief,' he said – and he sounded just like my dad, when he gets impatient in a shop. He pointed up to the ceiling. 'That's your problem,' he said.

'Where?'

'There.'

'What?'

'Look at that pipe. Shocking.'

It looked perfectly all right to me, but we all did our bit by tutting a bit, and shaking our heads. It was a big, thick kind of duct thing, and it ran along the top of the wall, and then upwards through a hole. Spud stretched up and tapped it, with his spanner, and Ben said, 'Ooh! That's the wrong gauge.'

'You bet,' said Edgar. 'Way too small.'

'Tiny,' I said.

'Lucky we're here,' said Spud. 'They can't take the strain, you see – got a lot of people here, have you?'

The boy blinked, like we were stupid. 'Thousands,' he said.

'Really? Big event?'

'It's standing room only!' he said. 'We've got Snowy on soon, and we're beyond capacity at the moment—'

'Ah,' said Damien. 'That's what's done it, you see. Too many people! – but you leave us here, and we'll do you an E.D.C.'

'An E.D.C.?'

'Emergency De-Commission—'

'Can you radio base, Stag?' said Spud.

'Roger,' said Stagger – and he made his transistory-thing crackle.

'In position,' said Damien.

Edgar had an idea then, and grabbed a locker. He dragged it from the wall while Vicky and the twins got down on their knees. I followed suit, and we started to lay our tools out, like we had a big, long, important job and had to start at once.

'OK,' said the boy, looking after us. 'I'll come back for you.'

Even as he said it, the corridor filled up with yet another load of kids. This time they were in those flowing Arabian robes, looking really exotic, and they were all giggling with excitement. Our guide was swept away with them, and we were on our own at last! Vicky darted off the way we'd came, as did Ben, and I realized then that they were checking all the doors.

It was the twins who found it.

'Here!' they said, hissing it quietly.

I was right next to Vicky, and she grabbed my hand. She was dead scared, and I could feel her trembling. We huddled together then, all nine of us, and looked at the sign. The words were spelled out in black and pasted where you couldn't possibly miss them:

★

43/2F KATKAT MADAMBA
DO NOT DISTURB

Edgar went to knock, but Ben got hold of his wrist and held it.

'Oh God,' he said.

'What?'

'What if she won't help us, Edgar? What if she just says no?'

# Katkat

## 12.18
## Dressing room

I didn't hear them at first.

I had my headphones on. I had my eyes closed. I was in the middle of a nightmare, doing my best to blot out everything, and if they'd arrived any sooner they would have bumped right into Jun and two nurses, because I wasn't well . . . I'd passed out, don't forget – I had literally fainted in the garden. Yes, I'd come round and everyone had been so, so nice, but there wasn't time to relax or get over it or deal with it in any way! The show had to go on, we all knew that, so I was trying not to think about the boy, the face, the eyes or any of it, trying not to think about my voice and what was happening to it.

'Focus,' I kept saying – but how could I?

I could hardly even speak, let alone sing – and I didn't want food or drink, so as soon as people came I wanted them to go again and leave me in peace. The more you try to be calm, though, the more frantic you get – so I'd sent everyone away and I was sitting down praying my throat would relax and knowing it must – that this had to be the terror and the tension, because after all, any minute I was going to be on-stage in front of millions and millions: who wouldn't be scared? But I have to admit this, I'd been sick as a dog, and this was a being alone like I'd never felt before. This was being boxed up in a little tiny room in hell, with me hardly able to breathe, and knowing for sure that the moment I went to the mic I'd be sick again. So I sat there clenching my fists, breathing deep . . .

The music I was listening to must have ended.

That's when I heard a tapping, and it turned into hard knocking: *BANG, BANG, BANG!* So when I looked up the door, it was shaking, about to burst the lock. I had some crazy idea that it was him again, come to find me, but I knew that was stupid, so I wiped my eyes and swallowedand I tried so hard to speak: 'Come in!' – and it was so hoarse and crackly still.

Then I remembered: I'd bolted myself in.

I flicked it back, and in they came! – a whole army, so you can imagine the shock. This huge gang, steaming in at me in big orange life-jackets with thick gloves and masks over their faces, and they just kept coming, one after another, forcing me back till there wasn't room for all for us. Two of them jumped up on the make-up table because the room was small . . . And just as I went to scream, or reach for the panic button on the wall, off came the hats and goggles and I saw it was Vicky, and Ben Gallagher, and Edgar, and all the others I recognized one by one – and in a weird way they looked more scared than me.

Vicky grabbed my hands, which were up around my face, I think, and pressed them together, tight and she might even have kissed them.

'Katkat!' she said. It was more of a hiss, really – and her eyes were big and bulging. 'Thank God we found you . . .'

I couldn't say a word. I tried again, but I just couldn't – my throat was now totally blocked.

'We haven't got long,' she said. 'Have we? And this is an emergency.'

I kept looking from one face to the next, and there they all were gawping at me – every single eye fixed on mine, and of course there were mirrors all around us so it looked like there were hundreds of them and I was totally surrounded. I thought, What can they possibly want? – but all I could do was open my mouth, and shake my head.

Vicky went on – urgent and slow, and she wouldn't let go of my hands. 'We. Need. Your. Help,' she said. 'Honestly, Katkat – we wouldn't crash in like this if it wasn't major, would we? But we have discovered a terrible wrong, and you've got to put it right – right now. There's no time to explain, and even if there was you might not believe us – so

I'm going to show you something . . . someone, in actual fact – a person. A human being, OK? And then you have to do the hardest thing in the world. You have to trust us.'

I was against the wall.

I could not move back, and they came even closer.

One of them produced this little laptop. Ben took it and pushed his way towards me, so he was right in front. I could see him fiddling with a memory stick, and I think time must have stood still, and I felt hands on my shoulders sitting me down, and before I knew it the screen was up against my nose.

I don't know what I expected, but I know I couldn't move, and once again I tried to speak, and absolutely nothing came – I'd been struck down mute, and I could not utter a sound.

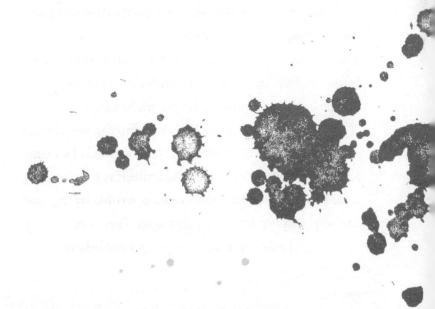

# Spud

## 12.22
## Continued ▶

I was right next to her.

I'd given Ben the laptop. I put my hand on her shoulder, just to comfort her, I think. I wouldn't have dared, normally, but she looked so scared – she looked really ill, actually, to be honest – like she should have been in hospital. We were pressing in on her, making it worse, and she was wearing this little white dress which showed her bones, so I just wanted to calm her down a bit – and what I felt was a skeleton.

She was like paper and sticks, and her cheeks were sucked in. She has the most beautiful face, does Katkat – and her hair was done, and she's wearing tiny silver earrings, as lovely as a model or a film star, even . . . but wrong. She'd had time away from school, and everyone knew why, but never talked about it. Now she looked half-starved, like some poor, cornered animal that was too sick to eat and couldn't speak up to say, 'Help me. This is wrong.'

She looked like death.

# Katkat

## 12.23
Continued ▶

I remember Ben's hand.

He pressed a key on the laptop, and the screen was so close that all I could really see was blue – and then I found myself looking at trees, and sky and a kind of paradise. I could hear the cheering of the stadium crowd, and I felt sicker than ever, but I couldn't stop looking at the screen, and the tiny little shacks on the grass. In the next slide I saw it was actually a school, and Ben clicked again to show me the kids, playing basketball.

There were close-ups then, one after the other, following a little boy who was running and jumping – and he did look familiar, but I didn't know why. I think the screen was getting bigger or I was leaning forward, but I still couldn't place him. He was with his friends, having the time of his life, and he had the loveliest face I'd ever seen, with the widest, happiest smile, which got happier and wider in each picture . . .

So when Ben clicked again, I was waiting for that same

face, as if he was there to bring me luck, or give me hope – and I was smiling back. So what I saw then didn't seem real, at first. It was like an awful trick, or like I was in a trance having some horrible flashback, because in a split second that beautiful boy had changed. He wasn't there any more, and what was standing in his place was my ghost, straight from the lodestone, and the garden.

He'd found me again, by magic – found a way in. He was there inside the laptop, gazing out at me, with his wasted face and hungry eyes – and I heard an awful noise then, like a groan of pain or fear, and I was the one making it.

He looked at me harder than ever, and once again I couldn't tear myself away, much as I wanted to. Why not? Why couldn't I smash the laptop to the floor, or turn my back, or cry for help? Why couldn't I run? Because I saw then, right out of the blue, that his face was like mine. He had just the same eyes, and because my hair was scraped back you could see my skull. My skin was stretched, just like his – so it was as if twins who'd never known of each other's existence had suddenly come together.

I said, 'What's his name?'

Just a whisper.

'Jamie.'

'Who?'

He was thin. Sick. Starved. Ugly, and all but wrecked – and we could have been brother and sister. I knew, then, that wherever I went he was going to find me, and reach out to me. I could hear the words in the silence, even though he didn't say them. '*Tell the truth,*' he was saying, through the pain. '*Stop running, Katkat – stand still, and face yourself. Stand still, and tell the truth.*'

That's when I closed the laptop.

When I focused again, they were all still looking at me, and I can't remember who said it – Vicky, or Ben, or one of the twins. Eleanor, maybe, or Edgar. Spud or Damien or Stagger, standing at the back. Maybe they said it together, all of them, with one voice:

'Will you help us, Katkat?'

And suddenly I could speak loud. I could feel my own voice, rising up in me, stronger than before – so I nodded once, then twice. And I tried it out, by saying the one, simple word I needed to say – the only word possible.

'Yes.'

# Edgar

**12.58**
**Continued ▶**

She came up with the idea then – by herself. We had a minute, I guess, to talk it through and it sounded just about mad enough. Because that's what had brought us this far, and kept us alive – madness, with a fair bit of good old-fashioned stupidity, and luck.

We stripped down to our boiler suits, and did a radio test. What then? – we had a good old-fashioned hug, knowing this was the final, final sprint.

Vicky and Eleanor stayed with Katkat.

I went with Stag, Spud and Damien. We made straight for the stage.

As for the twins, and Ben, they set off on the most dangerous part of the mission. They had just two weapons: The memory stick. And Katkat's pass:

## ACCESS ALL AREAS

# Polly & Molly

**12.47**
**Continued** ▶

We set off up some stairs and after a few wrong turns and doubling back, we found a sign to 'Zone E Backstage' –

That looked promising.

Moments later, Edgar checked in.

'Come in, twins, over,' he said. He was very calm and very quiet.

'Receiving,' we said. 'Over.'

'Where are you? Over.'

'We've found one of the tech stations,' said Ben.

'Any luck? – over.'

'We're about to find out. We're getting our bearings, all right? – over and out.'

He stopped a technician. 'Which way to the grid?'

The man's eyes narrowed. 'The grid. At this time?'

'Yup. Got a problem.'

'What area?'

'Projection.'

'That's access seven – what's gone wrong?'

'I don't know,' said Ben. 'Software I imagine, and Snowy's on—'

'In ten minutes, don't tell me. The grid's closed, so you'll have to go through control.'

Ben nodded. 'It's only just been reported.' He fingered the radio again, and listened in. 'Shit,' he said. 'They want a manual check. We need to get up high, and—'

'You've got clearance?'

We flashed the pass. 'Is it far?' said Ben.

'I'd take a buggy. Green zone, level seven. Then you're climbing.'

I drove.

This is Molly, and it was a quick, easy-to-operate electric car that skimmed us out of the backstage area, to a two-lane tunnel that dipped under the auditorium. The one security post hardly glanced at us, and we were soon on the far side of the stadium where the walls turned green. We ditched the vehicle by a bank of elevators and, flashing the pass again, found ourselves rising, slowly, to floor seven.

'You think we're close?' I said – this being Polly.

'I hope so,' said Ben.

The doors opened, and we stepped out into a carpeted corridor: it was totally silent.

'Why's it so quiet?'

'It has to be.'

'Why?'

Ben stared around him, listening. 'This is the operations area,' he said. 'All the servers will be here, you can hear them – the whole matrix. Everything's hard-wired to this floor – cameras, lighting, sound. The problem's going to be getting in, and getting up.'

'And look at that,' I said. 'No entry.'

'We need a code.'

'How?'

We'd come almost at once to a pair of steel doors, and they were shut tight against us. A small box stood to the left, requiring a pass-number. Worst of all, there was a camera above, staring down at us. I tapped in a number – this is Molly – hoping to buy some time, but the doors were thrown open into our faces, and I knew we'd been caught.

We hadn't, though – this is Polly again. A crowd of executives poured past us, into the lobby, and I saw Ben flinch to the side as if he'd been struck. He just managed to turn his back – for in the centre of the group was a silver-haired woman in a coat of golden silk. She had a  mobile phone pressed to her ear, and we saw that all-too familiar snarl of a smile.

'It's about to start,' she cried. 'What?' She stopped. 'Reception's bad,' she said. 'Wait, they're taking me down now – I've just checked, and it's fine . . . Nothing.' It was Helen Lockson. Her eyes bulged, and she started to laugh. 'Stop worrying,' she said. She sipped from a wine glass. 'We'll be backstage afterwards, so call me then. No, we're on track, darling – that's what I'm saying. The band's ready!'

I looked straight into her eyes. 'Excuse me,' I (Polly) said.

'What?'

'We need to get through.'

'Oh. Am I in your way? – so sorry . . .'

'Yes.'

She was slightly drunk. She smiled, and noticed Molly. We watched her eyeballs swivel, and she stood there trying to recall when and where she'd last seen twins. We stared back at her, and Molly took the door.

'Enjoy the show,' we said together – and we ducked past her, taking Ben with us.

# Edgar

## 12.53
## Continued ▶

Five minutes later, they still hadn't checked in.

'Where are you, Ben?' I said.

Nothing. Only interference, so I said it again: 'Ben! Polly – come in, please! Molly?'

At last, I heard a very soft voice. 'Getting close,' it said.

'Is that Ben?'

'Yes.'

'You're cutting it fine, buddy. Problems?'

'Just a few.'

'What?'

'Where are you? Where's Katkat?'

'I'm backstage,' I said. 'There's kids everywhere, it was easy. The band are on their way, but Katkat's switched off. Are you in the grid yet?'

'Edgar, we can't find it–'

'You need to, Ben. Is there no one to ask?'

'It's a maze all right? – and we've got to keep moving . . . there's cameras!'

# Vicky

They'd come for Katkat, and we left the together, holding hands. I was on one side and Eleanor on the other.

We moved towards the stage, and people stood back to let us pass. We were fast-tracked down a private corridor, and soon the rest of the band were gathering. I knew a few of the faces from the books and magazines, but all I could think about was Katkat, and I could feel her fear. There was a sound, like waves breaking on a shore: a kind of surging roar, and it got louder with every step. It was the audience, of course: twenty thousand people, hungry for the first glimpse of Snowy.

We came to a bridge.

That took us to a platform, which was bathed in soft, white light. It was curtained off, but so close to the stage we could hardly hear each other. Katkat stepped onto it, and I was about to follow with Eleanor, when I felt a hand on my shoulder, and we stopped dead.

It was Jun, the bodyguard, and I thought for an awful moment he'd discovered the plan. He put his mouth to my ear, though, and said: 'Sorry.'

'What?'

'Artists only, OK?'

'Oh,' I said. 'I thought—'

'She's fine, yeah?' He put his thumbs up. 'She's good to go.'

'Where's Snowy?' shouted Eleanor. 'Is he here yet?'

'He's ready,' said Jun. 'Feeling fine, and ready to go.'

'Good.'

'We have our final meeting now, so . . . where are you watching from?'

'I don't know,' I said.

The audience howled again, and we stood there in the hurricane. When the noise subsided, I said: 'We didn't think. We don't have tickets!'

Jun smiled. 'You're lucky, then,' he said – and he held up two thin slips of paper. 'Side of the stage, you won't see nothing. You get yourselves out front, yeah? – with the VIPs. I got two seats left, down in the front.' He winked at us.

'Thanks for helping.'

If he noticed our hands shaking, he said nothing. He just handed us the tickets, and turned to Katkat, who was cowering, holding my arm.

'You OK, baby?' he said.

Katkat nodded, and Jun crouched down low. He looked at her, hard, right in the eyes.

'You were sent to us, baby. You know that.'

'Yes.'

'The gods are watching. Aren't they?'

Katkat nodded.

'Get out there, girl, Africa's weeping. Let's wipe away the tears.'

He was wearing a tiny earpiece with a wire that disappeared under his shirt. I saw him finger it, listening hard, and the audience started to chant. It was one word, over and over – slow and menacing: 'Snow-y! Snow-y!'

There was a stamping too, as if an army had arrived and the stage was under siege.

'It's cool,' cried Jun. 'We're waiting for you.'

'The Snowman's here! This is the big one, guys. We're doing it, yeah? We're doing it!'

# Ben

**12.57**
**Continued ▶**

Edgar was yelling, but I could hardly hear him.

'It's the fifth song!' he said.

'What is?'

'"Tell the Truth!"'

'Edgar,' I said. 'We're going—'

'What?'

'We're going in circles, here—'

'Where are you, man? You need to be up there!'

'We know that!'

'Hurry!'

We'd totally lost our bearings, but we had to keep moving in case Mrs Lockson came after us, or raised the alarm. We'd sped down the corridors, knowing everywhere we went there were cameras tracking us, and there were so many doors into studios and offices . . . what we needed was grid access, and that meant finding stairs, or a ladder.

It was Polly who saw the sign: two words only, in red –

It was screwed to what looked like a fire exit, and we hauled it open together: the roar of the crowd poured over us. Everyone in that stadium knew the time, and knew that the moment was close, and as we clambered up the steps we could hear a chant and feel the whole place vibrating. Soon there was a slow, rhythmical stamping, and it grew louder until it was lost in a hurricane of whistling. When we reached the landing, there was a metal gate barring our way.

'This is it. We're in the roof.'

'Is it locked?'

'It can't be.'

We got it open together, and it was like pushing out onto the deck of a ship in high seas – we could barely move forward. We just clung together for a moment, looking at a narrow steel walkway, which stretched off into darkness.

We were up in the roof.

That's when I looked down, and wished I hadn't,

because beneath us was a sea of tiny lights, as nearly twenty thousand people held up tiny flames. Were they phones or lighters? I didn't know, but it was a carpet of fire. The chant had focused on the one word, over and over and there was a thudding, like a heartbeat: all those people, stamping again – faster now – in perfect time. I knew that we had to move, and Molly went first, thank God, because she saw me lose my nerve. I was clutching the rails, and Polly stayed behind me. We were on a kind of latticework of mesh and metal, suspended in thin air – narrow catwalks between the steel bars of the stadium grid.

This was the time for concentration.

I heard my radio screech, but I couldn't hear anyone's voice. Molly led us to a spider's web of scaffolding, and that was when the crowd started to howl. I grabbed Polly's hand, and we pushed on together.

Fire exploded below us, all around the stage – lightning started to flash. One o'clock, sharp: they were playing the Liquidator ad, right on cue and right around the world. We peered down, and saw giant screens filling up with foam, and the foam boiled into a letter 'L'. There were speakers everywhere, so the sound was deafening, and I got transfixed – hypnotized, almost – as the word started to form:

**'LIQ . . . UID . . . AT . . . OR . . .'** – I couldn't take my eyes off it.

Thankfully, Molly was more focused. She grabbed me, and pointed. She'd seen the beams of light, and traced them back to their source.

I saw it too, for when the screens turned purple, the projectors cut down straight through the darkness, clear as lasers. Eight machines in all, I counted them – wired in series, no doubt, with the master in the centre, taking in data and pushing it out. They were bolted to a bar ten long metres below us, and all I knew was I had to get to it.

Polly was shouting something, but I couldn't hear what.

I peered down, checking the access. Clearly, you'd need a harness. If you had to work on that particular bar, you'd work off a crane. I could see two, right beside us, but they were chained up out of use. The only way down was the emergency way, by means of a steel ladder, and the rungs were the width of your foot. Then there was a step across the void, and we'd have to hold each other like a human chain.

One slip would be fatal.

There was no point trying to speak: it was telepathy now. I ditched the laptop, so as to be hands-free, and looked up at the twins. I'd forgotten they were gymnasts, of course – and all I knew was that we ought to give up now, or try something else . . . because we were about to risk our necks.

# Polly & Molly

## 12.59
## Continued ▶

Ben put the memory stick into his mouth.

We dried our palms, and I realized my heartbeat had slowed, the way it always does before any serious manoeuvre – so had Polly's, of course, and we were thinking the same thing: it's just a series of moves, and you stay in control. If there was no drop, this would be easy, so forget the chance of falling, and say to yourself, 'We're just above the mat.'

Don't think risk: start the movement.

Don't even plan, for it plans itself, and it's all about what's within reach and what you can hold.

Polly nodded, and I swung myself over the rail, and found the first rung, top of the ladder. Ben came next, pushed by Polly, and I got his wrist. I held it hard, fingers wrapped right round the skinniest part: an unbreakable grip – and I jerked him towards me.

Seconds later, we were hanging in the air, and we

worked our way down together, step by step. We had to move fast, so when I jumped, I screamed. Nobody could hear, and it was such a long leap into nothing – and I caught the bar, swinging under it. I got a knee up and over, holding fast, and the bar was firm and I was safe. I was upside down, looking at Ben above me – and I nodded to him, and he let himself go.

I caught him, both wrists this time, and he kicked once over the void and was still, eyes wide open staring into mine. Polly came next, and that meant the two of us could lift him, and we set him firmly down just under the projector. He grabbed at the rail beneath it, and swung onto the platform where he needed to be.

No time to rest. So much to do.

I remember the heat, as if we were close to a furnace. The projectors were above us now, and they were smouldering – they could set fire to your clothes. We watched Ben, for he was the one squeezing into position.

He got under the main projector, and rested.

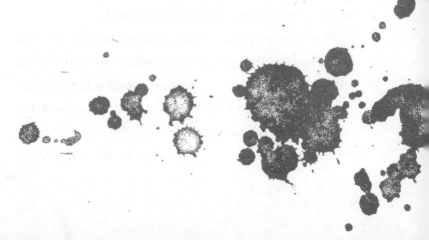

# Ben

## 13.02
## Continued ▶

I put my hand to my mouth.

It was shaking, so I should have waited – but I didn't. I had time, but I was panicking. I couldn't believe I wasn't dead, you see and my brain was flashing and fizzing, and I should have just sat there, eyes closed, and calmed myself down. Instead, I took the memory stick between my finger and thumb, and I could see the socket where it would go, and once I'd plugged it in I could over-ride the data input, and if the panel wasn't too hot I could take control, easily. Every file and photograph would be there, ready to show, and I was in good time. I think I might even have smiled with relief, and I know I clicked the radio, and said to Edgar:

'Ben, here.'

'Oh God, man—'

'In position, over. Ready to go.' But I was shaking, worse than ever.

'Ben?' shouts Edgar. 'They're on! They're coming!'

He shouted something else, but that's when Snowy appeared on-stage, and the crowd went berserk. The lights spun, and it was like being electrocuted. I nearly fell, and I grabbed at the bar with both hands – and, oh God, oh God . . . that's when the memory stick spun sideways, into space, and I watched it fall in slow motion out of my reach and down into the darkness.

# Polly & Molly

## 13.02
## Continued ▶

We saw it coming.

I (Polly) was closest, but I still had to dive. I lunged out, and felt Molly's hand on my wrist. I'd leaped so far I was off the bar, stretched out in space, and she swung me round, all in one movement, as we'd practised at our gym club. I caught the stick in my right hand, and came up behind her. I found the bar again with my left hand, and she steadied me.

I took it then – this is Molly – and clawed my way up to Ben.

His mouth was open.

So was mine.

Polly joined us, and so was hers, and we watched him plug the stick carefully and snugly into its port, our hands cupped under it just in case it fell again.

There was a hammering of drums then, and the first song exploded under us.

# Eleanor

**13.02**
**Continued ▶**

It was all absolutely too much.

Front row seats, maybe just six metres from the stage – I could have clambered over the barrier and touched him! Not that you wanted a seat, of course, because as soon as the band came on everyone was standing. The band poured on, and fanned out over the stage – I saw Jesse on sax and Tomaz Papidou on the keyboards. There was the little Indian sitar-player, waving at us, and he went to his special carpet to the side – and I saw the singers then – Katkat, all in white, looking so tiny and lovely and frail. People I didn't know and people I'd seen in the books, and everyone was screaming – I was screaming, but I couldn't hear my own scream.

Vicky grabbed me, and we were off our feet suddenly, because the whole crowd was moving forwards, jumping over the chairs and balancing on them somehow. We were part of a surging sea!

Where was Snowy? Not on stage! – we had to howl, and howl, and at last there he was, moving fast like he was late, with his hands in the air – and a dozen spotlights caught him and followed him right to the front, glowing white – luminous, like an angel! I almost managed to touch his shoe, but we were carried backwards and all I could do was wave.

The advertisement thing finished.

Would he talk to us? No. Snowy never, ever talks to the audience because what's there to say? – he's just there to play music.

The lights crackled into red and the drummers hit a mass of drums that crossed the stage. Six, heavy beats, and the first song hit us like a train, wham! I caught it right in the chest, because music can be like that – it can blast you off your feet.

Snowy grabbed his mic, and his weathered old face burst up onto the big screen behind him – so handsome and wise. We all knew the song, obviously, so we sang it back to him:

'Oh! My! Is this a new sensation?'

We almost missed the next few words, but whoever was on volume control found more from somewhere:

'Oh! Why? Is this an estimation?
I am here and you are here and we are here together now –
What's it going to be, my love? – it has to be elation . . .'

In came the drums again.

They were like cannon – it was a total war zone. Jesse Shangri-La strode forward then, into a pool of silver and his saxophone soared. The camera zoomed into the golden mouth, then cut to his hands flying up the keys! We got a close-up of Snowy as he smiled out at the world, and I think I fainted for about two seconds and then I swam to the front again, dragging Vicky.

There was Snowy, ready for the next verse, putting the mic back into its stand, and I saw Katkat in the middle of her trio, ready to sing. She hit the chorus, and wow! – it soared up over us. They all danced together, and did I forget why we had come this far, and why we were there? Yes – I did. I admit it, because I was just dancing.

The first song melted into one even faster, and Vicky managed to grab hold of me so we stood there hugging – then, thank God, they slowed down for a love song.

'Roses' was next – I didn't see  the first bit because I was crying too much. The whole stadium went quiet, and when I wiped my eyes Snowy was under this pink spotlight, with his little mandolin, and someone wheeled out a wheelchair with Rosie in it! – laughing! Snowy knelt beside her, and his voice was so pure – so delicate – I think everyone was in tears. When he got to the last verse, I heard a voice in my ear, and it was bloody Stagger! – I'd forgotten all about the radio . . .

'Close now, guys,' he said.

'Shut up!' I said.

'Come in, Vee, is she there? – over.'

'Who?' said Vicky.

'Katkat! – who do you think? We can't see her. Over—'

'Are you ready, Ben?' said Edgar. 'Tell me again, buddy – where are you, man?'

'We're standing by,' said the twins.

'Ben,' said Edgar. 'If you can hear me, man – I love you.'

'She's there,' said Molly. 'Look. Katkat's coming down.'

That's when the drummers started what is, seriously, the most famous introduction in modern music. The stage disappeared under this kind of blizzard of white snow. There were bombs going off, and gongs were crashing, and some great big bell began to toll. That was the cue for the children! All those lovely little kids we'd seen backstage, they ran through the snowstorm towards us in their bright kimonos, and saris and furs and stuff – the children of the world! – and spotlights swirled over them so they glittered and shone.

I saw Edgar then – with Spud, Stagger and Damien. They kind of scuttled into position like they were Katkat's personal guard, just in case anyone tried to silence her, I suppose – but she didn't need them.

She was moving too, down the steps – she'd seen them, I think, and she moved slowly, as if she was in a dream, or sleepwalking.

Snowy had turned, and was holding out his hand.

She was heading towards him.

# Ben

## 13.23
## Continued ▶

I was hands-free, head torch on.

It was easy to see the panel, and the options were there:

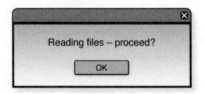

I clicked return.

'I confirmed, and the machine paused, thinking hard.

Files ready – play sequence?

OK

I was about to go for it when I heard Vicky's voice in my earpiece – I could just make it out over the music, because she shouted loud:

'Give her time, guys,' she cried. 'She's taking the mic. Wait for it – wait . . .'

# Vicky

## 13.23
## Continued ▶

Snowy had once called this song 'the world's fist, hammering on the door of fate'. Every percussionist was working at it, and the opening was ten times longer than usual.

Who cared? It could go on for ever, for the children were dancing now and so was the world. We heard rhythms from the jungle, the deserts, the steppe and the street. The children had made a star, which spun round Snowy, and a slender platform rose up on hydraulics, and extended out, over our heads.

'Tell the truth!' he cried, as he climbed onto it. He beckoned Katkat, and she moved towards him, eyes fixed, mic in her hand.

The crowd took up his words, and chanted them. When he reached the end of the walkway, he couldn't start the lyric. Katkat was behind him, pushing her hair back: in less than a minute the music would be sucked clean away into silence, and it would be just her, pouring out her soul.

At last, Snowy managed to sing:

'It can be a pressure, yeah? – like weight on your heart.
No one does it for you, girl, coz no one plays your part.
Close your eyes and block your ears – we do it all the time.
Then one day something happens and you realize it's a crime.
You lived your life lying –
Turned away from all the crying,
Tried to say it was unreal, oh no,
You never made the deal, and so,
The wise man and the beggar say you've got to walk the line now.
They put their arms around you, and you light up like a sign now.'

The whole band sang the chorus:

'Tell the truth, please, baby! – the lies won't do.
The water's coming down,
And the lies are showing through.
Tell the truth now, children – shout it from the mountain
Cos truth comes from the deepest well and rises like a fountain . . .'

That's when the guitars and keyboards screamed like brakes on a truck, and everything went slithering into slowness. The choir took up the refrain, and that meant

Katkat had to walk out, past Snowy, to the very front. The children raised their arms: there were a hundred or more, mixed in colour, creed and costume – and they were ready now, for the final chorus.

Their voices were as clear and pure as a cathedral choir. The stage turned violet as the chorus came to its close. Every face was luminous, like apparitions or ghosts – mouths open, eyes staring.

We saw that Katkat was in position, and the screen at the back threw her image up vast and spookily gorgeous. Katkat Madamba – our schoolmate – exquisite and starved and elf-like, with the whole world waiting as she found her strength. She made them wait longer, and at last there was silence. If anyone in the crowd had made a sound, he would have been hammered unconscious – it was like pain, and the seconds passed: one, two, three, four . . .

Then she opened her mouth, and sang.

I said, 'Go!'

And Edgar repeated it. 'Go, Ben!' he cried, and the twins echoed his command.

'Go!' they said, way up in the roof.

'Go!' I said, again – and Ben must have smiled to himself, and pressed the final command.

The screen flickered.

It cut to black, and then fading up out of that blackness we saw the emaciated face of our friend, Jamie Song, huge and accusing. He gazed at us, eyes burning, right behind Katkat, and the world gasped.

Katkat clutched the air. Her hands went up, and her head was on one side. Oh God, the torrent of song was almost unbearable, and it was like she was conjuring. A miracle was taking place – that's the only way I can describe it. I could not believe that such a sound could be coming from this tiny, slender little girl who'd been sitting in my classroom. The sound was too full, too deep, and it was as if she didn't need to breathe – the song was, what? – spring water, pulsing out of the rock, or dawn rising over the cityscape. I don't know. When she did stop, the earth stopped with her. It ceased turning for a moment.

My heart stopped as well, reluctant to break that silence by beating.

Her mouth was open. Jamie Song's mouth was open behind her. His face was full of pain, and when the image became Katkat again, we saw the same pain in her eyes, eyes that were bright as torches. They were brother and sister, and Snowy was gazing at her, absolutely stunned.

Katkat said, 'Stop the show, please. I need to say something.'

# Katkat

## 13.31
## On stage

'Stop.'

I had the mic in my hands, and the lights were in my face – but I was calm. When I faced front, I could see only darkness, so I said the simplest thing: 'What you're watching,' I said, 'isn't the truth. If you want to the truth, it's going to hurt. I'm thirteen years old,' I said, 'and I haven't ever, ever told the truth – I've forgotten what it is. The boy you see behind me – that's Jamie Song. And he is the only truth worth hearing today . . .'

The crowd was silent, and the words just came to me. I hadn't written anything down – they were there, in my mouth.

'That little boy is eight years old,' I said, 'and something terrible has happened to him... Our sponsor today exploited him. It's exploiting us – and it tried to silence Jamie.' That's when I felt the screen behind me change. I turned, to see the front page of the newspaper:

# LIQUIDATOR KILLS!!!

## BILLION-DOLLAR DRINKS SCAM LEAVES AFRICAN CHILD DYING.

### Trials were a farce: addiction cover-up exposed.

The page seemed to ripple and enlarge, so everyone could read it, line by line. The whole band was reading, absolutely still, and the world stood for longer and longer, taking in the truth.

'Look at what you're holding,' I said.

How many bottles had been given away? Millions.

'Look at what you're drinking, because I need you to know what I know . . . that we are addicted to everything wrong in this life. Look at me . . .' I had my skinny anorexic arms out. 'Laugh if you want, because . . . this is what we do to ourselves, guys – some of us. We turn ourselves into skeletons, while a big, rich company sucks our blood, and takes our money. It carves up the world, and ruins us.'

Ben threw another image of Jamie onto the screen.

I said, 'That's all they want: our money. And they have no mercy.'

He put up the image where Jamie was looking at us, trying to speak. Then he put up that monstrous, killer-email from Helen Lockson herself, and I didn't need to say any more.

**From:** Helen Lockson
**Sent:** Wednesday 11 June, 2014 11.38
**CONFIDENTIAL**

Jamie Song will be dead this week –
he can't last without treatment, and
only I have his records. Ignore all
calls, refer correspondence upwards.
We will bury him. Literally.

# Vicky, Stagger, Ben, Edgar, Eleanor, Polly, Molly, Spud, Damien

## 14.02
In the stadium

Snowy came back up to the platform.

We thought he was going to take Katkat's microphone, but he didn't. You could hear the murmuring of the crowd, and there were a few voices calling out. Don't forget, most of the audience were holding Liquidator bottles at this point. There was probably a bottle in every home too, all around the world.

We will never know what went through Snowy's mind, or the minds of the other musicians. He stood there in the spotlight, arms useless at his side, and the children of the world watched, because they were all stuck on stage, unsure of the cues. Jamie's image was up there again, but then it faded into one of the first, when he was on that volleyball court outside his school, in a Liquidator T-shirt. He had his arms round his friends, full of joy, and we zoomed in on the smile this time, which got bigger and bigger.

The silence stretched, and there is nothing like a silence in which everyone knows that everything's gone totally, helplessly wrong.

Snowy looked almost broken. He pushed his hair back, and he turned to his left and right. Someone in the crowd shouted something, and there was a shushing, as if we needed to hear what on earth he might find to say, if he ever spoke again.

Would he talk to us? No. He just reached for Katkat's hand, very slowly, and led her off the stage.

There was an intermission.

All over the world commentators came on to explain the strange turn of events. The Liquidator commercial wasn't played, but the front page of our paper was transmitted again. Then, after twenty minutes, Snowy brought the band back on stage, and went to the microphone where he bowed his head.

He thought long and hard. He looked out, and he still wasn't sure. This was the man who never spoke in public, and never, ever talked at a gig, but at last, he said something, in that deep, slow, frightened voice.

'We're going to play on,' he said. 'I was set to cancel, but – I don't think so. We're going to play now, guys. Aren't we? And it's going to be a better set than the one we planned. But I'm telling you something . . . I'll tell you now. This isn't for the sponsor, because that's ended. This isn't even for you out there. No . . . we're going to play for the little boy sent to us today. A little boy called Jamie, and for his family, and his people.'

He paused.

'Why is Africa weeping?' he said. 'I don't think I've ever asked, and now I'm not sure it ever was. I think maybe Africa's angry. Angry with fools like me, and a world that doesn't change. Africa's angry – so let's tell the truth.'

He spun round, and then he turned back as if he'd forgotten something.

'This is the beginning,' he said. 'We're just starting.'

And what did he do?

He played for three hours without a break, and when the band left the stage we howled for more until we had no voices to howl with. We brought them back on by stamping and chanting, and they played for another hour.

They finished with 'Tell the Truth' – the thirty-minute version – and the children sang again and sang their hearts out, before the great, great solo. Our friend Katkat sang it uninterrupted this time, and at the end we felt the wonder, and the power, of silence.

And that is how the story of Jamie Song came to be known, and how a very great wrong was put right. We do not claim much. Only this: that a blow was struck that day that broke many things wide open, and truth had its moment.

# Epilogue
# (Vicky)

Vicky here, just finishing off.

It's the end of the story, you might say. What else can there be? Well, just a handful of little threads that we ought to have stitched and tied. You can probably guess most of the outcomes, though.

First: Snowy threw a party – and who was the guest of honour? It doesn't take much imagination to know that it was an eight-year-old Kenyan boy called Jamie Song, who's getting stronger by the day and learning English, fast. Yes, he came out to the studio with Tilda and his whole family – they hired a bus. Rosie was there, with Mr Ahsan and Michael. We even pursuaded dear old Colin to take a day off and join us. Together, we had a picnic that went on way into the night, singing songs and playing music. We talked. We said the things that needed to be said.

What about Liquidator and the Locksons?

It would be nice to say they're all bankrupt and the managers in jail, but of course the world doesn't work that

way. The drink manufacturers launched an instant fight-back, and there were all kinds of news programmes in which they made apologetic statements, promising massive enquiries.

Their shares went down. The drink was withdrawn, and the posters disappeared as if they'd never existed. Eventually the company put out a press release telling the world that it had uncovered 'deeply questionable decisions made by junior directors'. They said that 'in the light of internal investigations, working practices will change immediately. Customer health must be our guiding light'.

Did we believe them? Well, Ben told me that the company had been hammered, so it would have to transform itself. My dad reminded me that it takes an awful lot to beat a multi-billion-dollar multi-national company, and that we'd made an impressive attempt. Of course, we'd wanted to see Mrs Lockson in handcuffs, weeping – but that didn't happen. Eleanor and I visited the Aspire building last week – that, you may remember, is where Lockson and Lockson were based. There was a large sign, saying 'Offices To Let' – for those wonderful lawyers in their diamond-glass building, with their state-of-the-art coffee machine, have packed up and gone elsewhere.

Has my dad reformed, and found a job as an investigative journalist? Has he finally given up alcohol, and is he now a happy man? Well . . . I have to tell the truth, and the answers are no, no, and partly. He's writing a book, which is good, but he still says he won't work for the newspapers. He drinks, but he's keeping it more under control than in the past – I hope. Perhaps I'm fooling myself, just as he's fooling himself, but our household is definitely brighter. There's more laughter, and that's nice.

I know the world's problems aren't solved in a week.

I know, for example, that there will still be a hundred people in that hospital corridor, waiting for doctors who simply can't cope. I replay the scenes, and I remember those blocks of flats in the rain, and the lonely playgrounds. I remember that journey we made, and the despair we encountered, and I remember the families crammed into tiny rooms, sleeping in shifts, and the eyes watching as we drank our tea.

Oh, the problems of the world . . .

How nice it would be if our teacher Mr Millington had issued us all with magic wands: 'Go out and put things right,' he might have said. 'Go on, children! Scatter some magic dust and make the world happier.'

Which brings me to the very last few pages, and the Friday before half term.

# Vicky

## 16.00
## School

Imagine my excitement when I heard Mr Millington wanted to see me, privately, after school. Imagine my imagination as I speculated on what he might want to say, because – don't forget – he'd been the one to tell me what a bitter disappointment I was, and how I wasn't fit to represent the school.

Four o'clock was the appointed time, and I walked up the corridor five minutes early. 'Late', after all, is a four-letter word. I was surprised to find Ben there too, waiting with Edgar.

'Good,' said Mr Millington. 'Come in – all of you.'

His office was its usual neat self, with nothing on the desk except a computer. He sat in a hydraulic chair, whilst we took grey, plastic ones.

'The first thing to say,' he said, 'is well done. That's been said, of course, but it's worth repeating. You achieved a great deal: all of you.'

'It wasn't just us,' I said.

'I'm well aware of that,' said Mr Millington. 'Where's your tie, by the way, Edgar?'

'In the wash,' said Edgar.

'Oh. And your blazer?'

'In the bin.'

'Oh. You'll need one after the holiday, or you'll be on report again. Anyway – there are other matters to discuss. I think you know what I'm about to say,' he said.

'I don't,' said Ben.

'Don't you?'

'No idea, sir.'

'Oh.' He paused, and moved his mouse.

'Why don't you say it?' said Edgar. 'We'll help you if we can.'

Mr Millington's bald patch turned slightly pink. 'The work-experience programme has ended now,' he said. 'Triumphantly, in fact – it's earned the school a lot of very good publicity, and I think everyone did well. Unfortunately, however – from an administrative point of view – you three have something of a problem.'

'What's that?' I said.

He smiled. 'You haven't completed your placements.'

'How's that?' said Ben.

'You didn't actually put the time in. You gave up your time, of course. But you didn't do enough hours in your respective places of work, so I can't sign you off.'

Mr Millington paused again, and we simply stared at him.

'You were with Stems and Petals, Benjamin – one day and a half.' He was looking over his spectacles at his computer screen. 'Edgar, you were taken on by that . . . gymnasium, that fitness centre. One day only, and I've had no paperwork at all. While you, Vicky, were in specialist catering and were "let go" on your first day.'

Still we sat there, in total dumbstruck silence.

'Now that doesn't mean disaster,' he said. 'I am not preaching a counsel of despair, because there is always a way out of these situations. What it means, if I can just come behind you, Edgar . . .' He'd stood up. He moved towards his shelving unit, squeezing round the back of Edgar's chair. He took down a box file, which I recognized at once. He'd used it at the start of the project, and I could see the same sticky label with his own capitals in red felt tip:

## PLACEMENTS - YEAR 8

'Are you going to ask us to do it again?' said Ben.

'Yes.'

'You're joking,' I said.

'I'm not. You've failed the module.'

He opened the box. 'I want to move fast,' he said. 'Choose another firm, or company, and you can do a totally new placement next term – with some of the younger children. We're extending the scheme, you see. So you could make up the credits that way, and if you're successful this time, we can issue a certificate.' He smiled again, and sat back down. 'How does that sound, Edgar? I do want to be supportive, you see.'

I don't know how long the silence lasted. I remember noticing the tick of Mr Millington's clock, and the click of his knees as he stretched his legs. Ben and I both looked at Edgar, and though I'm not a mind-reader, I swear he was wondering how easy it would be to pick up the monitor and smash it down onto the man's head. He was thinking how nice it would be to wedge it tight to his shoulders, so his whole face was jammed up into the electronics and he was peering through the glass. Ben and I could then plug it into the mains and fry him.

'We do the whole thing again?' I said, at last.

'Yes.'

'Another project,' said Edgar. 'Of work experience.'

'Exactly.'

Ben went to speak, and thought better of it. We sat in silence again. That's when the giggles started.

'Are you all right, Vicky?' said Mr Millington.

I wasn't. The giggles got worse, and I couldn't answer him. I laughed louder and louder, and I saw Ben's lips twitch as well. He was grinning at Edgar, and that meant there was no hope at all, so I put my head back and roared – I could not stop.

Mr Millington tried to say something else, but Ben and I were laughing too loudly to hear. Edgar was cracking as well, and when he finally gave in we actually clutched each other in full-on, uncontrollable hysterics. Half a minute it must have lasted – maybe longer. We struggled for self-control, but Edgar fell off his chair, and we all erupted again.

At last, Ben sat up straight, and we managed to control ourselves, and I managed to say: 'We'd love to, sir. We really would . . .' After all, why not? What else did we have to do? And the best thing was, it would get us out of school and give us an adventure. I wiped my eyes, and asked the obvious question: 'What placements do you have?'

Mr Millington couldn't look at us. 'This is serious,' he said. 'If you can't behave better than that—'

'I'm sorry,' I said. 'We're serious now.'

'We are,' said Ben.

'Totally!' grinned Edgar, and that nearly set me off again.

'So what have you got, sir?' said Ben. 'What's in the magic box?'

Mr Millington lifted up a piece of paper. He put his reading glasses on, and showed us a list. 'At the moment,' he said, 'I have several to choose from. They're all challenging, and they require smart, creative young people. People with a bit of . . . initiative.'

He licked his lips.

'That's the question, isn't it?' he said. 'Can you show initiative?'

# Acknowledgements

This book took a while, and many people helped me – both strangers and friends. Thank you to my family, of course. To Louie North, Helen Macdonald, Mike Smith, Mike Hemsley, Gill Binks, John Dryden, Christian Wakefield and Edward Moore. Alexander and Thomas Ward offered ideas, as did Caitlin Mantz. Plot details were endlessly churned by Michael Gee and Jane Fisher, and the children of British School Manila were inspirational. My agent, Jane Turnbull, got behind it from the start and is embedded in the final draft – as are the dedicated team at David Fickling Books: David and Rosie, with the support of Sue Cook, Linda Sargent, Joe Brady and Bella Pearson.